Momentum

Momentum

SACI LLOYD

Holiday House / New York

Library of Congress Cataloging-in-Publication Data
Lloyd, Saci.
Momentum / Saci Lloyd. — 1st ed.
p. cm.
Summary: With energy wars flaring across the globe, oil prices gone crazy,
regular power cuts, and soldiers keeping the Outsiders in check, Hunter, one
of the privileged of society, is fascinated by the Outsiders, so when he meets Uma
he is quickly drawn into her circle of the poor and disenfranchised.
ISBN 978-0-8234-2414-6 (hardcover)
[1. Energy conservation—Fiction.   2. Rationing—Fiction.   3. Protest movements—
Fiction.   4. Social classes—Fiction.   5. London (England)—Fiction.   6. England—
Fiction.   7. Science fiction.]   I. Title.
PZ7.L77874Mo 2012
[Fic]—dc23
2011022056

With thanks to: Veronique Baxter, Rachel Wade, Uly Lyons, Herick Moukodi, Mat Clark, Dan Edwardes, Ibrahim Abu Asheegh, Salim Ataig, Karen Selby, and all my colleagues and students at NewVic.

Pronunciation note:

家 [jee -uh]: The Family. The global social network portal owned by Chinese media corporation Futurax. Estimated global membership: 4 billion.

FOR ALL THE OUTSIDERS

One

High on the edge of the apartment roof, Hunter *knows* what to do. He's set up a good base to jump from; he's positioned his toes just over the edge; he's relaxed, his knees are slightly bent, and he knows to throw his arms forward and make the jump with his whole body in order to maximize the distance. And also he knows to keep it simple; that all he's got to do is focus on the other rooftop, five meters away. It's all about momentum. Focus on the target, not on the ground or the drop.

He gets it, he really does. *So now, Hunter boy, bend your legs, relax, and throw your arms....* He shivers, suddenly aware he's been standing up there a long, long time. A gust of wind catches the side of the building, swirling grit and plastic around him. He glances down, at the fourteen-floor drop between his building and the next. He feels fear. He likes it. He hates it. *This is bad for you, this is illegal, this will hurt.* It's like facing a mirror. *This is who you are today.* Ah, what did he go and look down for? He blows out his cheeks. It's just not going to happen, not today. Fool.

Hunter eases himself down onto the roof, pulls out a stick of gum, and leans back on his palms, drumming his heels over the side of the South Quay Estate building. Gutted, rotten, ruined, the apartments lie open all around him, their secrets exposed for all to see. Not that anybody's looking. Nobody comes here. Or nobody that he knows. Not even the slum, the favela people, live this close to the water. His father would kill him if he knew he was here. But he's never going to know and, anyway, right now, who cares? The pain of the missed jump is fading, and Hunter scans the desolate estate, visualizing all the intricate drops, climbs, runs, twists, vaults, and leaps, scattered like jewels in the concrete sprawl below. Hunter smiles. This. It's the ultimate high. And it's all his.

For a moment, he savors the silence. Just a few blocks to the west, the wealthy city apartments of St. Katharine Docks stick up out of the dreary skyline, sparkling in the late afternoon sun. But here, there's no hum, no thrum, no flicker, no vibration of man-made energy. Nothing. Hunter stretches, feels himself as he really is; a delicate shell of blood and bone strapped aboard a stone ball as it rotates on its axis at twenty-three and a half degrees, spinning around an exploding helium bomb. But so quiet, on mute. Perfect engineering.

In the opposite building, three men dressed in dark gear step out onto the twelfth floor. One waits at the top of the stairwell while the others proceed along the corridor. They walk lightly, with purpose, coming to a stop in front of a red door, the third from the end. The first man steps forward, peers through the security eyehole set into the door. His eye appears, massive, a fish-eye, to the boy staring back at him through the lens on the other side of the door. His pupils dilate. Only a thin sheet of wood separates them. The man presses his ear to the door for a moment before pulling back with a shake of his head. He signals to his partner.

And then together they shoulder-charge the door, smashing the wood clean off its hinges as they explode into the apartment. But the boy is ready and, taking advantage of their momentary imbalance, he hurdles over their bodies, landing on the exposed concrete of the corridor before twisting on his heel and setting off toward the stairs. The man standing there shouts, raises his gun, but the boy is no longer running toward him; swinging himself high onto

2

a metal ceiling rail, he is now high on the ceiling. His feet connect with the man's head, smashing it back against the wall. A second later he lands on the stained floor before executing a vault over the stair rail to the floor below in one fluid movement.

Landing on the lowest step, he then sets off along the corridor toward the far side of the building. On the floor above, the two men race out of the apartment, shouting, and their calls are answered by more men from below, now scaling the stairs. The boy will be trapped between them. He hesitates for a fraction of a second before changing direction. He races directly at an apartment wall and springs up, catching a water pipe before smashing feet first through a narrow window block above the door, propelling his body through the glass shards, and coming to land inside the hallway of the gutted flat. The men flood down the corridor after him, Koch-MP7 gunfire shattering the door frame. A beat, and then suddenly the balcony door flies open and the boy rolls out on to the terrace, spinning over the ironwork railing before sliding down a pipe on the outer wall. Seconds later, the men appear on the balcony, their gunfire echoing around the ragged estate walls.

And now Hunter can see everything. On the walkway of the building opposite he watches as the boy desperately zigzags across the rutted surface, high-velocity bullets raking the wall behind him—and in a last-ditch attempt to escape, he hurls himself inside a disused lift shaft. Hunter gasps. The boy is like an animal; a human animal. And then, suddenly Hunter catches sight of the armored jeep below, the Caveirão, the death wagon. Kossaks! Heart hammering, he flattens himself against the roof, grips the edge, the brick crumbling beneath his fingers. He can't let them see him. But the boy, where is he? Hunter wills, he screams him to escape.

And then there he is! Launching himself from the lift shaft, he flies out into the air, aiming for a scaffolding rope hanging over the edge of the building. His body arcs outward, graceful, a beautiful curve, high above the earth, and for one shining moment, there's nothing else, just the boy and the sky and the curve. The rope is barely there. But as his body begins to loop downward, the boy

3

snatches the rope clean out of the air, grasps it tight, and the forward momentum swings him in a great arc across the front of the building. In great swinging leaps he propels himself across the shattered walls, a horizontal run that defies the laws of gravity, before he disappears around the northernmost edge of the estate block.

Keeping low, Hunter scrambles across the shattered tiles to the opposite side of the roof. He can't lose sight of the boy. He's now reached a fire-escape ladder and is hurtling downward, descending in great leaps—but beneath him a Kossak soldier suddenly emerges from a second-floor balcony. He lifts his gun. The boy hasn't seen him. Hunter screams out, but there is no sound. He shouts, but there is only silence. If they hear him they will kill him too. They will find out only later who he is.

And then a sharp metallic flash cuts through the air, but it is the soldier who falls, red pumping from his shoulder. Hunter twists his head. What was that? He sees a flicker of movement from a doorway somewhere below in the estate—and a shout is carried up on the wind. The boy's head snaps around. He stops dead, before suddenly reversing direction again, now climbing back *up* the fire escape with breathtaking speed. But the Kossaks are closing in. There are too many of them. Gunfire and shouts ring out around the enclosed walls. Hunter half-closes his eyes, he can't watch. How can this kid make it? Impossible, but with a final desperate leap the boy throws himself up from the top of the fire-escape steps, catching hold of a roof-gutter pipe by the tips of his fingers.

For a terrible moment, he hangs there, his fingers gripping the buckled plastic as he desperately tries to find a foothold, some way to lever himself up—and then he's done it, he's on the roof! Without pausing for a beat, the boy starts to run across the tiles. Directly toward Hunter's building. Building speed; muscle, sinew, bone, tensing and bunching for the jump between the apartments. And as he reaches the edge, as he launches himself into blank space, the boy throws his arms forward; his whole body a single thought, a single move. Forward! His body battling gravity soars through space.

Hunter gasps: he's going to make it! And then suddenly the boy's body distorts, as if ripped apart. It collapses; the arms slumping motionless, the legs skewing to the side. All movement checked, all momentum destroyed; red holes spatter across his chest—and all energy and grace blown apart, the boy's body drops out of the sky like a stone.

Hunter crawls to the edge of his building, straining his eyes to see where he fell. To him it feels like *his* heart has stopped beating, as if he himself is lying dead on the street. To the Kossaks it's just another dirty Outsider kid down. To the girl, Uma, stashing her crossbow in the basement apartment below, it's another wasted life. She glances up for a second, catches sight of Hunter and freezes. Who's that? Did he see her? Is he a Kossak spy? She'd better check him out, just in case. She makes a soft hissing noise and the dog guarding the door lifts her head, fixing her with clear blue eyes.

Uma jerks her thumb toward the roof. "Lyuba. Follow him. Find out where he comes from, yes?"

The dog stretches, rises to her feet and, pausing at the doorway, listens intently with red-tipped ears.

"Wait! Don't go till you're *sure* the Kossaks are gone."

The dog sighs.

"Don't think I didn't hear that, buddy."

But Lyuba is already gone, a silvery form slipping into the shadows.

Uma drags her sleeve across her cheek, wiping away a tear. Filthy pit of a slum estate; stupid dust always getting in her eyes.

Two

Two hours later, Hunter steps out of the madness of the Oxford Street night market into the filthy 家 Bar, and a surge of relief washes over him. Home turf! He pauses in the entrance to allow his eyes to adjust to the trash-littered, puke-stained gloom and wonders if it's more disgusting in here than usual, or if he's just being picky tonight.

The place is live, that's for sure. At least a hundred boys are plugged into their RETScans. Yelling and shouting, they batter their cars around the Monte Carlo track in Ultra Vivid 3D. And over by the far wall, he can just make out a group of girls through the pulsing light as they flirt with a bunch of SIMboys, giggling and screaming over the pulsing MumbaiCore music.

"Hunter!"

He turns. A skinny kid with a shaggy, half-grown-out Mohawk stands in front of him, hands on hips.

"Oyo, bro, whe' you been?"

Hunter frowns. "What?"

"I buth yu, bu' you don' get back to me."

"Leo, mate...I can't—" Hunter's rib cage rattles as a bassline drops into subsonic overdub, and so he grabs the boy by the shoul-

6

ders, pushing him back through the doors and on to the street. The sound mutes instantly as the door swings shut.

Hunter leans forward. "What're you saying?"

The boy sticks his finger in Hunter's chest. "Man, da Thoothie gir' yu lik'th here. I been buthing yu!"

Baffled, Hunter stares into Leo's face, peering through the ultra-lightweight lens postitioned over his friend's right eye. What's this boy on? Then a smile spreads across his face. "Suzie? *Suzie's* here? Leo, my man, are you on the Xtra again?"

The boy brings his palms down hard on his cheeks, creating a deep, hollow pop. "Ye'thir, I ith!" And then he bursts out laughing.

Mala Xtra noodles. Super Numb Spicy. You've got to love 'em. From Sichuan province, first created to cover up the taste of rotten meat, the original Mala's been ramped up to mutant strength in some crazed hellhole biochemist lab with truly godlike results. One pot will fire you down to hell, two will chill you up to heaven and three will blow your frontal lobes clean out of your skull. Leo Wellington Santiago da Silva is a strictly three-pot minimum man. Leo is now doing a kind of moonwalk shuffle out on the sidewalk.

Hunter shakes his head. "I'm starving. Let's go out back for something to eat where it's quiet. I got stuff to tell you."

"Thtuff?"

"Yeah, Leo, big thtuff." Hunter cuffs him round the head. "And lay off that poison willya, you fool? I need the Silva brain online."

Leo replies by way of a gentle headbutt and scuffling. They push against the door. It opens and the 家 Bar sucks them back inside its slimy, vomit-coated gut.

Some half an hour later, slouched down in a busted armchair in the back canteen, Leo's fingers whiten as they crush an empty Coke can on the chipped tabletop. His face has lost its crooked grin, his Mala buzz has worn off, big style.

"Bad," he says.

Hunter nods. "I know."

"No, you don't know. You're telling me like this is some cool thing. But me, I know this stuff. I lived in the slums, an' it took me long enough to get out. What you mixing it up in there for, bro?"

"I'm not mixing it up. I was just there was all."

"Doin' that Free Runner foolishness? Citizens don't jump, that stuff is strictly for the Outsider kids, an' you know it. Any Kossak sees you down in the slum doin' that, he takes you down. He shoots first an' he finds out you're some candy-ass rich white boy later."

Hunter bats his rice carton to one side. "Yeah well, at least I'm alive. Not plugged into the 家 twenty-four seven like a braindead dingus."

Leo's mouth curls into a sneer. "What's a dingus?"

"You."

"That word don't even exist and even if it did I ain't one."

"Are too. An oxygen-starved dingus brain is all you've got left. A blob of mush stuck on to a spinal cord. Man, you can't even go to the toilet without your RETScan to show you what to do with your hands."

Leo leans forward. "I *know* what to do with my hands. Believe."

Hunter laughs. "Okay. I'll give you that. But serious, when was the last time you went naked...just, I dunno, walked down the street without your RET?"

Leo frowns, reaches up to tap the slim semi-transparent head-set that runs from his ear across to his right eye. "Dunno. Why? I *love* it. Everybody loves it, 'cept you, you freak. It hooks me into the 家, which makes reality way, way cooler and it ain't hurting anyone. It's what you're doing that's messed up. You keep on jumping down in the favela like you do and you'll get more in the way of reality than you can deal with. If they don't shoot you, the Kossaks'll bust you for sure, and it'll be on your Citizen record for, like, a million years. Even a Tech 1 Class god like you has got to keep your ID *clean*, Hunter."

"What's so bad about being dirty?"

They both glance up. The girl who leans over the table is so hot, it's like there's a pheromone steam rising off her body.

Leo swallows. "Nothing, Suzie. I was jus' telling this idiot here...that—"

Hunter cuts in. "I've got to live my life through a RETScan lens like everyone else if I want to be normal."

Suzie lowers her gaze, fixes him with violet eyes. "Oh, Outsider talk? How very illicit. But you didn't answer my question, *Hunter*."

Hunter frowns. Man, this girl is beautiful, but the boy...the Kossaks...he just can't play these games tonight. "Leo says I've got to play the game if I want to keep my ID status clean...and I was saying that there's got to be more to life than...not being..."

"Dirty?"

He feels the blood pounding in his temples.

Suzie smiles sweetly. "Such as?"

Desire is exploding through every vein in his body. She comes even closer. What is that scent? It's like a drug. But something's wrong, something about her, he knows he's meant to want her, he *does* want her, but it feels wrong right now. His body, his heart won't jump. He looks down at his hands.

She pouts. "Nothing to say? Not even gonna try?"

He blows his cheeks out. "Nah."

Suzie leans in so close he can feel the heat coming from her body. He can't breathe. Her hair brushes against his cheek. "Forget it, then, Hunt. Although I *thought* me and you had something going on."

She turns and walks away. After a few seconds, Hunter twists round, gazing after her as she saunters down the length of the bar before disappearing into the crowd at the far end. He shakes his head. He's blown her off. Even though he's just done it, he still can't believe it. He's been working on this girl for months. Not looked at anyone else. A former heat-seeking deadly missile, in the space of one minute, he's turned himself into a burning wreck, a smashed-up, flaming hunk of metal lying out in the Nevada desert. When he turns back to the table, Leo's eyes are bugging out.

"What you do that for? If you didn't want her, I woulda stepped in. You loser. You pretty-boy loser."

Hunter runs his hand through his hair, trying to get his focus back. "Leo, I'm serious...I'm trying to tell you something here. I saw a boy killed tonight. Doesn't that mean anything to you?"

Leo hammers his fist down on the Coke can. "You had it and you blew it, man. That girl was totally *there*—an' she's got that hot friend Louise. It's Easter break just starting an' we coulda had ourselves two weeks of good times, an' now—"

"*Leo!*"

Leo sighs. "Yeah, Hunter, it means something. But once you go caring about shit that ain't your shit, you're on a one-way ticket to the metropolis of Shitsville. I got enough trouble of my own. I feel bad for the boy, but he's an Outsider. He chose the life. So let it go, man."

Suddenly all the lights and sound cut out in the bar. For a long moment the room breathes in pitch-black silence. In, out, in, out. Waiting patiently. This is a room of people used to being plunged into darkness. A boy screams, a kind of fake horror-film scream, and all the kids around him laugh. Then silence again. In, out, in, out. Suddenly the energy surges back—the Monte Carlo racetrack resequences in full Immersion Mode and the heavy bassline drives out from speakers once more.

Hunter grabs his jacket. "What's going on? That's the fifth cut today. I'm getting myself home before the tube runs out of juice. You coming?"

Leo shakes his head, his fingers reaching for the power switch on his RET. "Nah, man. I've got this new program, *Hell's Kitchen Backroom Brawler*. Learning me some killer moves. Why don't you jump in with me, I mean we need the practice. It's the London 家 fight finals tomorrow."

Hunter shakes his head.

"Why not?" Leo looks hurt.

Hunter stares at his friend, his best friend. *Because it's not real, Leo. Because even though you're stripped to the waist in a Hell's Kitchen backroom bar and the blood is oozing from your smashed-up face, you don't feel any pain, you don't feel any real fear. And that doesn't do it for me anymore.*

He smiles, rubs his belly. "Nah, I'm a bit slow after that egg-fried rice. Get Mei Mei, she's always up for a rumble."

Leo nods. "Okay. But you're still up for the finals tomorrow? You ain't gonna bail on me?"

Hunter grins. "No way. Tomorrow, my place at nine. For sure."

At the bar exit, Hunter pauses. A light rain is falling and Oxford Street shimmers in the market lights. Pulling his jacket collar tight around his neck, he steps outside, turning left toward Bond Street tube station. The ye shi, the night market, glows and flutters around him, cheap glitter tat, girls laughing, arms interlinked, air sweet and heavy with jalebi and donuts frying and the manic beat of MumbaiTech and all around hundreds of bodies pressing, moving forward.

Hunter cuts through the crowd, moving to the outer edge of the pavement to take his chances with the rickshaws and scooters that weave and thread their way along the main drag, their tiny electric-engine hearts driven to bursting point.

And then he stops. He feels something behind him. Like someone's looking at him. He turns, but sees no one. Just the street, full of people as usual. Hunter shakes his head. Why would anyone be watching him? He jerks his jacket collar just a little tighter and hurries on.

Lyuba waits until the boy moves on a few paces before uncurling her tail and resuming her graceful stride along Oxford Street.

Three

Night is falling as Uma walks along the main drag of Little Rome in the Bow favela. All she wants to do is get home after the day she's had. Around her the street is waking up. . . . There's a fifty-speaker Baile on tonight, the biggest club night of the month, an all-nighter, and all around her the roads are choked with people getting ready—hefting stoves, sacks of flour, cases of beer, speakers, live chickens. This is a proper favela party, East End style.

As she reaches the crossroads, soft Arabic music begins to flow from Mr. Ali's shisha bar and Uma smiles despite herself. Mr. Ali is one of her favorites. But today she doesn't stop to say hello, today she just wants to get home. So she keeps her head down, doesn't look up as the two graceful forms twist and leap over the tenement buildings above her, moving from wall to wall, roof to roof. But Mr. Ali sees them. Glancing up from his tea counter, he cups his hands around his mouth. "Eh, gatos! Wha' you got for me today?" After this he bends over laughing, wheezing, flecks of spittle flying into an iron water jug boiling on the ring in front of him. Uma blinks as she walks by, thinks about maybe skipping her early morning apple tea from Mr. Ali's from now on.

In a few paces she draws level with a bunch of shouting, laughing boys bunched in a tight knot around a table football game. One of them looks up, a short, stocky boy with an immaculate flattop. He grins as he catches sight of Uma.

"Hey, girl, you comin' out to dance wid me later?"

She shrugs. "Maybe, Fats."

The boy staggers backward, miming an arrow breaking his heart into pieces. Uma rolls her eyes; when will Little Fats give up? She can't take him and his gang seriously, in their pinstripe jackets and massive gold chains. But in his own way he's a sweet guy; she's known him since they were both little kids, and it's a game they've been playing for years now. He never stops asking and she never stops saying no. Waving her hand, Uma turns from the old Roman Road onto a side street and the bustle of the main drag fades away sharply.

"Uma!"

She looks up. The two jumping figures are directly above her. The nearest one, a girl, in a Raiders baseball cap and old skool Timberlands, drops from the roof of the library before sliding down a lamppost, coming to a stop in the dirt directly in front of her.

Uma's face softens into a grin. "Damn, Rose, you're almost free-styling these days."

The girl points upward. "Nah, it's Ray Ray you want to watch. Look at him now."

Uma lifts her gaze again. A young boy, maybe ten, eleven years old, pauses fifteen meters up on the exterior of an old car-park block, sizing up his next move. A beat—and then he executes a shimmering series of jumps across a concrete ramp that curls around the building.

"How's he doing?"

Rose sticks her hands in her back pockets. "Y'know. Couldn't wait 'til the stitches were out to start jumpin' again. I told him, Younger, this is your face, you gotta give it time to heal. But he don't care."

"Is this the last operation?"

"Nope. Not by a long way. That last one was just to ease the pressure, y'know?" Rose turns abruptly away, waves her arms in a signal to her brother to come down. Uma knows not to ask any more questions. Rose is her best friend, but it's strange sometimes the things people can't talk about. Because they're too big, too close. So she never asks how Rose gets the money to get her kid brother onto the operating table. I mean, she knows Rose is a gato, a thief; half the favela kids are—but Uma can only guess what danger her friend has to get into to raise the kind of cash Ray needs. And Rose takes a fierce pride in never talking about it. Of course, everyone in the favela looks out for the pair of them, but in the end the buck stops with Rose. She's all her brother's got.

Rayshimmies down a drainpipe, arms loose, feet gentle, and rolls onto the ground in a pure, fluid movement. He turns to face them, a laugh flashing across his shortened, bulging face. Dusting off his fatigues, he gives Uma a shy nod and then, as if unable to stand still for a second, darts forward and signs something to his sister, his hands blurring with the speed of his words.

Rose rolls her eyes. "Yeh, yeh, go!"

He gives her another bright grin, turns, and runs directly at the brick wall bordering the street. Using his landing foot as a spring-board, he propels himself upward, catching the top of the wall with his fingers before flicking his body over to the other side. Rose watches him a long moment, sighs, then takes out a khat leaf pack from her pocket. "I ain't even sure that boy's fully human."

Crunching a leaf in her mouth, she offers the pack to Uma. "Wanna hang tonight? I do hear tell one of the Kray Brudders has been an' stolen a gallon jug of white lightning from his dad's stash. Oirland's finest. Eighty percent proof."

Uma glances down. "No. I don't think tonight. I-I...just saw the Kossaks take a kid out down by the river."

Rose sucks in a breath. "Who?"

"Don't know...No one from round here. I-I tried to help, but—"

"He was alone?"

"Yeah."

"But what was he about, running in alien territory without backup?"

"Yeah, you're right, he deserved to die."

Rose puts her hand on her friend's shoulder. "I ain't saying that. But *alone*? This ain't on you, Uma. I mean, there's rules."

Uma shrugs.

Rose smiles. "Ah, a little magic joos will fix you. You *got* to come clubbin' tonight with me."

Uma gives her friend a sly grin. "This wouldn't have anything to do with Wu being back from Paris, would it?"

Rose staggers back like she's been shot. "Suspicious old tart, that's youse. Come to the dance and we'll drink to the boy in style, right?"

Two hours later, the Baile is in full swing, but Uma is still home. Her apartment block faces the party and the blast of the sound system echoes around the inner courtyard, but something's wrong. London is in a blackout again, and peering through her window she can just make out her neighbors moving back and forth, speaking in low and urgent tones. And if that wasn't enough, her aunt and four guards have just rocked up. Uma watches as one of them settles on the flat roof of an old electricity substation, semiautomatic trained toward the perimeter, where the slum turns back into the mainstream.

Suddenly Uma hears voices coming from the next room. Ah! This is her cousin's room, maybe she'll hear something now. She clambers onto her mattress roll and, swinging her dark, heavy hair back, she presses her ear against her bedroom wall. It's her cousin Guido all right. But it's so hard to hear him in all this crazy noise. Frowning, Uma blocks out the Baile speakers, forcing herself to focus only on Guido's deep, muted voice.

"I don't like it, I think we should move. Something's going on. All the power cuts we've had today and the Kossaks raiding the favelas like crazy. They almost shut down the Bow Baile, 'cept they knew we'd riot if they did."

Another voice cuts in. A well-modulated, decisive tone. Uma's heart lifts. This is her aunt Zella. Now she'll find out what's going on for sure.

"I agree, but we can't move yet. I've just had information that the boy Uma saw gunned down by the Kossaks is one of ours, from the Old Kent Road favela. We must stay to attend the funeral."

Uma chokes back a gasp. The boy was an Outsider?

Guido's voice rises. "Who was he?"

"Shafi Haque. Fourteen-year-old son of Bangla-climate fugees. They've already been through so much, Guido. There's nothing for it, raids or no raids, we are Council members and must attend his funeral ceremony tomorrow at dawn."

Guido sighs. "If we must, we must. But we move as soon as the funeral is done, yes?"

"Agreed. And then stay out of London till whatever has stirred up the government blows over."

Uma hears Guido's heavy boots start to pace the floor. "What about Uma?"

"She goes where you go. How it always is."

"She's so young for this."

A pause. "So are you."

Uma jumps from the mattress and walks over to her bedroom window. She shivers; the favela seems so vulnerable, with the power-slashed dark city pressing in all around them; the only bright point, the soft glow of the solar-powered Baile dance floor. This is all she knows. When Mr. Ali rolls up his shutters as dusk falls and the exotic music steals into her room, that's her world. And she loves it. She's more free than any of those Citizen kids, those *Sleepers*, with their perfect ID cards out there in the city. She's got friends, real friends, people like Rose she'd trust with her life, she has the Dreamline, she has her cousin watching over her. Her whole life is here, in Bow favela.

Her sharp ears catch a sound at the door. Heart lifting, she turns, hoping to see Lyuba back from following the boy. But no, it's another guard, taking up position on the front step. Reaching into her backpack, Uma slots a new bolt into her crossbow, zips the bag up, and leans against the deep-blue wall of her bedroom. It's studded with rough star shapes, a design that she and Guido painted when she was a little girl; a wall of heaven to keep the monsters away. Uma smiles, taking comfort in the touch. She takes a deep breath. She's got to stay calm, conserve energy, remain alert, just like she's been taught.

On the west side of the city, the Battersea Power Complex shimmers as evening falls. Stepping out of the elevator on the seventh floor, Hunter waits impatiently outside his front door for the retina scan to authenticate his ID. As soon as the lock releases, he strides into his room and flicks on the wall monitor. Has the boy made the news? Hunter knows there's no way, favela kids dropping to their death isn't a major story, leastways not in the Citizen world he lives in, but he does it anyway.

He frowns as the screen fills with a shot of some kind of power station. Boring. No boy there. He flicks to another news channel, then another—but they all seem to be carrying the same breaking story. Hunter settles on Channel One. The coverage has now switched to an aerial shot of a nuclear power station and Hunter recognizes it immediately; the whole of London is in love with this place. It's Bradwell B, the first of the new South East nuclear reactors to come online. Five years overdue and six billion over budget, still it's the answer to everyone's prayers! The end of the endless energy cuts in the capital. The opening ceremony last year was like they'd found the crock of gold at the end of the rainbow. People were weeping in the streets.

The shot now cuts to a close-up of a group of handcuffed people, heads smothered in hoods and jackets, as they are pushed into the back of a high-security police van. Underneath, the headline rolls by.

Outsider group arrested. Sabotage operation on Bradwell B. As of 16:00 hours the nuclear reactor shut down as "safety precaution." Power cuts predicted in London area.

Hunter grins. His dad is going to be well pissed. And then, as if on cue, the screen dies. He stands still for a long moment, waiting for the Battersea apartment's backup power to kick in. It won't be long. This place is state-of-the-art, it comes equipped with a huge solar energy storage unit in the basement.

Stepping up to his bedroom window, he looks out over the black city, willing the lights to come back on, for the thousands of rows of panels on the Battersea Estate to spark back to life. And then suddenly he needs to forget it all. It's too big.

Hunter turns in the dark, reaching for his bedside cabinet. His eyes light up when he finds the disk. Ah yeah! *Berlin Brawler.* Leo'd be proud of him. He checks his RET battery meter—enough juice for a couple of rounds—and positioning the eyepiece over his right eye, Hunter loads the fight program. Bye-bye, reality.

A few seconds later a soft laser beam streams directly onto his retina and Hunter crouches down low, body tense, as his room dissolves into a battered Berlin tenement building.

On the far side of the grimy tenement room, a white-blond street fighter rises from the trash-covered floor, sizing him up. And then without warning he lunges forward, taking Hunter's legs out from under him, kneeing him in the gut as he drops.

For a second, Hunter lies on the bare tenement boards—as the adrenal dump of a cocktail of emotions flushes into his body, the age-old chemicals designed to make him faster, sharper, stronger—not lie on the ground, like a flatfish. Come on, Hunter, fight it! He clenches his jaw. This is why people lose fights, because they're not used to fear anymore, because they don't know how to handle the adrenalin.

He forces himself into training mode, wills himself to remember what he's meant to do with fear chemicals. Act! And he suddenly laughs out loud. Do it!—jump up, move! He drags himself to his feet.

"Whoah, not fair, not ready!" he shouts, before falling into a crouch, ready for the street fighter to make his next move. But he won't go down so easy this time.

On the other side of the gated complex, the dog watches the moving shadow of the boy. He's a shallow fool like all the rest, but he has a good heart. Lyuba can see hearts very clearly. Lyuba doesn't listen to what people *say*, she watches their bodies, their eyes, their faces, their flow.

Four

Hunter thumps his hot pillow for the last time and admits defeat. He can't sleep. Actually that's not true. He *can* sleep, but every time he falls into unconsciousness, he falls for real—plummeting down from the roof edge, clutching and clawing at empty air as the ground rises up toward him. The boy won't let him be. Hunter curses; why can't he be more like Leo and shrug it off? But then Leo wasn't there, didn't see it happen before his eyes.

Hunter pulls himself upright, gazes around the spartan white walls of his room. He thinks about going to the gym. Maybe that'll fix him up. He rolls his shoulders, feels the stiffness, the pain in his arms and torso after yesterday's action. He trains nearly two hours every day, but somehow it didn't prepare him for real danger, for the real thing.

And then a new thought hits him like a cold slap. Is the boy's body still there? Are the rats working on the corpse, right now as he's lying here in bed? Going for the soft parts, the eyes, the lips, first? Oh God. Block, block. Hunter glances out of the window. Still dark. But it'll be just light by the time he gets himself out east. He has to go back, he has to see.

Slipping into the dark jeans and old Abercrombie sweatshirt he always wears for jumping, Hunter creeps out into the hallway, pausing only for a moment outside his dad's room. As usual it's like there's nobody there. The only signs of life are three toes poking out from under the duvet. Hunter grins, resists the urge to pinch. Two minutes later and he's walking out of the main exit, zipping up his thick leather motorcycle jacket; his dad's from back in the day—and Hunter feels good in it—although he can hardly imagine his old man burning rubber round London. Or any place for that matter. Once out in the underground garage, he eases his bike out, careful to avoid his dad's prized Mercedes Electro Class 4. Ten years old and counting. Only the super-rich can afford a brand-new car since the oil crisis, and it'd be instant death to scratch the thing. Hunter's taking no chances. Whatever he was before, his dad's now turned into a major-league old fart.

He wheels the bike all the way through the security barriers, before sparking the engine into life and setting off toward St. Katharine Docks. Soon he is on Millbank, roaring toward the West End with the whole road to himself. There's Westminster Bridge off to the right, looming, a black outline blotting out the gray dawn light. Hunter gives it a half-salute, like he always does, before twisting the throttle, throwing his body to the right and rolling the scooter into a banking curve as he approaches the Houses of Parliament. Bridges are good. Bridges get you across the water, safe. Hunter loves bridges almost as much as he hates the water. No, that's not true, he doesn't hate the water; he's completely, stone-cold terrified of it. But then everyone is, underneath. Water is the beginning of every living thing. We all come from it and we'll all return to it in the end.

Down on the Thames, the chill dawn air rises, shrouding the funeral boats in a thick haze as they make their way toward Tower Bridge. Uma shivers in the bow of her boat.

"Take this." Her cousin Guido reaches sideways, wrapping his jacket around her shoulders, and Uma nods her thanks, drawing the fabric close around her body. Ever since her mum went, he's always been there for her, even though he's only a few years older. To her left, her aunt Zella stares directly ahead, scanning the river for other boats. Uma looks toward the bank, trying to make out Lyuba as she keeps pace from the shore.

She closes her eyes. It was terrible, back on the Millwall Dock. The mother and the father of the dead boy, Shafi. They were weeping, screaming, grabbing at her, like she could give some of him back, the last person to see him alive. And her unable to tell them anything, to give them any comfort. Their fourteen-year-old boy shot from a rooftop by the Kossaks. And no justice, not now, not ever. What could she say to make that better?

Uma opens her eyes, casting a sideways glance at Zella. Upright, calm, focused. Uma sometimes stares at her aunt, straining to make out a few lines of her mum, but with not much joy. Her mother's face, well, the last time she saw it, beautiful, tired, but with kind lines—it couldn't be more different from this closed-off, hard face beside her. But maybe Zella had to become this way...maybe she was a girl once, too, laughing, playing in the sun. Uma sighs. She doubts it, somehow. She played hopscotch with her once, had to teach her all the rules. How can you not know how to chalk a few boxes on the ground? The woman studied neuroscience at Cambridge; she's a legendary code-maker, mind like a steel trap, and she can't play hopscotch. Go figure. Uma fights to keep the tension in her body under control. They desperately need to hurry; this funeral must be done and all of them gone as soon as possible after the sun rises and mainstream London wakes. She knows Guido and Zella are desperate to go undergound as soon as this is over.

And then her heart lifts as she catches a glimpse of Tower Bridge up ahead. It's the closest bridge to where the boy Shafi died. Traveling up- and downstream, at least fifty other favela boats are silently converging on this one spot. She can't see them all yet, but she knows they are coming. The Outsiders honor their dead. And the bridge and the river are special, linking this boy through the water back to his home in Bangladesh, where his village has all but slid into the sea.

On the Victoria Embankment, Hunter races along the road running parallel to the river; the cold air smacking against his face, the
buildings a blur on his left-hand side. He grins. This beats lying in
that sweaty bed and that's for sure.

The horror of yesterday is beginning to fade and he breathes
deep. *What's up with me? I didn't make the boy fall. I didn't make the
Kossaks into the nightmare they are. I didn't do any of it.* And as he
speeds along eastward, he counts off the bridges in the brighten-
ing sky. Like he always does. Blackfriars, Millennium, Southwark,
London—then the flat gunmetal gray shape of HMS *Belfast*—and
now Tower Bridge, looming up ahead on the right. Hunter laughs.
No RET, no 家. London as it really is. His. Naked. Real.

Suddenly he becomes aware of the boats, their dark shapes
swarming up the river from all different directions. Hunter frowns,
easing off the throttle. They're heading toward Tower Bridge. Something's going on under there, down by St. Katharine Docks. He's got
to take a closer look before he goes to the favela. Taking the slip lane,
he turns left, cruising onto the bridge before parking his bike on
the narrow pavement beside the nearest tower. Keeping low on the
concrete, Hunter crosses to the rail and leans over the edge, peering
down at the boats rocking below on the tide. What's going on?

Near the base of the bridge, Uma grips a flower garland with one
hand and the rough wooden edge of the boat with the other. All
around her, people are crying. But she sits dry-eyed, staring down
at the swirl of dark water, a model of perfect self-control. Uma swallows, clenches her fist—willing herself to stick to her vow, made
when she was eleven, on the day her mum was jailed—that the
Kossaks would never, *ever* get another tear out of her.

Then finally the moment comes that they've been waiting for.
From the east, the sun climbs above the skyscrapers of Canary
Wharf. And as the first rays cut through the dawn sky, hundreds of
voices burst into song.

Leaning over the bridge railing, Hunter's heart flames as the slow, strange, savage music rises; it's so full of longing and pain. Tears spring to his eyes. There's nothing manufactured here, nothing synthetic, erased, or enhanced. It's just raw grief. These must be the Outsiders. They can't be anyone else. He knows he is trespassing on some private grief, that he should leave out of respect, but it's so powerful, so real, it draws him in—and almost against his will, he leans farther and farther over the edge of the railing.

And then, like buzzards, the military choppers are upon them, dropping out of the sky and blotting out the new sun with their black, bloated bodies. Hunter stares, slack-mouthed. For a second he can't understand what he's seeing. But Uma can. For the Kossaks to blow precious fuel on a chopper raid, it can only mean one thing. They're coming for them, for the Outsiders. And they mean business.

Five

Hunter forces himself to move. He can't be caught here. Kossaks are pouring on to both ends of Tower Bridge, moving fast. He's trapped. *No!* There's one way still left. Up. For a second he scans the stone towers rising fully fifty meters above him. His eye travels upward, over the arches, ledges, windows, bars—all the way up to the horizontal metal girders that link the two towers together. He'll be safe there, as long as he can keep out of sight of the choppers. No Kossak would ever follow him so high. He swallows. Is he good enough to make it? He *has* to be. The truth of Leo's words comes crashing over him, that the Kossaks will shoot first and ask later.

And that's when his body takes over. Turning, he races toward the nearest tower, summoning all his energy for the jump. He's got to catch on to the ledge at the apex of the stone arch and use it to lever himself upward. Propelling himself forward, his palms, his fingers slap on to the cold stone, gripping tight, until, grunting with strain, legs kicking wildly, Hunter hauls himself up onto the ledge and flattens himself against the ornate stonework, barely three meters above road level. Within seconds the soldiers arrive beneath him, but all their focus is on the boats down on the water.

Hunter grabs an iron hook set into the tower wall and uses it to straighten his body. Above is a set of three windows. That's his next goal, to get past them. Extending his arms to their maximum reach, he fastens his fingers around the lowest wooden ledge and lifts himself up until he is level with the first set of dark window-panes. Drapes hang down, blocking the interior. He thinks about smashing the window and climbing inside. But he can't risk the noise. No, he's got to keep going. One window down, two to go. Hunter reaches for the next ledge. And when he's climbed that, the next. And then his heart fails him. Looking up, he sees above him a solid overhang; two carved stone bars that run across the face of the tower, bulging out at least thirty centimeters from the wall. He'll never get past them. But he has to.

Gunfire, screams erupt below. Hunter reaches up, grips the upper bar, and then starts to raise his body, his whole weight hanging from his trembling fingertips. For a few seconds nothing exists except this lift—this gasping, muscle-busting lift. Inch by killing inch he rises—hoisting his head, his chest, his thighs past the stone bars, he continues to lift himself until he is able to rest his knees on the lintel above. Gasping for breath, his body a trembling mass, Hunter pauses for a second. A stab of euphoria floods through his chest. He cuts it off. *Move!*

On the Thames, Uma crawls across the bottom of the boat as a burst of gunfire erupts into the water by her side. Guido's been hit! Shrugging off the jacket he lent her, she grabs her own shirt at the shoulder and yanks hard at the fabric until the sleeve is ripped clean off. Then she takes her cousin's arm and raises it, wrapping the cloth tight around the oozing patch of red on his shoulder. Another barrage of gunfire sweeps toward them. Terrified, Uma stares up at the bridge. Two choppers hover over the Thames, Kossaks are swarming all over the area, and military speedboats are closing in from all sides. How can they escape this?

She raises herself again. A body floats past, facedown in the water. Uma watches it a moment then lunges forward, retching into the river. Why doesn't her aunt tell the others to lay their weapons down? And then suddenly Zella is there, kneeling on the wooden boards by her side.

"Uma. Uma!" She shakes the girl. "Listen to me. I don't know how they know we're here. Somebody must have tipped them off.... I'm going to have to give the order to surrender."

Uma wipes spew from her chin. "You can't do that!"

"I've got to. We're dying here. This isn't a battle we can win."

Uma stares down at Guido's pale face. "But we never surrender."

Grim-faced, Zella twists the girl to face her. "I've got no choice.... But, Uma... I've got something they can't have. You have to take it and get away from the Kossaks."

Uma gazes at her aunt, blank. "And go where?"

"Up there." Zella points to the bridge tower. "It's the only way. Climb as far as you need to be safe. Go silent, like you know how. I'll create a diversion while you're in the water."

Guido stretches out his hand. "No, Zella. I'll do it!"

Her eyes sweep his blood-spattered arm. "You can't."

"It's only a flesh wound, I can make it—"

"No!"

"You can't send Uma—"

Zella chops the air. "Silence! I must. You are injured and I can't climb like her. She's the only way." She reaches deep into her pocket and a moment later pushes a small metal case into Uma's hand. "Do not let them get this. Ever."

Uma shoots a terrified glance at Guido. He leans forward, his eyes burning into her. "Do as Zella says, Uma. Remember all you've been taught."

She nods, and he crushes her to his chest for a moment.

"Go!" Zella screams.

Uma tucks the case deep into her pocket and in a flash she's over the side of the boat, disappearing underwater in moments. Behind her, Zella's face twists in agony as she watches her young niece swim for her life. And then she pulls herself upright, grabs Guido's gun, and unleashes a spray of bullets at the Kossak lines.

Underwater, Uma kicks hard, speeding her body forward through the dirty, swirling current, driving herself to stay under till

26

her lungs are blown. She wills herself forward until, chest screaming, she is forced to surface, coming up only a few meters from the
sheer stone base of the bridge. Snatching a swift breath, Uma dives
again and a few seconds later she is out, above the lapping waves,
body bunched against the stone, seeking out her next move.

Her expert fingers move along the cracks, they find a hold,
just a tiny gap in the stone, and she slides her body sideways and
upward; moving diagonally like a lizard across the wall. In less
than a minute, she reaches the road level. Shouts and screams and
smoke and gunfire sound all around but she doesn't stop to look.
Her only business is to climb, her only goal is the gilded tower roof,
the metal girders, fifty meters above her. Peering through the railings, she sees a scooter parked at an angle, and using that as cover,
she vaults over the iron bars and in seconds she is running toward
the arched-door lintel at the base of the tower.

High above, Hunter raises his body up over his arms for the
very last time and hurls himself on to the metal girders that span
the two towers. And then he lies there, gasping, for a full two minutes, a trembling ball of adrenalin-pumped muscle. *Oh God. Oh
God. Oh God. Is he safe? Don't just lie still, idiot. Check.* Forcing himself to uncurl, he creeps to the edge of the walkway, peering down
through the latticed metalwork.

A bullet ricochets off the steel girder and he flings his body
backward in shock. What the—? And then someone is upon him.
A blur, an arm, a palm smacking into his nose, followed by a boot
kicking down hard. Hunter falls onto the metal struts under the
weight. Pinned down, he frantically squirms to get out from under
the body, this body that's come from nowhere. He gets an arm free,
swings his fist into something soft. He's rewarded with a grunt.
Hunter bends his elbow again, balling his fist tight when suddenly
he feels the cold razor on his neck. He freezes, squeezing his eyes
shut against the stroke.

A sharp intake of breath.

"You?"

Hunter swallows. What?

The blade moves directly over the artery as it pumps a wild tattoo in his neck.

"What is your name? Tell me or I cut."

"Hunter... Nash."

"Why are you following me?"

He gasps. "What you talking about...? I'm not—"

The blade pushes down and Hunter's eyes fly open, staring up into the girl's face, into the most enormous, darkest eyes he's ever seen. "I-I've never seen you before in my life."

"You're lying."

"No." He scans her features desperately. No. Never. Pale skin, dark hair, full lips drawn tight....

"You were at the South Quay Estate in Wapping yesterday, right? Deny that and I'll kill you now."

He frowns. "I—don't want to. I was there."

"Doing what?"

"Practicing... jumping."

"Liar!"

The razor bites down on his neck, piercing the skin. He bites back a yell. "I'm not lying. I was trying to... jump the roof—I go there cos no one knows me."

"Why not? Where do you live?"

"Battersea Power Apartments."

"A *Citizen*? You people don't jump in the favela."

Hunter's eyes blaze. "I do."

Suddenly the pressure on his throat is gone. Uma straddles his body, knees either side of his hips, her eyes boring into his. "But that doesn't explain what you're doing here now. Tell me the truth."

Something drums and clangs feverishly in Hunter's ears. He can't tell if it's coming from the outside or from the blood in his veins. He can't tell what's real and what's not. And then, blades whirling in the sucking updraught, a chopper materializes in the sky behind them, catching them both in a great swirl of wind. Uma throws herself flat, measuring the length of Hunter's body, and for a second they lie there, pressed together, unable to move in the force of the energy. From the nearside door of the chopper a Kossak soldier moves into position, covering them with his semiautomatic. A bullhorn order cuts through the air.

"*Citizens! Lie on the ground facedown immediately. Legs spread, arms out. Failure to comply will be met with deadly force.*"

A rope snakes down from the chopper and four soldiers begin their descent. They'll be on the walkway in a matter of seconds. Uma closes her eyes. She's got to do something, now. This boy's an ID Citizen, there's a chance he can talk his way out of this, that he'll not be searched. A massive gamble, but what else can she do? Nothing. She snatches the metal case from deep in her pocket and pushing it into Hunter's hand, she leans forward, whispering in his ear. "Don't let them take this...Hunter. *Please.*"

His eyes widen. What has she just given him? He's in so much trouble, but at least he's a Citizen. He's got a chance of getting out of this alive. It's *her* who's in trouble now. *She's* the Outsider. She can't just drop an illegal package on him. He won't take it. And then, almost without knowing what he's doing, he closes his fingers around the case. Immediately Uma rolls away from him and as he turns to lie facedown on the metal girders, Hunter thrusts the metal disk deep into a rip in the inner lining of his dad's old leather jacket, just as the soldiers' boots touch down beside him.

Six

Leo stalks down the King's Road in a mean mood. Normally he avoids high streets and shopping malls; the 24/7 adverts are too much for his brain, but this morning he can't. His RETScan is exploding with subliminals. It hurts. And what makes it worse is that idiot Hunter, whose dad can afford a NON COMmercial stream import, hardly uses his, while he, Leo da Silva—lover of Virtual Reality, most cunning Fox's Fox of Code-breakers, Bare Knuckle Beast of Battersea and general all-round genius—has to put up with this madness on a daily basis due to his low-end piece of garbage RET.

It's early. Leo doesn't do early, but if he doesn't get to the supermarket now and take his place in line, all the stuff'll be long gone. His brother Paolo's coming home from the rigs for a few precious days off and Leo doesn't want him getting back to an empty fridge. He hardly gets to come back at all with the new seventy-hour week, so when he does, Leo reckons he owes Paolo a full fridge of his favorite stuff: pizza, spicy chicken, and beer, crates of beer. And if Leo wants to be sure of getting that today he's got to line up for it. The Bradwell B shutdown has gotten people all panicky *again*.

As he passes a McD's on the corner, the Golden Arches spin across his lens, taking a 3D chunk out of his visual cortex forever. The color yellow will never be as yellow again. But Leo smiles suddenly, a wolfie smile, he's just worked out what'll make him feel better. He'll wake the fool up, that'll teach him not to turn hot girls like Suzie down and mess up Leo's Easter break plans. He winks at an old lady as she comes out of a Tea House. She frowns back, but it's lost on Leo. He grins, flicking his RET to connect as he crosses the road.

High above the Thames, Hunter and Uma lie facedown on the narrow bridge girders. All Hunter can see is a pair of boots, inches from his face. Solid, steel-toe-capped boots. The soldier bends down over him.

"Name and ID."

He forces his voice to stay calm. "Nash, Hunter. ID number: 5044F/VV09."

"Prove it. Show me your card. *Slowly.*"

Hunter slides his hand into his pocket, extracts his ID, and reaches up to hand it over to the officer, just as a piercing ninja-attack scream cuts through the air: *AAAAeeeeeeOOOOuuuuiiiiaaaaaa!*

The cold, blunt barrel of the Kossak's semiautomatic jabs him between the shoulder blades, and Hunter freezes, arm midair.

"What is that? Answer me now."

AAAAeeeeeeOOOOuuuuiiiiaaaaaa!

The barrel presses harder. "Last warning."

"It's my . . . friend Leo. That's his ringtone."

The officer narrows his eyes. "Boy, you are in some serious trouble . . . don't be messing with me. Cut him off and hand your card over."

Ask any cop here about fighting armed kids in the favela and he'll tell you that to make it from rookie to veteran cop is all about staying alive. Because here in the London favelas, or in any of the former First World city slums for that matter, the difference between a living veteran and a dead rookie is the split second it takes to think twice about killing a kid because you don't know if he's armed or not.

Hunter reaches up to power off his RET, but his trembling fingers slip and he presses the connect button by mistake.

"Goooooooood morrrrnnnnnnninnnnnnnng, fa–vel–a–do!"

Hunter squirms. "Leo? Man I can't—"

"Talk? Aw, why no, amigo? You in bed dreaming 'bout free running, my little Outsider brother?"

A cackle of laughter distorts the line.

"Leo!"

"C'mon, wakey wakey, Kossak-hater!"

Hunter twists to face the officer. "He's only jok—" And then he blacks out as the rifle butt descends on the side of his head.

Twenty minutes later Hunter opens his eyes slowly. Where is he? An ambulance? Raising himself with a grunt, he glances out of the window. Looks like he's on a slip road leading to the bridge. The soldiers must have carried him down here. The road in front of him is lined with handcuffed people, all being herded into the back of a line of armored jeeps. He can't see the girl anywhere. Over by a concrete bollard a bunch of kids around his age are lined up on the ground, all their possessions laid out on the pavement in front of them. He scans face after angry face, but the girl's not with them either.

A wave of guilt washes over him. The only reason he can think of that he's not over there is a stupid piece of ID plastic, something he didn't earn, that he takes for granted. They must have found it on him after they knocked him out. Well, his dad earned it all right; a lifetime of slaving for City Hall has raised him and his family up to the highest Tech Class, the level with all the security and access benefits. But still, that's his dad, not him. And then with a stab of panic Hunter suddenly realizes he's not wearing his jacket anymore. He jerks himself up into a sitting position. *Oooof arggh.* Big mistake, the white ambulance interior spins.

The military paramedic in the front seat glances at him via the rearview mirror. "Best keep still."

"Am I . . . under arrest?"

"No, your ID checked out. Why didn't you tell us you was Tech Class one."

"You didn't exactly give me a chance."

32

The soldier cocks an eye. "Oh, a comedian?" He jerks his head toward the armored jeeps. "You wanna go for a ride in the big vans?"

Hunter shakes his head.

"That's a nasty bruise you got yourself there, so I'd stay still and rest up while you can. Your father's on his way. I reckon he's going to have something to say about you fooling around on the edge of slumland at dawn. If you were mine I'd thrash you to within an inch of your life."

Hunter steadies himself on one elbow, resuming his search for his jacket with minimum movement. Suddenly his eye falls on a stripe of red leather sticking out from under a blanket.... Is that it? He shifts the blanket slightly with his sneaker. Yes. He lets out a slow breath.

"I'm cold.... D'you reckon I could put my jacket on, sir?"

The soldier shrugs. "Sir? That's better. But you can get it yourself, dog nuts."

Head swimming, Hunter reaches over and drags the cold leather onto his shoulders. Then he slips his hands inside the pockets and stealthily feels through the lining for the package. His fingers inch forward... till he feels a rectangular shape under the surface. Relief floods through him, but he's careful to keep his face blank for the paramedic, who still watches him via the mirror.

Hunter glances through the window once more. Where's the girl? He scans all the remaining lines of prisoners, but it's no good. How is he supposed to get in touch with an Outsider girl? Kids like him just can't walk into the favelas. All he can do is go back down to the South Quay Estate and hope to cross paths with her there. Ah, who's he kidding? It's impossible.

He blows out a breath. Now everything is over, his body is shaking. He can't seem to stop it. And he feels tired, the kind of tired that sucks and drags you down. But somehow Hunter fights it. He's not sure he wants to fall into the sleep that'll follow.

Evan Nash jumps into the front of his Mercedes, fires it up and floors it. He is so angry he could rip the wheel off the steering column, but instead he limits himself to a brutal twist, spinning the tires in a feral curve as he screeches out of the Battersea Power Apartments. What is his stupid son playing at? What is he thinking? He isn't thinking, that's the problem. The boy never stops to think; he's just like his mother, always rushing into things, never slowing down to work out what he's doing to others. To him. His father. His heart, pounding hot in his chest, suddenly tightens. The boy. The only thing he's got.

Once on the Embankment, Evan runs his fingers across his cheek, rasping gray stubble. He forces himself to calm down, to *breathe*. This is what he does best. Be calm. Evan is the *go-to* guy in any city energy breakdown. And since oil prices went crazy, it's been one crisis after another. His squad is the first one they call out when the hospital generators go down, when the tube cuts out, when the depot freezers die and food lies rotting inside. For ten long years, he's been on the front line, sparking up the connections when the juice runs out. The energy gap they call it. Some gap, feels like the Grand Canyon. The country's so far behind other wave and wind nations—it's been stumbling along for years on crazy expensive gas from abroad and bits of old nuclear and coal. And now... just when the first of the South East nuclear power stations comes online and he can finally, finally take a breath, those *Outsiders* go and damage the reactor and God knows how long it'll be before Bradwell B is back. The other nuclear power stations are still a year or two from ready at best. Anger floods through him again. He's got a lot of respect for the Outsiders and the way they make their own energy, but this nuclear attack is so mindless, so stupid.

Suddenly a sign flashes up ahead. He's approaching a checkpoint. Evan glances ahead, whistles. This must have been a massive operation; all of Tower Bridge is a sea of flashing lights and military vehicles. A few minutes later he comes to a stop, fixing on his best, most assured Evan Nash smile as he climbs out of the car. The one he's perfected over ten years of practice. *The smile of a man in control.* But as he slams the car door shut behind him, he suddenly feels a wave of deep dislike for this Evan Nash control freak and his stupid dogface smile. Who the hell invented him?

Seven

An hour later, the Mercedes is traveling westbound, back toward Battersea. Inside, the atmosphere is not good. Hunter stares stonily out of the window, letting his father's words roll over him. Let him shout. More police choppers are in the sky, traveling upstream toward the Isle of Dogs, to the east, where the slums are thickest. Hunter frowns, shakes his head.

Evan, mid-rant, notices the head shake. "And what are you doing that for? The Kossaks—I-I don't always like their methods either, but they've got to be tough. If the Outsiders won't play by the rules then—"

"It was a *funeral*, Dad. I saw them from the bridge. They were singing when the police opened fire."

"Hunter, they sabotaged a reactor. Our whole infrastructure is built on oil and we need a plan to get past it. You name it, it's oil. Prosthetics, batteries, shaving cream, painkillers, cameras, plastic packaging, candles, heart valves, cosmetics, detergents, fishing line, preservatives, carpets, glue, hair dye, ink, nail polish, shampoo, insecticides, shoes, toothpaste...."

Hunter shuts his eyes. Not this again.

Pulling up at the lights, Evan twists in his seat. "Look at me! I'm not sure what the hell you think you were doing down there in the first place. I don't really buy this insomnia dawn bike-riding tale you're spinning me, but I can tell you one thing for sure... If I catch you anywhere, and I mean anywhere, down near the favelas or the Outsiders again, I'm taking that scooter off you. Got it?"

Their eyes lock for a moment. Then Hunter nods and drops his gaze. First rule of engagement. Withdraw when you are outmatched. Smile. Nod. Pretend. Live to fight another day. The lights turn green and Evan sighs, accelerating up through the gears as they near Battersea Bridge. Beside him, Hunter slumps into his seat; his head is banging, but now the danger is over, he's starting to buzz. That was no 家 Bare Knuckle Bout. That was the most real he's ever felt. And that girl.... He fingers the case through the lining again. He can't wait to get back home and see what's inside. After all the trouble he's been through to protect it... he's got to take a little look. Plus, *come on*, he's never going to see her again.

Once they are home, it's another long, long hour before his father is done with him and Hunter can finally escape to his room. Locking the door, he activates the window tint before taking out the case. A dense, cool metal container, it slides open easily to the touch, to reveal... what? A tiny, wafer-thin, curved shard of... glass? China? Shell? Hunter picks it up, looks at it from every angle while holding it up to the light. It has a faint mother-of-pearl sheen, and at the wider end he can just make out a miniature symbol, some kind of swirl, maybe? Activating his RET search function, he runs the object past his lens and after a few seconds a molecular image appears onscreen and an audio commentary begins.

"The double helix structure. DNA is a nucleic acid that contains the genetic instructions used in the development and functioning of all known living organisms. The main role of DNA molecules is the long-term storage of information. DNA is often compared to a set of blueprints, like a recipe or a code, since it contains the instructions needed to construct other components of cells, such as proteins and RNA...."

Hunter frowns, flicking the search function to mute; he can listen to this later... So what if it's the DNA symbol... what's it for? An app, a program, a data hold? If it is, it's no hold he's ever seen before, made for no reader he's ever seen either. Hunter snorts out a breath. What an anticlimax. Maybe the girl was just winding him up, teasing him.

Suddenly there's a knock at the door; his old man *again*. Now what? Hunter quickly drops the shell back into the metal case and roughly stuffs it under his pillow before crossing the room to release the lock.

The door swings open to reveal Evan standing tense on the threshold, hands on hips.

"Why's this door locked?"

"No reason."

"If there's no reason then why do it?"

Hunter opens his mouth for an angry retort—*to get some space from you*—but suddenly a bright shaft of sun bursts through the clouds. It floods the hallway with light, catching his father directly in the face and throwing all the lines, the gray, the sag into sharp relief. Hunter shuts his mouth with a snap. The man looks *old*.

"Dunno, Dad. No reason. Just let it go, yeah?"

Evan sighs. "All right, then, I'm leaving to pick your scooter up from the police compound. Don't even think about leaving the house. There are raids everywhere."

Hunter fixes on his best Hunter Nash smile. "Course, Dad."

Up on the twenty-fourth floor of the Central Military HQ in Vauxhall, Commander Clarke of the 5th Military Police battalion gestures for the other two soldiers who stand alongside him to leave the interrogation room. He waits till the door slams shut before bending over the man, who lies slumped, strapped to a metal chair. He is so close his face almost touches the other's beaten, pulped cheek.

"Oh, come on, Guido. We know you know. Don't make us hurt you. Because we can hurt you very badly and you *will* talk. Everyone does. It's just a question of when. So who shut down the reactor?"

A burst of sunlight cuts into the room as Guido forces open a swollen eye. "You."

Clarke smiles. "Us? Ah, interesting, so it's *our* fault?"

Guido nods. "I'd bet every dollar I had that you've got technical trouble down at Bradwell. But of course you can't admit you messed up, so you've got to blame someone...and so you make up this story, that it was us who sabotaged the plant...."

Clarke pushes the metal chair back. "This is not the time for an Outsider lecture; we're trying to keep this country moving forward."

Guido frowns. "Your progress is not our progress. It's only for people who look and sound like you. Anyone different you hate."

"At least our way is realistic."

Guido snorts out a gob of blood from his fractured nose. "No, it's not. All your cuts are about hatred for the poor working people and the immigrants.... The only justice you offer is for Citizens who do what they're told. But we want an end to your system forever." Guido's eyes close in pain. "Your progress smiles only at the powerful. The common people, the natural world, it kicks in the guts."

Clarke scans the man's dark face thoughtfully. Big words. But in his experience, often the ones who talk the loudest are the most scared. It's worth a try to see how the man reacts under real pressure. He smiles. "How d'you think you'd look without an eye?"

Despite himself, Guido flinches.

"Half as good looking? A quarter? How does it work, *looks-wise*, d'you think?" Clarke spins Guido around to face a cracked mirror on the wall. "Take it all in, my friend, because this is the last time your face is going to look like you, Guido. Unless, of course, you help us. We know there's a lot of interesting stuff in that head of yours. And don't think you'd be the first, we have dozens of informants inside the favela...you'll be among good company." Clarke stands up. "Or is it time for the guards to come back in? But this time, I warn you, we will hurt you for real."

Guido swallows.

Twelve floors below, Uma sits in the corner of a crowded cell. Around her women are going nuts; chanting, shouting, screaming, banging on the cell doors. But Uma sits perfectly still. She's just seen Zella being taken from the opposite cell and dragged away by soldiers. Uma rips at the skin around her thumbnail. Why have they taken only her? And what's her aunt going to say when she finds out that Uma's given away the package? She frowns. Suddenly she can't bear it anymore, the questions, the images in her head. She wants them gone and now. Clambering to her feet, she hurls herself through the crowd, banging her fists in a wild tattoo on the steel bars, before turning to join in the rolling chant that bounces around the cell walls.

"Free us now! Free us now!"

Over in the Bow favela, it's a war zone. Anybody who hasn't gotten away in time stands in the streets while the Kossaks trash their homes and businesses. But Rose and Ray Ray are long gone. As soon as the raids began, they took to the rooftops and they are safe now, if being two orphan teenage kids hiding out in a half-demolished terraced house on the Isle of Dogs, while their own apartment is being trashed by military police, can be classified as safe.

In the old house, Harry's place, Rose glances down at her little brother. He's stretched out asleep on a ratty pink sofa beside her. She envies him. She is restless, but there is nowhere to go. The Thames is rolling by so close; it feels like she can almost touch it—partly because the house stands only paces from the riverbank, but mostly because a great chunk of the front wall is missing. Only some steel cables running from the roof supports to the ground prevent the rest of the housefront from collapsing.

Rose shivers and looks round uneasily at the great piles of rusty, disfigured tools, weapons, pram wheels, syringes, jewelry, bones, and who knows what else that crowd the long sideboard—all the things that Harry collects from the Thames. It's all part of the service, he says, a ten-thousand-year-old job to gather up the weapons and goods offered to the river since man first came in contact with the water. Rose wrinkles her nose. Some of it's pretty whiffy. What did she come here for? Healing? She fights down a growing feeling of nausea in her belly.

A skinny, impish old guy in ratty discount store pajamas clatters down the stairs, pauses in the doorway. This is Harry. He senses the girl's anxiety and quickly crosses the room, laying his hand on her arm. Warmth immediately spreads through her shoulder. Bending over her, Harry begins to sing, sending out all his kindness and strength. *This girl is troubled.* His melody is more like a scent; healing shapes of the past and the present and the future rise and curl in the air. Just like all the things he's gathered from the Thames and all the offerings people have made. Harry sees it all and honors the forgotten. He lives on the edge of the favela, between the slum and the city and the river, between worlds.

All of a sudden, Rose loses her fight with nausea. Overwhelmed, she stumbles to her feet, barely making it to the front door. She bends over, emptying the contents of her belly on the doorstep. Gasping for breath, she fights down the sickness, the fear. The fear that she's lost her home forever.

Eight

Night falls over the city as the countdown to the finals of the 家 London Bare Knuckle Bouts enters its final minutes. The virtual stadium hall, marked off into countless fight squares, glows under the arc lights. The tension is high, the mood is good. Fifty thousand kids are online and ready for action. *Chu hai*, getting high. There's a lot at stake.

Over the past decade, London has taken a massive slap in the face; she's a city helplessly clinging on to to her old status in the face of her Fifth World rivals, Beijing, Delhi, São Paolo, Mumbai, Shanghai...all the big cities from the new powerhouse nations of the global south that have joined together to grab the remaining oil reserves. So tonight is a chance to make it right. The chance to represent the city and to win at something.

In his bedroom, Hunter jogs from foot to foot, trying to keep his body loose, his mind light. By his side, Leo stretches out his hamstrings. He is already *inside*. Hunter breathes deep. He can't even believe he's in the same room as this Brazilian idiot after what happened yesterday on the bridge—let alone be about to get hammered by some monster from Hornchurch.

In his fight square, Leo unbends and checks out the other fighters. *He can win this.* He half-smiles. He didn't spend years in the favela for nothing. I mean, these 家 guys, all spending hundreds of hours in their funky gear, thinking they're great fighters. They're such a joke. But Leo knows you can't know how good you are 'til you're tested in a fight. A real one. And he's been in plenty of those back in the slums. And that's where his advantage is. These people actually believe there are rules. And so when they get into a fight with a brawler, a real street boy like him, they freeze. They don't know what to do. That's his plan tonight. Plain and simple. He's gonna fight street style, play dirty. Allowing himself a small da Silva wolf smile, Leo turns and nods at Hunter, who has just entered the fight square.

"You just watch my back. I'll do the lead work, okay?"

Hunter groans. He knows this look in Leo's eyes. The boy is the world's worst fighter, but somehow in his tiny mind he's Bruce Lee. "You're not planning new moves are you?"

"Trust, bro."

"Ah, Leo—"

But then a deep conch-shell blast reverberates around the massive hall, signaling the first round. It's too late now. Shaking his head, Hunter crouches down, eyeing the back of his crazy friend. The last time Leo developed some new moves they spent thirty-six hours in the hospital ER.

On the twelfth floor of the Central Military HQ, Uma's cell is suddenly full of soldiers. Without a word, they cut through the crowd and grab her. The favela women try to protect her, holding on to her body, blocking the way, but they are no match for the armed guards. A soldier flings a rough cover over her head, and she is dragged through the doors and down a maze of corridors. A buzzer sounds, Uma can hear the metallic pistons of a lock releasing—and suddenly she is outside. She feels the bite of cold air and up ahead is the sound of a running engine. Suddenly she's pushed forward again, a hard shove. Uma's hands fly out in reflex, slam onto cold metal. Is she back in a jeep again? She's pushed inside, her head cover is roughly pulled off, and the armored door is slammed shut behind her. For a second she lies still. Then hands are on her, grabbing at her arm.

"Uma!"

She stares up, blinking. Zella! Uma falls forward into her aunt's arms. And then the jeep gears engage and the vehicle starts to move forward. Uma peers around the interior.

"Why's it only us?"

Zella presses her lips against Uma's ear. "Shhh. Whisper in my ear only. I don't know. . . . It's not just this reactor break-in. . . . They seem to have inside information. First they know about the funeral and now they're singling me, *us*, out."

"Why?"

"Don't know. You've still got the package, right?"

Uma's tongue sticks to the roof of her mouth.

"Uma. Answer me. You've still got it, right?"

"No. No, I . . . I had to give it to someone."

Her aunt draws her head back in astonishment. "You . . . *what?*"

"I had to. The Kossaks busted me."

Zella forces her voice down to a whisper again. "Why didn't you hide it?"

"I couldn't. A chopper came out of nowhere. I had a gun in my face before I could move."

"Who did you give it to? Which favela?"

Uma closes her eyes. "None. I-I gave it to a Citizen."

A hiss. "*What?*"

"I had no choice. Look—I can get it back . . . I—Lyuba can lead me to where he lives."

Zella's fingers dig into her arm. "Do you have any idea what you've done?"

Anger begins to build. "No. You didn't say, you just shoved the thing into my hands and told me to climb the bridge."

"And ordered you to never ever let it fall into Kossak hands. You've just given away'—Zella presses her mouth against Uma's ear even closer—"the Encryption Codes . . . the system we use to encode and mask all our information on the Dreamline. There are only three copies in existence, and I am one of the Keepers. If the Kossaks get hold of just one of them, they will be able to decipher all our messages, locate all our people, destroy our global network. We'll be completely exposed. Hundreds and thousands of names, lives—"

Uma's stomach drops. "How was I supposed to know? This is the first time I've even heard of it." Suddenly her anger boils up. "And if it was so important, why did you trust me with it?"

Zella's eyes blaze as she tries to get herself under control. A long beat as she stares at her niece. "I had no choice."

"And neither did I. The boy was the only way." Uma's voice cracks. "You have to believe me." She folds her arms around her body, stares at her aunt, head reeling. She always knew Zella was a senior figure...but to function at this level of danger, this was insane....

Zella drops her head in her hands. "I only had the Codes on me because of the reactor break-in. Normally they are safely hidden. But I knew I had to move them because of the intensity of the Kossak raids."

All Uma wants is to feel her aunt's arms around her, for her to tell her it's not all her fault. But Zella sits cold, interior, calculating. After a minute she lifts her head. "I guess they're moving us to another prison. Probably Belmarsh. Obviously they know who I am, and with your family background...this might just be a precaution. It may be nothing to do with the Codes. We've got to keep calm. Don't give anything away. You especially. You're a minor—there's a chance they'll let you go after questioning."

"What if they don't? Can't you get a message to Guido?"

"No! Even Guido doesn't know about the Codes, that I'm the Keeper....You must tell no one...until we know what's going on. It's bad enough there's two of us. Even I don't know who the next person in line is. It's on a strictly need-to-know basis."

"Why?"

"The less people know, the less they say under torture. It's horrible, but it works. And if the Keeper is *compromised*, if I think I'm going to break, I must enter the Dreamline and lock the Code program down—and then, whatever happens...I can't reveal what I don't know. No matter what's done to me."

"But if I get the Codes back it'll be okay?"

Zella looks down. "As I say, it depends on what happens to me next. If it turns out they do know I'm the Keeper and they question...*force* me...if I think I'll break, then I've got no choice other than to lock myself out. That means the Codes must move on to the new Keeper immediately."

Uma frowns. "But if they release me and I get them back from that boy, how will I know if that's happened...y'know, that you're in trouble...and I need to find the...next person?"

Zella's voice trembles. "I don't know. This has never happened before—but the answer will be inside the Codes. The program will lock down, but there will be directions inside for finding the new Keeper... *if you know how to look*." She grips her niece's hand tight, raises it to her face. "But you promise me that if you think that's happened, that you will tell no one, that you will do everything you can to follow the trail?"

Uma feels her aunt's hot tears on her hand, and she pulls back, staring at her, wide-eyed. She's never seen Zella like this.

Slowly she nods. "I promise."

A wave of pure fear crashes over her. How can she hope to keep such a vow? And then she pushes it down. She's going to get the case back from that Hunter boy. Zella isn't going to break, she's too strong—she's going to be questioned and released like she always is—and soon everything will be back to normal again.

Suddenly the jeep slams to a halt and after a few seconds the back doors are thrown open. Two soldiers jump inside. The nearest one grabs Zella, bundling her toward the exit. Uma throws her arms around her aunt, gripping for dear life, and the guard staggers off balance. For a moment they all tangle and roll on the metal floor. Then the other soldier steps forward, breaking Uma's grip with a savage kick to her elbow. Uma screams in pain as Zella is dragged away and she catches one last glimpse of her aunt's face, a sheer brick wall behind her, as the jeep doors slam shut. Uma hurls herself against the black reinforced metal, but it's no use, she's trapped in here, and outside walls all around. This is Belmarsh for sure.

In the 家 Bare Knuckle fight square, Hunter is laughing so hard, his ribs hurt. He knows he shouldn't—but Leo's opponent, the *Essex Slumdog*, has now got him in a kind of raised headlock and is slowly twisting him off the ground. It reminds Hunter of this time when he saw a guy kill an octopus on a beach in

Greece—he kind of turned it inside out from the head outward—and this is what's happening to Leo right now. This woman's raised *hard as nails* to a new level. She's a beast. It looks like Leo's eyes are going to ping clear out of his skull.

Hunter's done everything he can, but this is Leo's round, he can't jump in and help. It's against the rules. The lady's blonde ponytail swishes in the stadium lights; her docker's arms bunch like a bag of coconuts—and the online 家 audience, all ten million of them, roar their approval. *La Slumdog* lifts him higher and higher and higher…until, with a yell of triumph, she flings Leo Wellington Santiago da Silva clear across the glowing fight square and into the watching crowd. Hunter stares at Leo's flailing body for a moment before his lens flickers and blurs—

—And the next thing he's doubled up, laughing, on his bedroom floor as Leo lands in a crumpled heap on his bed. Hunter stays down on the rug, trying to get it together for Leo's sake…and it's a long moment before he dares to look over at his friend; his strangely quiet friend. Suddenly he stops laughing. This isn't right. Leo is never quiet. But he is right now. Hunter scrabbles to his knees. "What're you doing?" Then his stomach drops. "No!"

But Leo doesn't respond. He's lying on the bed perfectly still. He's not cussing and moaning like he usually does when he's thrashed in a Bare Knuckle Bout. Instead he is staring, entranced, at the tiny, curved shell in his hand, his forefinger tracing over the symbol at its base. And then he lifts his head, wearing the most intense expression Hunter's ever seen on him. "My brother, how did you come by this?"

In the armored jeep, Uma strains her ears, desperately waiting for the soldiers to return. But what can she do? Nothing. She hears the crunch of boots across gravel and then the van doors are flung open again. A soldier makes a grab for her arm and drags her forward. She hasn't got the strength to fight him. Hands clawing at the jeep, Uma is lifted clear of the vehicle. And then suddenly there is a savage leap and growl, claws and flashing teeth…and a snarling Lyuba is there, grappling and dragging the officer to the ground.

The Kossak falls, bellowing in pain, and in a flash, too quick for thought or fear, Uma breaks free. Running full tilt across the stone courtyard, she leaps over a set of spotlights before plunging onto a dark lawn. In twenty paces she reaches the outer wall. A flying cat leap, a blur of bricks and mortar and she hauls herself to the top. For a second she pauses. Where is she?

And then she sees, or rather feels the Thames running near. Guards shout from the courtyard below. With a great scrabbling leap, Lyuba runs up the wall to join her, frantically scratching for a hold. Uma grabs the dog by the scruff of her neck before turning to throw her over the other side of the wall and then following her down.

Where's the river? Straight ahead. A siren breaks through the night air and Uma races for the water, feeling her way down the dark backroads until she emerges on to the bankside. There's no other way. She jumps and the river gulps her up like an eel…the dog crashing into the water a few seconds later.

In the black river Uma dives, kicking ferociously, desperate to put as much distance as possible between her and the shore. The current is fierce, dragging her body downward, but she won't give in, she won't be taken under. Calling Lyuba to her side, she forces her arms to pull back, her legs to kick, again and again.

After ten minutes she finally turns to look back toward the bank. There are lights there, but no searchboat on the river, at least not yet. They probably don't think anyone would be crazy enough to jump in. She read once that in all the history of convict chases in London there's never been a case of an outlaw making it across the river alive. Uma turns her body round; even if there's no search boat she can't take any chances, she's got to put much more distance between her and Belmarsh. But there's no way she can last much longer in this freezing water.

And then she catches the glint of a mast; a boat is bobbing on the tide over to her left. Heading toward it with heavy strokes, she finally comes alongside and drags her soaking body inside, hauling Lyuba in behind her. Untying the mooring rope, she throws herself under a tarpaulin and lies there like a dead person, letting the tide carry her upstream. She can do no more right now.

Nine

Some thirty minutes later, Uma's boat bumps up against a pontoon stretching from the dark bank deep into the Thames. Shivering, Uma drags herself from under the tarpaulin and scans the Embankment for any sign of the police. Where is she? She frowns, it seems she's been carried a long, long way upstream by the tide. A series of poured concrete buildings...the old London Eye over there...light still flickering in a few pods...this must be the Southbank. Uma lets out a breath. At least she's got a chance here. This is a meeting place for good Citizens out for a drink and karaoke. Decent people with solid ID. Not the sort of area where the Kossaks want to be seen beating young girls up.

After one final check, Uma slides over the side of the boat and motioning for Lyuba to follow, she clambers onto the wooden boards of the pontoon. Lyuba bounds forward, barking in joy as her paws hit solid ground.

Uma waves her arms. "Shhh. Is that your idea of secrecy?"

She looks down at the dog; the dog looks back, head cocked.

"Well, what're you waiting for? Lead the way. To the boy."

Lyuba trots forward lightly on the muddy planks and Uma follows, her sneakers squelching. Who knows how far she's got to go tonight.... She's so tired she could fall down on this rotten pier and fall asleep forever, but she can't allow herself to give in to the shiver in her bones. She's got to get the Codes back.

Sitting on the edge of his bed, Hunter chews the side of his thumb, scanning Leo's face for signs of explosion. Now he's told him about the girl, the package, the Kossaks. But Leo for once is thoughtful, quiet. Hmm. Silence from Leo is bad. Hunter stares at the delicate object in the palm of his friend's hand. "But how do you know this is Outsider work for sure? What d'you really know about them?"

"Well, for one because you just told me the girl came from the funeral by the bridge. Only the Outsiders throw ashes on the river like that."

"But you knew it was their work before I told you about her."

Leo shrugs. "Well that's cos of the symbol. See?" He traces his thumbnail across the base of the shell. "This here's the double helix, y'know—DNA. The origin and circle of life."

Hunter nods. "I know, I looked it up. What's it supposed to mean?"

"It's to do with us all being made of the same stuff. Equal, or some such fairy tale. Outsiders use it on all their documents." Leo shakes his head. "But as to what's inside here, I don't know. It's some kind of data storage for sure . . . and that's what's weird because the Outsiders normally never back up *anything* on hardware. All of their communication is encrypted on the Dreamline. That's why the Kossaks can never bust them."

"What's the Dreamline?"

"It's their global communication system. We use the 家 and they use the Dreamline. Allegedly. Nobody knows for sure."

"I've never even heard of it."

"That's because you ain't an Outsider. It's completely hidden inside the net."

"Did you pick all this up when you lived in the favela?"

Leo shakes his head. "No. Hardly anyone knows this stuff, even there. But back in the day I used to hang a lot with this ID gato kid, Rama. He was into scamming people's 家 accounts, picking up passwords, second-life info, whatever he could make money off.... Anyways, I used to help him out a bit."

Hunter frowns. "But why's this Dreamline so difficult to find? I mean, if you know your way around the net, you can find anything, right?"

"Nuh-uh. The Outsiders hide the Dreamline in the Darknet—"

"Woah. Back up. What's the *Darknet*?"

"That's the part of the net that Citizens like you never go to. All of you guys are splashing about on the surface with the 家, but the reality is the net is way, way deeper. About ninety percent of that place is off limits, *dark*, filled with old data, dodgy companies, lying CVs, terrorist cells, pedophile rings, covert police operations. You name it, it's down there."

"But what's the Outsider...communication system got to do with that?"

"The Dreamline? Nothing. The Darknet is just where they hide it, down in all the waste and rubbish, all the digital stuff we've chucked away. Those Outsiders are some kind of code geniuses, and unless you know the way, the Dreamline just ain't there. Invisible. Unfollowable. Unmonitorable. And of course the Secret Service the world over are crazy to hack it, to decode the system, but every time they as much as get a sniff of the thing, bam, it just disappears and all they're left with is a pile of Darknet data like some Honolulu tax returns circa 2000. Nothing. Rama was nuts about finding it. It's like the hacker's Holy Grail."

Hunter holds up his hand. "Wait, this Rama, I thought you said he was an Outsider?"

"No way, man. He was just living in the slum, getting by. It's like out here, you've got Citizens who are doing good, like your dad...and then there's the rest of us, scraping to make it through the day, working seventy-hour weeks, living on the second-hand market, yeh?"

Hunter nods.

"Well, it's the same in the favela. There's different people there. There's drug gangs like the Bessarabians, into heavy stuff, y'know...and then there's people who've fallen through the cracks, like Rama—his dad gambled his ID away and his mum had a breakdown, couldn't work, and so they ended up there...and then there's the Outsiders. Forget all this talk about them being crazy revolutionaries...they're mostly ordinary people. I mean, a bunch of them could probably get IDs if they wanted to, but they just won't play by the rules. They're all the ones who go on strike, who protest, who build their own power grids, who turn the parks into allotments. It's them who the Kossaks raid the favelas for."

Hunter sweeps his hair back from his face. "I thought they raided 'cos of all the drug and gang wars going on."

Leo grins. "Nah. Kossaks don't care if a bunch of poor people are killing each other, as long as they keep it inside the slums. Doing their job for them, innit?"

Hunter takes the transluscent shell from Leo's hand, holds it up to the light. "But we're not getting any closer to what's inside here. What I don't understand is if the Outsiders are so good at creating code, then why make a storage device like this? Seems too risky, why not just hide it all in the Darknet?"

Leo strikes his thigh. "Now you're getting it, buddy. My question exactly. In all my years I've never seen something *concrete* like this. Outsiders are some kind of paranoid psycho vigilantes about covering their traces. I reckon it's something they *got* to keep secret, off the Dreamline, for some reason. What did the girl say to do with it?"

"Keep it safe."

"And what are you gonna do?" Leo shakes his head. "I mean, you know you ain't never going to see her again. Not if she went in the back of a K Jeep."

Hunter exhales sharply. Leo talks so much rubbish it's hard to know how much to believe. And then Leo's eyes suddenly spark. "Of course, the only way to know for sure what we got here is to test it."

"What RETScan will sample that?"

Leo stretches. "No brand you ever seen, amigo. The Outsiders, they don't use RETS, they use implants to jump into the net."

"They don't use headsets like us?"

"Nah, gets in the way of free running. They use surgical

implants, bury them just above the eye, wire 'em directly into the optical nerves."

Hunter's eyes widen. "I thought only rich kids had those. My dad's been on the wait list for two years and nothing."

"Yeh, well. Outsiders don't wait for no imports. They make 'em themselves. Legendary technicians and programmers. And don't let all that poor slum life fool you, neither. Outsiders livin' the best life in the city, you ask me. The finest food, hundred percent energy, a massive clan to back you up and the best, and I mean the *best* parties."

Hunter sits for a moment in silence. "But what if the girl comes back?"

"Nash, you are an arrogant jackass if you think your charisma runs to an Outsider girl busting out of jail to track you across town."

"Not for me. But she seemed to think this thing was pretty important."

Leo shrugs. "True. Okay, so if it turns out it is for real, then we'll try and get it back to her. But how we gonna know what we got unless we test it? I could do it if you gave me some time. I'd have to create an external patch to mimic an implant, stick it over my right eye…and then all I'd have to do is swipe this shell over the patch to fool this shell program into thinking it was an Outsider implant. If I do it right it'll load whatever's in here. Rama did it once, reckon I could too." Leo rubs his nose. "Look, bro, this girl might just be yanking your chain, this thing might be nothing. But it's dangerous to go looking for an Outsider girl in the favelas, the Kossaks have got spy rings hooped all around those guys, and I ain't getting mixed up in that unless I know we got something for sure." He pauses. "An' speaking of real…there's another angle on this…I mean, look, Hunt, d'you know how much this thing might be worth? What the Kossaks'd pay?"

Hunter looks up sharply. "And what they'd do to me for having it in the first place? Just being on the bridge, I got a busted head and a formal caution. Next level is an ID mark or a prosecution for sure. And besides," Hunter sees again the red bullet holes flower across the boy's chest, "I'm not giving up the girl to a bunch of Kossaks. It's not…right."

"Hot, was she?"

An image of Uma flashes into Hunter's mind. Hot? No, well, *yes*, maybe...but more like just totally...different. He closes his hand around the shell crescent, slides it back inside its metal case. "No. Leo. It stays here. I made a promise."

Leo blows out his cheeks. "Oh, what?"

"At least for a while. I owe her that. After you can take it, maybe."

"After when? A week, a month? What's the point, man? The Outsiders will probably have completely changed up by then and it'll be worth nothin'. Let me just *test* the stupid thing."

Hunter slides his bedside cabinet drawer open, takes out a wooden box, opens the lid. "What did the Outsiders ever do to you that you wanna sell them out so badly?"

Leo watches as his friend drops the case inside the box before shutting the drawer. He loves Hunter, but the boy don't know, can't know what it's like, always living on the edge. Leo's only got his brother. He's only one month's salary away from being back in the slums, only one misdemeanor away from black worker status.

In the basement of Belmarsh prison, there is still another floor below. This is where the cells that don't exist are. Where Zella squats on the cold floor. Where the live cable spits blue and white sparks as water drips from the tap, centimeters from her bare feet. They have left her alone in the dark with the cable. They've given her an hour to decide if she wants to do it the easy way or the hard way. Zella doesn't know what the Kossak plan is—maybe they know about the Codes, maybe they don't. Either way they are going to try to break her. Zella knows herself, she knows her own limits. This ordeal...she may not get through this. The hour is nearly up and she must make her decision now. She has no choice. Squeezing her eyes shut she activates her retinal implant and instantly enters the Darknet.

Striding through a brightly lit lobby awash with advertising slogans, Zella takes the first left, walking along the plush carpet till she reaches the toilet block. Entering the fifth cubicle, she closes the door behind her before bending and swiftly unscrewing the door mirror. In a few seconds she removes the panel, revealing not the back of the toilet door, but a dark-lit passageway. Dank air wafts up from inside. The Darknet.

Zella steps through, the bare soles of her feet freezing on the cold tiles, but she keeps walking, and in a few minutes she arrives at an intersection where dozens of corridors converge. With expert eyes, she scans the maze of passageways before taking a deeply downward-sloping section, the lights flickering intermittently overhead as she navigates her way past towering piles of mildewed, molding data stacked up along both edges of the tunnel.

Zella marches on, taking turn after turn, following the signs only she can see, because she planted them there. The Keeper. And then finally, she catches sight of it up ahead. The Dreamline, a delicate trail, glowing gently as it curves a sinuous path through the garbage. As soon as she catches sight of it, Zella runs forward, reaching out for it with her outstretched hand. Warmth and light explode through her body. *Connection*. But there's no time.

At high speed, she scrutinizes line after line of data until she finds what she wants: the lock for the Code program. Zella pauses, looks down at her body, bathed in golden light. It is so beautiful here inside the Dreamline. All the self-sustaining systems they have built, the Fourth World knowledge they've saved; the blueprint for a free world, free of corruption and brutality. And all of it the Outsiders must hide because the brutal governments and their bloody tool the Kossaks can only ever see them as enemies, instead of the future.

With all her heart, Zella wants to stay here, inside, safe. But she can't. She must do this. Reaching forward, she deletes a single line of Code and immediately the golden warmth around her evaporates, replaced in seconds by the chill, dank air of the underground tunnel. Despite herself, Zella gasps. How easy it is to destroy something. She has locked herself out of the Dreamline, and the Code program is closed to her forever.

She cannot betray the movement now. With one last flickering pulse, the Dreamline fades beneath her and the only clue to the location of the new Keeper who can activate the Codes again is a faint, almost invisible trail hidden inside the transluscent shell in Hunter's bedside cabinet.

Lying in a shivering ball on the cold cell floor, Zella throws a silent, fervent prayer, straight from the heart, that Uma will find the new Keeper. That she will keep the secret safe. That she will live.

Ten

It's 4 a.m. and the moon is riding high in the clear night sky, casting long shadows across the road. After a heavy trek along the back roads with many detours to dodge Kossak roadblocks, Uma now crouches down behind the wheel arch of a pickup truck, trying to keep her shivering body under control. She forces herself to look carefully at the exterior of the Battersea Power Apartments. Now what?

She glances down at the dog. "You sure it's here?"

Lyuba sits down heavily, offended.

"All right, all right. Don't suppose you got his apartment number, did you?"

A yawn from Lyuba. Uma frowns, trying to remember his surname... he gave it to the soldier... up on the Tower Bridge roof... what was it? N something... N what, though? An image of the old rope-swing tree in Mile End Park comes to her mind. What's that? An *ash tree*. *Nash*. That's it. She scans the sparkling high-security complex and rolls her eyes, *little slummer rich boy*, up on the bridge, spying on our funeral. What a creep. He'd better have the Codes safe; that's all.

She's got to keep moving or it feels like she'll faint. First things first, she's got to get herself past the security guard. She needs to do this on her own. Bending down, the girl caresses Lyuba's soft head. "Go home now."

The dog gives her a long look.

"I mean it."

Lyuba takes a few paces before she stops, turns again.

Uma waves her arms. "Now, Lyub. I'll see you back at Harry's place."

Lyuba is not happy. But this time she leaves, obediently trotting away into the shadows. Despite herself, Uma smiles. No matter how down she is, Lyuba always makes her smile. It's like she's made from magic. Her cousin Guido found her, abandoned, after a favela shoot-out, and they've been inseparable ever since.

As she approaches the security gates, Uma drops onto all fours to slip under the barrier. There's no way the guard is going to let an ID-less, soaking-wet girl inside at this time without a lot of very boring questions. Carefully, she crawls under the barrier and as she wriggles onto the manicured lawn on the other side, she jumps to her feet and jogs toward the main building entrance. Up ahead, the main entrance doors slide open and a woman steps out into the night. Luck! Uma speeds up, throwing her shoulders back and smiling as she passes by.

With a last burst of speed she slips inside, the doors gliding shut behind her, and for a moment Uma leans against the glass panel, allowing herself to luxuriate in the heat of the apartments. Then, moving with casual purpose, she crosses the lobby to the address bank on the wall and taps in the name *Nash*. The digital screen flashes. Flat 759, seventh floor. Uma smiles grimly.

A minute later she's outside Hunter's front door. Her luck is gone again. Retina scan entry. What is it with these paranoid people? Who are they so scared of? Her face breaks into a sudden grin. People like her, basically. Uma sighs; well, if she can't get in the front way, she'll have to go in by the back. Her gaze moves over the balconies that line the exterior of the building.

Evan wakes with a start. What was that noise? He's fallen asleep again with his RETScan on and he opens his eyes to see a journalist standing in the middle of some jungle with the words *China and Venezuela oil deal leaves USA in the cold* rolling across his lens. Evan yanks himself upright, sighs, wondering if this is the moment that the first oil war breaks out between China and the USA.

Switching off his RET, he sits in the dark for a moment, listening. And then he hears it again...a metallic thud, coming from the balcony. Wrapping his dressing gown around him, Evan opens the balcony door, steps outside, and barges straight into Hunter.

Evan jumps back. "What are you doing out here?"

Hunter turns. "Nothing, Dad...I just heard something—"

"Yes, I did too."

"Anyway, it's nothing. A bird. S'gone now." Hunter edges toward the edge of the balcony, shielding it with his body. So his dad won't see the girl. The girl who just jumped off the edge.

"You sure?"

"Yeh, Dad. It flew off when I came out....Honest."

Dangling from the metal rail of the balcony, Uma feels like her arms are going to rip free from their sockets.

"Hmm. Some big bird, to wake us both up like that. Was it injured or something?"

"Nah...but it *was* big, massive, maybe like a falcon or something. Anyway it's gone...so..."

Uma grits her teeth. *Get rid of him.*

"A falcon?"

Hunter shifts position. Oh, he's got to do something and now. The girl's going to drop to her death while he's talking to this idiot about falcons. He hardens his voice.

"Dad, I've had it for one day. Quit hassling me all the time."

Evan's eyes blaze for a second, then he drops his gaze. He's sick of always fighting with the boy. That's all they seem to do now. He sighs. "All right, son. And get yourself indoors too. Cold out here." He turns back to his room, yanking the door shut behind him.

Hunter waits till his dad's bedroom light goes off before hurrying over to the balcony rail. Peering down, he can just make out the girl's fingers, wrapped tight around the metal grille.

"All clear."

Uma tries to swing herself up, but she can't build up any momentum from this hanging position. After a few seconds she hisses, "Well, don't just stare. Help."

Hunter extends his arm over the edge.

She shakes her head, furious that she needs to ask for help. "Further, you moron. You'll have to climb down here."

He freezes. "Moron? Did you just call me a moron?"

She can feel her fingers beginning to slip. "Just do it."

"I don't know if I can reach that far, me being a moron and all—"

"Just do it—"

But by now Hunter has climbed over the rail and taken hold of her by the waist with his right arm. "Up on the count of three, okay?"

Uma nods. And with his added strength, she is able to swing herself upward, grab the rail, and crawl back on to the terrace deck.

Hunter jumps noiselessly back over the edge, whispers, "My room. Don't want to wake my dad up again."

Uma rises to her feet slowly. Her legs feel like lead. Hunter follows her inside, locking the door behind them. For a moment they stare at each other in silence.

Uma tries to smile. "Hello again . . . *Hunter Nash.*"

His eyes widen. It's just too weird, her being here like this.

"How . . . did you find me?"

"I didn't. My dog did."

"Dog? What dog?"

"Lyuba, my dog."

"But how did your dog do that?"

Uma glances at him sharply. What is this, early reader book one? "Hunter . . . *my dog did it, okay?* Never mind how."

Hunter hesitates. This girl is making him nervous. "You know my name . . . so can I know yours?"

She shrugs. "I guess. Uma."

"What? Uma?"

"Yeah. Short for Malouma. After a . . . famous Arab singer."

Hunter shakes his head. "Never heard of her."

"No, well, you wouldn't...she was an—"

"Outsider?"

"Yes."

His voice drops. "You're one too, aren't you?"

Uma rolls her eyes. "Why? Turn you on, Sleeper boy?"

Hunter flushes. "Just asking."

She flicks him a cool appraising glance. "It does, too. Disgusting."

"Woah! I never said nothing. A girl jumps me on top of Tower Bridge, drops a secret package in my pocket, gets me smashed in the head with a Kossak semiautomatic and then drops onto my balcony in the middle of the night—and instead of grassing you up to my dad, who will one hundred percent call the cops on you, I'm standing here trying to be polite. So give me a break."

A pause. Uma rubs her arm. Suddenly she feels so light-headed. "Okay, okay. I'm sorry. Anyway, I don't need to bother you anymore. Or get you into any more trouble. Thanks for your help.... Just give me the package and I'll be out of here."

Hunter suddenly notices her wet clothes. "You're soaking. Do you want a towel or something?"

"No. Just the package." Uma holds out her hand. "Please."

Hunter frowns. "Won't you tell me what this is all about? I mean, I went through a lot to keep that thing safe for you."

Uma digs her nails into her palm to keep herself upright. "I can't."

"The boy who died, did you know him?"

A pause. "No."

"Why did they kill him like that?"

"Because that's how it is in the favela."

Hunter glances at her face. She looks so pale. A wave of pity, of anger at the brutality washes over him, but there's nothing he can do. She doesn't want his help. He's got to give the package back and let her go. He doesn't even know why he wants to know more, not after the trouble he got into today. Hunter crosses over to the bedside cabinet, bends down and slides the drawer open, reaching inside for the wooden box. He opens it.

It's empty. His hand jerks back. Has the metal case fallen out? Hunter reaches again inside the drawer, sweeping it with the flat of his hand. There's nothing there. This isn't happening. He pulls the entire drawer out of the cabinet, tips it upside down...nothing. This is literally completely impossible. No one ever comes into his room.

Uma frowns. "What's going on?"

"I put it here, right here. And now it's gone."

Her heart thuds slow. "Don't lie."

He whirls around. "I'm not lying, I swear. I put the case here about two hours ago right before Leo went...oh, no. *Leo.*" Hunter smacks his forehead.

"Who's Leo?"

"My friend....He was here earlier. He wanted to test it."

"You *opened* it?"

"I—we didn't think you were going to come back."

Uma stares at him, wild. "You had no right!"

Hunter glares back. "You had no right dropping the thing on me if you want to talk about rights."

"I *had* to. You were the only way to keep it out of their hands.... They treat Citizens differently...and I didn't know what was inside then, I swear."

"But you do now?"

A beat. "I can't say."

"Why not?"

Suddenly it's too much. It's all too much to handle. And before Hunter can move forward to catch her, Uma drops to her knees, collapsing cold on his bedroom floor.

Eleven

Hunter doesn't know what to do. It's not normal, having a passed-out girl in his room. On other days this might be like some kind of fantasy, but right now it's freaking him out. What to do? He touches her hand, she's freezing. Snatching up a blanket off the bed he bends over her. Her eyes flicker open, wide, frightened. He motions with the blanket. "For you."

Her eyes close again. He lays the cover over her, scanning her face for a moment. God, he's never seen anyone so pale. And then her eyes are open once more and she's staring up at him, her huge purple-black pupils contracting against the light.

He jerks back. "Want a glass of water?"

She nods. Hunter sneaks out down the hallway toward the kitchen, heart racing. This is just too weird....

In the room, Uma tries to pull herself upright. She feels so weak. But she can't be weak. A flicker of something close to panic rises in her eyes for a moment, but she pushes it away, dragging herself upright against the bed as the boy comes back.

"So, where is this Leo guy?"

Hunter hands her the water. "He...lives over in Lambeth, near Larkhall Park."

"How far?"

"Half an hour? Ten on the scooter."

"You sure he's taken it?"

An image of Leo comes to Hunter's mind. Traitor of a friend. He nods. "It can only be him."

"Give me the address."

Hunter pauses. "I don't want him mixed up in any favela thing. Leo's only just got his permanent ID status. I'll call him, get him to bring it back."

"No. You can't talk about this on the 家."

"Okay, then. I'll go and get it. Be back in an hour. You—you stay here."

Uma juts her jaw. "Oh, yeah, like I'm trusting you out of my sight. And PS, Leo already is involved, up to his thieving neck."

A sudden need to not let her go, to keep her talking, to keep her from leaving, comes flooding over Hunter. She suddenly strikes him as a pathetic figure, lost under the folds of the blanket.

He sticks his hands in his back pockets. "I'm not just gonna tell you where he lives."

"You have to."

"No, I don't."

Uma's eyes flash. "Yes, you do."

Hunter holds out his hands. "Okay, look, I'll take you there on the scooter."

She shakes her head. "No, I don't need your help."

"Yeah, you do. I know where he lives, what number, remember? And PS, it's a lot easier to get into people's apartments when you press the buzzer and they go, 'Who is it?', and you go, 'It's me,' and then they buzz you in. Unless you're addicted to climbing up the outside of buildings?"

Uma glances up at him. What's this boy doing this for? What does he want? She sits silent for a moment, her head still propped by her arm resting on the bed.

A scooter would be good right now.

Crouching on a filthy Mickey Mouse rug in the middle of his bedroom, Leo is transfixed, his RETScan laser light rerouted on to a transluscent digital patch above his right eye, the light hitting the patch before bending sharply downward again to hit his right retina. On the rug lies the Code shell, dropped to the floor as soon as Leo swiped the shell across the patch and went *inside*.

In the elevator, Leo stares grimly at the bank of numbers that run alongside the door. He's starting to really, really hate this whole experience. He can't exit on any floor and he can't get back down to the lobby. Why did he even come in here in the first place? He frowns, trying to retrace his steps. As soon as he patched himself inside the Code program, he found himself in some downtown financial building—a glass and steel bank skyscraper kind of a deal—and it felt like the right thing to do to check it out, so he walked in through the revolving doors—and right in front of him the lift doors slid open. It was the most natural thing in the world, to walk forward, to step inside.

But now he's been to at least thirty different floors and each time, all that happens is the doors glide open on to massive storerooms, bulging with papers, disks, addresses, files, phone numbers, emails, documents. He's in the Darknet all right. What a dump. Nobody comes here, least of all kids playing around on the 家. He's in a whole other place now. This is where all the years of data accumulate; all the secret passageways, all the dead-ends and lost files. On each floor, the information is packed so full, so high, so tight that there's no way to even step out of the lift. The elevator slows again and this time the doors open on a solid wall. Leo stares at the bricks, swallows. What if he can't get out again? He pinches his forearm. *Keep it together, boy.*

Leaning back against the wall, staring at the bank of numbered buttons, Leo forces himself to focus. This is Outsider coding, Leo; you've got to think like them if you're going to find any clues or direction in all this mess. He tries to drag up what he knows about them. Underground, international network, natural world, rebellion, new economy, global justice, free running… that's not much to go on. All that time he lived next to them and this is all he can come up with, apart from a few bits of Rama conspiracy theory? He was too busy trying to bust his way out of the slum to go near them. They were too dangerous.

But now, focus. Think like an Outsider. This building is a bank headquarters, right? On various floors he's caught glimpses of office workers, meetings, screens of rolling, flickering numbers. What would an Outsider be doing in here? This would be hell for them; they don't even use mainstream money; they've got their own currency. So, all they'd want to do is get out of here. So how would they do that? Leo grins. Yes. Only one way to go. Not through the main exit. No, an Outsider would go high, go stylish. Free-runner style. The *roof.* Leo's hand moves over the number bank, hovers over the top button. Presses it. Got to be better than here. The doors slide shut. Leo grins. Bye-bye, bricks.

The lift suddenly speeds up, accelerating with a turbo-charged boost, and Leo is hurled to the floor by the insane G-force. It feels like his head is being pulled off his neck. He spreads his arms and legs against the walls to stop himself from being battered from side to side. What is going on? And then, when he's about ready to puke his guts up, the lift decelerates with a smooth hum and the doors slide open on a black city skyline. A gust of icy wind blows grit into Leo's face as he lies, gasping, on the metal floor. But he can't stay here—there's no way he's making another trip in that death box—and he scrambles to his feet, stepping clear of the elevator. And not a second too soon, for as soon as his feet touch the roof concrete, the doors shut with a clang as the lift plunges downward again.

Leo looks around. Well he's made it onto the roof all right. It's huge, a wide stretch of railed concrete with a helipad landing area marked out in white and yellow lines over on the far side. Zipping his hoodie up against the bitter wind, Leo pads toward the guardrail, set some two meters back from the actual edge of the building. Suddenly a gust catches him, pushes him forward, right up against the metal barrier. Woah! Two hundred and twenty floors of heart-stopping drop appear before him; this ain't no joke. Leo plants his feet firmly on the ground and narrows his eyes....Now what? And then he sees it. The lime-green filing cabinet. Standing all alone on the far side of the roof, casual, as if that's what filing cabinets do all the time, hang out on skyscraper roofs. Cautious, Leo approaches. Seems okay. He moves in closer.

He circles it, but there are no clues, no marks, no warnings. It's just a totally average filing cabinet. He turns on his heel, glances around the roof once more. There's nothing else up here that even looks remotely interesting. He grasps the top drawer, pulls. But it won't budge. He gives it another yank, but it's stuck fast, or locked. He moves down to the next drawer; fastens his fingers under the metal catch, gives it a swift pull, but again it's locked…and the next one down again is too. And the next. Now he's at the lowest drawer. He reaches out and this time, ah, it moves.

Slowly, ever so slowly, Leo slides the drawer toward him. No problemo. Everything's cool. He lets out a breath, peers inside the drawer. There's a red cardboard folder inside, that's all, the kind people used in offices back in the day. Leo takes it out, eases back the elastic band from the top and opens it. Inside there's a single piece of legal paper, with two neatly typewritten lines in the center of the page.

To where Fleet-ditch with disemboguing streams
Rolls the large tribute of dead dogs to Thames.

Leo frowns. What is this, some kind of directions? This program is proving harder to work out than he thought. Here you're either on the inside or you're not, and he's not. He glances around the barren rooftop. He's going to need more time to hack this thing.…Maybe the best thing is to exit, go work out a solution in his room, and then come back later. This roof ain't going nowhere.

Leo positions his RETScan recorder over the paper and activates the lens capture. Then, closing the folder, he slides it back into the drawer. But as the folder hits the metal base, suddenly the drawer slams shut, as if pulled from inside by some unseen mechanism. His hand is trapped, caught between the sharp edge of the drawer and the main body of the cabinet. Leo gives a little tug. And then, from far underneath the building, the ground shudders. Leo pulls harder, but the drawer still won't open. Ah, it really hurts. Suddenly the building vibrates—this time accompanied by a growly subsonic rumble—and now the whole structure moves. It tilts. As the ground beneath it collapses.

The roof is no longer level. Leo kicks at the drawer, nearly cracking his own wrist bones in two. Damn! This is killing him. The shell Codes lie on the rug beside him in his room, but he can't reach them, he's trapped inside here. This ain't no 家 Bare-Knuckle Bout that he can exit by unplugging his RET. Sparks of pain shoot up his arm. Then comes another thundering boom, like the aftershock following an explosion. A long beat…and then, in front of Leo's horrified eyes, a rip, a tear begins to form across the surface of the roof. The same thing is happening to the next building, too. And then with a slam, the filing cabinet falls onto its side, pulling Leo down with it. This is embarrassing. He's being beaten up by a piece of office furniture.

A buzzer sound cuts across the roof. The earth shudders again, the roof slants another degree downward, and now the cabinet starts to slide. Leo tries to brace himself against the pavement, to stop the movement, but there's nothing to grab onto on the flat roof surface. The cabinet is sliding toward the edge with Leo attached by his lousy, stinking wrist. Oh, this isn't happening. In this world, if he falls it's going to hurt like he's falling for real.

The crack across the roof widens, metal struts scream under the strain as the building spasms in a series of massive tremors. The whole urban world is going down; every tower block buckling, collapsing under some great, unseen force. This whole program is shutting down for good.

The buzzer sounds again as Leo's building lurches once more; and as the roof angle steepens the filing cabinet begins to pick up speed, moving inexorably toward the edge. Leo rains down frenzied punches and kicks on the locked drawer, but the thing is clamped like a vice around his wrist. With his free hand, he claws frantically at the concrete, trying to catch hold of anything that will slow him down, but the surface is smooth. There's nothing to slow him down.

Buzz! Leo grimaces. What's that? The door? Who the hell is at the door? He's powerless. He's trapped in another world. Another fast meter of slide. Oh, man, he just caught a glimpse of the ground below. Distant crisscrossing city streets, two hundred and twenty floors down.

On the front step, Uma steps back from the door intercom, turns to face Hunter. "Now what? That's three times."

Hunter glances at the upstairs window, trying to work out what to do. Leo's bedroom light is on, so why doesn't he answer? He knows Leo's security number...but he doesn't want to bust in on him like this—

The cabinet is nearly at the building edge. Leo throws his arms out wide, desperately spreading his body as a counterbalance, but his weight is not enough, the angle is too great. He's going to fall. He screams.

Hunter stares up, wild-eyed. He can't delay anymore. He punches in Leo's security number, the lock slides back and he races upstairs, shoulder-charging the flimsy apartment door—and with Uma close behind, he crashes into Leo's bedroom—a wild pit of wires, readers, cables, disemboweled machines, noodle pots and grubby under-pants, HaiCore techno booming off every surface. At the center of all the madness lies Leo, stretched out on a rug, screaming, clawing at the fibers, his face twisted in terror. Uma pushes Hunter aside, grabs Leo by the shoulders, scanning his face intently. Then in a movement too quick to follow, she presses down on her right eye as she activates her retinal implant, plunging deep into the Darknet after the boy.

Leo's body plunges over the side of the building. Down, down, down, the streets, the cars, the hard earth rushes up to meet him. He braces himself for the collision, the spike of stone and steel through his guts. And then, impact! His body contorts with pain—but somehow he still falls. He is underwater. He's still alive.

Uma catches sight of him as he plummets downward and she dives after him. Down, down, down, diving deep into the dark river. And then, with an explosion of light, the Dreamline flashes into life beneath them.

Spiraling down toward it, Leo makes a frantic grab at the glittering lines of Code and symbol. And as his hand enters the golden stream, a tremen-dous shock jags through his body and for a long, timeless moment he can't feel where he begins and ends. He's shattered apart, he's a spin and spiral of subatomic particles, the hub of a great dancing pattern. And then blackness envelops him again as his body drops clear through the Dreamline. Seconds later Leo hits the riverbed, striking the soft, slimy, treacherous base with tremendous force, a great cloud of mud billowing up around him. And then he lies there like a dead man.

Uma is down by his side in seconds. She's got to get him out of here. Reaching forward, she shakes his shoulders, hard.

Leo's body twists.

She shakes him again. *Leo! Come on. Up!*

She crouches over him, desperately trying to keep her footing on the riverbed. She's going to have to lift him herself. Fighting the swirling current, she grabs him, and clutching him to her chest, she kicks furiously upward, forcing them both to rise. Up, up they climb. She can't do this. He's too heavy. But she has to. With the last bit of will, her heart bursting with effort, Uma reaches, grasping, stretching for the air as she explodes out of the water.

She's made it! But as she breaks the surface, a searing flash of light burns a fiery trail across her retina, a diamond shape blazing momentarily before it fades to a blank, as Uma collapses in a heap on Leo's bedroom floor.

Twelve

Leo bolts upright, trills a high, girly laugh, and then slumps back onto the floor. But he's okay. He's breathing. The idiot has oxygen in his lungs again. Uma struggles to her knees, glances at Hunter. Something ripples near his mouth. Despite herself, Uma feels an answering twitch on her face. She can't help herself. And as Hunter starts to laugh, so does she; pure relief washing over both of them.

Leo's eyes flick open in disbelief. "Amigos... what just happened?"

Uma grins. "I followed you *inside*. From the idiotic way you were screaming, I knew you were in danger near the Dreamline. We protect it well, it's death to go near it if you don't know what you're doing."

Leo rubs his face. "Notnidiot. Vey vey clevaboy."

"So clever you were about to get yourself killed. Your sensors were pushed to overload... and I don't even know how you got close without an Outsider implant."

"Rama's method. Faked it with a patch." Leo gingerly rubs his swollen wrist. "Hunter, is this her?"

Uma rolls her eyes. "Yes, I am her. And I'm guessing you're the thief Leo."

He props himself up on one elbow, smiles. "Yeah, baby, I am."

She holds out her hand. "Give it back, right now."

Leo tries another smile, this time at Hunter. "Sorry, mate."

Hunter snorts. "Loser. Do as she says."

"All right, be cool. I just been through a near death here." Leo sits upright, starts to scan the floor. He pauses, thoughtful for a moment. "But I got to tell you, Uma, I don't think you're gonna be able to get back in there. That world proper crashed...it was like someone had pulled the plug on the entire program."

Uma lifts an eyebrow. "What, just because it crashed on you? It's meant to do that with trespassers."

Leo starts searching. He lifts up a corner of the Mickey Mouse rug. "Nah, I'm serious, I've done enough hacking in my time to know a lockout when I see one. Someone or something has closed down access to that whole program."

Uma gives him a sharp glance; he's serious....He can't be right...but on the other hand, someone who knows how to mimic an implant clearly knows what he's talking about. She holds out her hand.

"Hand it over."

Leo shakes the rug and the shell falls onto the lino. "Ah, there it is!"

Uma snatches it up. Pressing down lightly above her right eye, she powers up her retinal implant again—she's got to check this out right now. Preparing her body to go *inside*, she falls into a tense crouch. One second, two, three—but her implant is not activating. It's a void. She reaches up, pressing the skin harder. Nothing. Turning away from Hunter and Leo, she whispers a password, then another. Nothing. A cold, cold breaker of fear crashes over her.

Uma licks her lips. Why isn't it working? The flash of light as she surfaced the water with Leo...what was that? Again and again, she tries to reboot, but the transluscent lens fixed over her pupil remains dark.

She turns to Leo. "My implant won't boot up. Can you patch me in with your system?"

Leo shakes his head. "Sorry, but that thing's blown big time."

"Can't you make another one?"

"If you give me a few days, yeah…" He narrows his eyes. "Why? What's going on with your implant?"

Uma frowns. "I don't know.… I was pushing it so hard to get us both up out of the water and…when I surfaced, with you…there was a flash of light across the lens and—"

"What color?"

"What color what?"

"The flash…was it a kind of yellow-gold or more metallic?"

"Metallic. Really sharp."

"Followed by a diamond in the center of the screen?"

Uma nods.

"It's blown."

"How d'you know for sure?"

"I worked on a hundred of these with Rama. I know."

Uma stares at him in dismay.

Leo shrugs. "But you can easy get one of your people to fix it, right?"

Uma shakes her head, numb. Zella's words—warning her to tell no one—roll around inside her head. What is she to do? She can't check the program herself, nor can she ask any Outsider for help. She's stuck. But if Zella *has* locked herself out, that means she must act immediately, that she must find the new Keeper. But how is she going to do that? Uma bends over, folding her arms around her chest. It's all too much.

Leo swallows hard. What *has* he done? He frowns, trying to retrace his steps *inside*. The collapse started when he captured that piece of paper from the filing cabinet. That was when the foundations started to shake. Maybe it was him that caused the program to lock down? What was on the paper? He grabs his RET from the floor and pulls up the shot. The two lines appear on his lens.

"Listen, I dunno, but I—I found this *inside*, just before it all collapsed."

To where Fleet-ditch with disemboguing streams
Rolls the large tribute of dead dogs to Thames.

"Does that mean anything to you?"

But Uma is curled up tight, miles away. Leo glances at Hunter. "I'm trying to help..."

Hunter shakes his head. "Leave it, Leo."

"Hold on." Leo activates a search. In a few seconds his lens flashes. "It's from something called *The Dunciad* from 1728. Alexander Pope."

"So what?" Hunter looks at the girl.

"It's about a river, er...the Fleet River in London."

"And again, so what?" Hunter moves over to Uma's side, reaches out a tentative hand to touch her arm.

"It was covered, bricked in, in the 1870s, it says here. It's a secret river."

"Look, Leo, man...just shut up, will you? You done enough damage for tonight."

"Fine...look, I'm sorry. I'm trying to fix up here...an' this message is the only thing we got from *inside* to go on."

Uma suddenly lifts her head. "You got this from *inside*?"

"Yeh, I told you, from the filing cabinet...on the roof."

"A river? Where?"

Leo scans his lens quickly. "The Fleet. It rises in...Hampstead, near the ponds, and then runs down into the city. Used to be called *the river of wells*...and, uh...it flows through Kentish Town, King's Cross and Clerkenwell, before coming out into the Thames at Blackfriars...."

Uma sits very still. Is this it? Zella said that even if the program shut down there would still be some kind of directions to the Keeper. But what's she supposed to do with a massive stretch of stinking underground river? "Is that all? I mean, wasn't there anything more specific? Y'know, like a place or a time, something like that?"

Leo shakes his head. "No."

Uma tries to remember Zella's words clearly. If the worst happens, then she's got to get the Codes to the new Keeper, even though she doesn't know who that is or where they are. What kind of stupid system is this? One that cuts out betrayal. You can't tell what you don't know.

"Say it again, slowly."

Leo scans his lens. "*To where Fleet-ditch with disemboguing streams rolls...*"

"Stop there!" Hunter mutters. "To where it *what*? Rolls? That means where it comes out, the mouth, y'know, where it *runs* into the Thames. Leo, search where the Fleet comes out. That's maybe where we're looking for."

Uma frowns. "But I don't understand. The river is underground, no?"

Leo holds up a finger, taps in a new search, waits impatiently as new lines of information start to roll onto his RET lens. "Says here...even though it's subterranean, the Fleet runs directly into the Thames through a tunnel at the Thameswalk exit of Blackfriars station, immediately under the bridge. Ding, ding, ding, jackpot!"

Uma chews her lip. "I guess it's possible."

Leo sticks his hands on his hips. "Possible? That's all you got to say about this genius code hack? I nearly died in there to get this for you."

"Me? The Kossaks more like."

Leo blushes. "Well, yeah. Sorry 'bout that. Was before I knew you."

She gives him a long, level stare. "Nothing new. There are spies everywhere in Bow favela." At the mention of the name, such a longing comes over her to get back there. When did she last sleep? Uma draws a deep breath, checks the time. 6:00 a.m. Well, this is the only thing she's got to go on. "Okay, Hunter, Leo...thanks for the longest night in history, but I'm going to say good night now."

Hunter stares at her. "Where are you going?"

She returns his look. "That's not your business."

"I want to go with you. I mean, you're going to Blackfriars Bridge, right?"

"You can't." Uma rolls her stiff shoulders. It's time to leave. This boy...well, he's just going to get in the way.

73

"But—"

"But what? We're done, Hunter. Thanks for taking the Codes for me, up on the bridge. I owe you for that. And for bringing me here...but this is my thing."

Hunter crosses his arms, stubborn. "How're you going to get there? The Kossaks are everywhere, ID checks all over. A reactor went down, remember?"

Uma curls a lip. "Yeah, and I bet you think we were responsible?"

"Well, were you?"

"No! We're not terrorists. Look..." Uma forces herself to be calm. "I managed just fine last night...."

"In the dark, yes. But it's going to be light any minute now.... And there's a hundred cameras and checkpoints between here and the bridge, I reckon."

"I'll be cool." Uma runs her hands through her hair. He's looking at her with that expression again. What is it? Kindness? *Pity?* Anger rises inside her. She didn't come here to be pitied by some Sleeper boy. Just because he helped her out once, he's acting now like he's got some rights over her. Her eyes spark. They're all the same, so arrogant, so smug! "Why don't you quit bugging me? This isn't some Sleeper thrill."

Suddenly Hunter grabs her wrist, his eyes boring into hers. "It's not that! I saw that boy die too. I saw him killed in front of me. I...I want to do something...to make it right." He drops his gaze. "I don't know what all this is about, and I don't need to know, but what I'm saying makes sense. We'll go on the scooter, with my ID status it'll be easy to get across town. At least let me do that."

Uma looks at him for a long moment. "But after that you'll go, right?"

His mouth twists in a crooked smile. "Yes. After I see you safely to the bridge I'll go."

Uma lets out a long breath. Can she trust him? No, almost definitely not. He's a Citizen. But right now he's offering and that's worth a lot when you've got nothing.

"All right," she says, abruptly. "To the bridge."

The blood rushes to his forehead.

Uma wags a finger in his face. "But after that you *will* leave—and I'll break both your legs if you think about changing your mind."

Leo bursts out laughing. "Uma, you are some serious *spicy* Mala!"

She turns to him. "You've got to promise me you'll tell nobody about this."

Leo swallows. "Okay."

Hunter leans forward. "For real. You got to make up for what you did before. That was messed up, man."

Leo holds up his hands. "Ai'ght. I did a bad thing. I swear on Paolo's life I won't let you down again." He glances out of the window. "Now you better get your little arses out of here before it gets rush hour."

Hunter nods. "Okay. But first I need just one more thing from you. I got to keep my dad chilled." He runs through a few storylines in his mind. There's no way the old man will leave him be unless he can come up with a damn good excuse . . .

Deep inside the Kossak military headquarters, an activation alarm is triggered and a monitor crawler moves into position, settling itself over Leo's network line. This Citizen has just accessed a high-security area of the Darknet, a hot spot zone for the Dreamline. The security breach is noted. This Citizen is now under surveillance.

Thirteen

In Bow favela, the armored jeep swings onto Roman Road just as the first rays of the morning sun hit the long lines of south-facing windows of the estate earthships. Screeching to a halt, the back doors of the jeep swing open and a body is pushed out onto the rutted pavement. The Kossaks are doing this all over the London favelas—dropping beaten and bruised men and women as a warning to the Outsiders. *Look what we will do to you if you mess with us.* Then the engine guns and the death wagon accelerates away, leaving behind the pungent stink of hybrid fumes. And on the road, after a long, painful moment, the body moves. A man. His fingers stretch over rough gravel, his legs bend and then with with a groan, he summons up all his strength to push himself to his knees.

Guido takes a moment to absorb the pain, wiping the sweat from his bruised forehead before hauling himself to his feet. Scarcely glancing up, he staggers across the deserted road to Ali's shisha bar, but when he gets there, there is no bar, just a gutted shell. Guido sways for a moment on the threshold. What? Lifting his heavy head, he looks along the street. The place is a mess. Vegetable plots flattened, the well filled with rubble, pigs and chickens running loose all over the street. Goddamn Kossaks. But right now he hasn't got the strength. He has to get his body stitched up, he's got to rest, but most of all he has to find out what's happened to his little cousin Uma. Rubbing his hand over his shaved head, he forces his brain to think.

A flicker of movement overhead catches his eye. Maybe it's a gato kid . . . or at least someone who can take a message. Guido takes a breath. "Hoi!" Silence in the deserted favela. It's like an old Wild West town after a shoot-out. And then he sees the boy loping sideways along a series of drainpipes.

Guido cups his bruised hand around his mouth. "Ray Ray, is that you?"

The boy slides down the final meters of pipe and comes to land on the sidewalk. His eyes grow big in his pinched face as he takes in Guido's appearance.

"Ray, where is everyone?"

The boy throws his arms wide, pointing in all different directions.

Guido nods. "You got to get me some help. Is Rose close?"

He nods quickly.

"Tell her to come now, yes?"

Ray Ray rises up, brushing the dust from his pants. Holds out his fingers to indicate time.

Guido sighs. "Thirty minutes? Okay. Be as quick as you can."

He slumps against a busted door frame. What a life. His dad, a hospital porter, was one of the first to be relocated, soon after the mayor slated the whole south side of Bow for demolition. It was the same plan all over London, all over Europe and the United States— the idea was to pull down whole projects, tower blocks, estates— and rebuild them from scratch to make them carbon zero. And so, all over London, the councils forcibly moved the people out of their homes, hundreds of thousands of them, and then started to bulldoze the old buildings. But they'd hardly even got started when the oil crisis hit. It came out of nowhere—a small dip in production, and suddenly the world went into panic mode with prices soaring like crazy. In no time there were lines at the pumps. People were thrown out of work practically overnight, and the country was on its knees in months.

Guido frowns, his gaze resting on the smashed-up solar roof panels his people had scrimped and saved so long to buy. They started to come back when the oil war broke out in Iran. Ordinary men and women like his parents who couldn't afford to live anymore, people thrown away by the harsh new government laws that were brought in to *restabilize* the economy.

The trickle soon turned into a flood after years of nothing but endless cuts, always hitting the poorest and the weakest—and anyone who thought about going on strike could forget about keeping his job. The government cut society in two, setting rich against poor—and whipped the so-called Citizens into a frenzy of anger against anyone who was different from them. That's when the ID system came in. If you had the guts to fight for your rights or protest the cuts you lost your ID. And without an ID you couldn't work. And if you didn't work there was no safety net anymore. You starved. And then the Citizens hated you even more.

And so people fighting just to put food on the table came here and built a new life. They rebuilt the zero-carbon estates, block by block. They hammered up solar panels and wind turbines and planted reed beds and brought the ground back to life, where once there were only needle-strewn dogshit parks and parking lots. They brought life and markets and music back. The Outsiders. Guido shakes his head. God knows where the Citizens think they get the right to look down on them. All cities, even London, started in mud, right?

"Guido. Can you hear me?"

His eyes flicker open. Rose bends over him, her face full of concern. "Jeez, Guido, you bin dancin' with them Kossak boys again?"

Despite himself he smiles. "Don't. Hurts."

Rose glances at his busted head. "Got to get youse somewhere's safe. Can you walk?"

"Just . . . but, Rose, I need you to do something for me." He flicks a cautious glance at her face. He doesn't want to ask her to do this, but she's all he's got right now. "I need you to try to find Uma."

Rose sucks in a sharp breath. "Wasn't she arrested with all of you?"

"Yes, then she was separated and driven with Zella to Belmarsh . . . but the prison-watchers have just got word to me that she never got out of the jeep at the other end."

Rose swallows. "Where d'you want me to look?"

"Along the Kossak security route, their jeeps always go along the river." Guido draws a breath, stretches out his hand. "Can I trust you to get a crew together? Check the river, all the bridges . . . y'know—in case . . ." He blocks his mind against the thought.

Rose slips her hand into his, her white palm disappearing in his great brown paw as he struggles to his feet. "Okay, but first I'll take you down to Harry's place on the Isle of Dogs. A bunch of us are hiding out along there."

Guido nods, and as he rises he lets out a tiny *fsssst* between gritted teeth. That's the only sign he'll show of the pain. They raise 'em tough in Bow favela.

In the Battersea Apartments kitchen, Evan Nash cuts his toast into severe triangles. He glances at his watch. Five past six. He smiles to himself, the boy deserves an early wake-up call after yesterday's stunt.

He cups his hand around his mouth. "Hunter! If I have to call you one more time I'm going to finish this bacon myself." After a long silence, Evan flings down his napkin and stomps down the corridor toward Hunter's room. Opening the door, he stares at the empty bed for a moment, then looks around the room, peering out toward the balcony. Suddenly all his anger dissolves and he takes an uncertain step backward, half stumbling as he sits heavily on Hunter's bed.

After a second he reaches over to the bedside table and picks up an antique, silver-framed photo. Hunter and his mother laughing, the boy brown as a berry, the woman caught a little off guard, her mouth a surprised O.

He remembers it so clearly; it was that hot May, the one that took everyone by surprise, and Rula had said, "Right, c'mon, we're going." "Where?" "To the beach! Quick, before we stop to think about it." That was the last year before gas prices went crazy, and you could still do stuff like that. Evan smiles, he remembers it was a hot day, his bare feet burning on the sand, but he can't feel it, the heat. He can't get the feel of warm sun on his body somehow. He frowns, catching sight of himself in Hunter's bedside mirror. A man in a suit sitting on his son's bed, trying to remember what the sun feels like. Ridiculous.

His earpiece buzzes. He glances at the number. Relief floods through him. "Hunter? Where are you?"

"Yeah, that's the thing... I'm at Leo's. He's had one of his flip-outs."

Evan narrows his eyes. Is this another line? When did Hunter get so sneaky that he has to question everything he says? Evan sighs. He's not sure what he thinks about Leo. Hunter's only known him a few years, but the two are inseparable. The boy is definitely a bad influence, a crazy ex-favelado, but on the other hand he's got something, a spark, something that Hunter comes alive to. Something that was missing for a long time.

Evan glances at his watch. "Look, Hunter, is it serious? If it is— well, I can't take him to hospital like last time; work is ringing off the hook after this reactor thing."

"No, Dad, I reckon he'll be cool if I stay with him a bit."

Evan taps his teeth. "Put Leo on for me. I want to talk to him myself."

In Leo's bedroom, Hunter's eyes widen. "Ah, Dad, you don't need to—"

"Just do it. I want to hear how serious it is from him."

"Okay."

Hunter flicks his RET to speaker before turning to Leo and bugging his eyes out, spasming his neck in sharp jerks from behind the lens.

Leo smothers a laugh. Hunter flicks him on the ear, mouths, *I'm serious.*

Leo's voice becomes faint. "Yeh, Mr. Nash? Oh yes, it was pretty bad but I'm restin' up now." Pause.

"Nah, it's not a hospital thing." Pause.

"I know it's a serious thing." Pause.

"Yes, I'm takin' the medicine. And I'm gonna spend the day in bed." Leo pats the mattress, winks at Uma. She rolls her eyes.

"Yessir. I will most def call you if I feel any badder. My brother's not back for a day or two . . . so thanks for letting Hunter stay." Pause.

"No, sir, I will not let him out of my sight—I'm keeping him rooted right here. I know how you feel 'bout the Kossak raids. Bye." Leo disconnects before dropping into a deep bow. "And the Oscar goes to Leo da Silva for his breathtaking performance in Epilepsy, the Bitter Truth."

Hunter blows his cheeks out. "Cheers. Thought he wasn't going to go for it at first."

Back in the bedroom, Evan gazes around his son's room, the early morning sunlight spilling in from the hallway window. The apartment seems suddenly so quiet, so empty.

Gray morning light creeps under a concrete underpass in the Isle of Dogs, barely illuminating the tunnel beneath. Rose leans against a wall as she waits for the Kossak patrol to pass. As soon as the jeep taillights disappear around the corner, she springs up, gesturing for the group to come out of the shadows. Not that they need any telling how to take care of themselves. Outsider in their blood, the best, the strongest, the quickest kids she could round up in the short time. The oldest maybe eighteen, the youngest no more than ten.

She scans their faces. "So, we'll split into four groups, yeah? Wu, you take the Bow Cru down to the Southbank. Little Fats and Joe, you go farther southside, down Shad Thames way, ai'ght?" She jerks her thumb toward a boy in a panama hat, cocked at an angle. "Pepe, you lot range over the Isle of Dogs—and me and the Kray

Brudders here'll take the north side from Westminster, all the way up to the Tower and Wapping."

Pepe tips his hat and Little Fats bends to tighten his trainer laces, his muscles bulging as he reaches down. "But, Rose, what if the Kossaks have her? What did Guido say to do then? Fight for her?"

"If you're outnumbered, then follow her, report home for backup. But, Fats, if you think you can win, then fight for sure."

The boy's mouth curls upward into a grin. He fingers the huge lump of jade on his gold chain. "If Guan Yin wills it, I'll take the whole lot of 'em on."

Rose holds up her hand. "Oh, and another thing. Today we go dark. No implants, no Dreamline, no nothing. Guido says it's too dangerous in these raids."

Pepe explodes. "What? That's insane. What them Kossaks so mad about?"

Rose shrugs. "Nuclear reactor down. They been waiting ten years for that dirty juice to come online. And now it's gone and London's in trouble again. Gotta blame someone."

"But we din't do it, I reckon."

"No, me neither. But tha's not our thing today. Today is Uma. We find her, we bring her back. Got it?"

And with that the circle shatters, each group flying in a different direction, leaving the patch of concrete under the flyover empty; the only thing left, a blue plastic bag that spirals and flutters up against the graffitied walls. From a distant rooftop, a sniper catches the flicker of movement, but by the time he's raised his gunsight to his eye even the bag is gone, lifted high above the favela by the cold east wind.

Fourteen

Closing in on Westminster Bridge, Uma grips the rear scooter bars tight as Hunter banks into a low curve. They are nearly level with the golden statue of Lord Shiva, who stands guard over the southern bank of the river. Ahead, one lane is closed, the Kossaks waving every suspicious vehicle over to the cordoned area. Uma's chest tightens, but for once, she's invisible, strapped into her helmet, looking for all the world like a Sleeper princess, riding with her Tech Class 1 boyfriend. She's the perfect Citizen. The girl she'll never be. The officers scarcely even glance their way. *What a life.* Uma flicks the helmet RET function on and Westminster recedes behind the fine mesh of the 家. Wind speed, temperature, contacts, friends, meetings, shops, people's IDs, CCTV footage, bars, credit scores, second-life info…you name it, it's all here right in front of her.

She can't help but grin. So this is what it's like, to be on the privileged inside. Pretty, yeah, very pretty. The Dreamline is spartan by comparison, although it's much…deeper somehow. She looks up at the Houses of Parliament. A gigantic sunflower hologram grows, unfolds, blooms and fades over Big Ben with the latest government slogan glowing underneath—*We're All in This Together*—Uma's grin widens. What a bunch of jokers.

Hunter feels the sway of her supple body behind him. Why won't she put her arms around him? He drops the scooter handles even lower as he accelerates past the Shiva shrine—that's got to make her come close—but all he feels is a slight tensing of her thighs on the seat behind him. Damn. And as he comes out of the curve, he catches a glimpse of the golden eyes of the god, immutable. But the mouth...is that a smile on Shiva's face? Hunter twists the throttle, spurting him forward through the crowd of bikes jockeying for position on the road ahead.

As they fly down the Embankment, the river rolling dull silver on their right flank, Uma sees yet another roadblock up ahead, but this time it looks as if the police are stopping *all* the traffic on the exit to Blackfriars Bridge. She taps Hunter on the shoulder and he nods, peeling off away to the outside lane before cutting down a side street and bringing the bike to a stop in a tiny alleyway.

Uma studies her RET for a second. "Good. I can cross the highway here and cut down left to Blackfriars Bridge along the Thames path."

Taking the helmet off, she shakes her head. "Shame I can't keep this thing."

Hunter opens his eyes wide. "No! It's Sleeper technology. Evil!"

Uma shoves the helmet in his chest. "Don't be an idiot. Anyway, thanks for the ride, but I got it from here."

Chest hot, Hunter watches as she stalks gracefully down the street. Is he going to run after her? Oh, man, he can't, it's too—he watches the bikes and scooters fly past on the main road—and then suddenly he's running, dodging the traffic like a madman, struggling to catch up with her.

"We said the bridge!"

Uma half smiles, but keeps walking, and they move on in silence, until rounding a bend in the path, suddenly the red pillars of the bridge loom up ahead.

Hunter pauses, shading his eyes. "According to Leo we're to look out for a ladder on the Embankment wall just before the bridge."

Uma points. "I see it...to the side of the first arch."

They break into a run. Hunter gets there first by a few seconds, and leaning over the edge of the Embankment wall, he peers down-ward. The ladder rungs lead down to the river, disappearing into the water about three meters below.

"There's something down there, maybe a hole..."

Uma clambers over, descending with quick steps. Behind her, Hunter hesitates, staring blindly at the brown swell of water, before he swings his leg over on to the first rung, joining her just above the waves. Peering downward all he can see is the top half of a wide circular hole, fenced off by an iron grille.

Uma bends as low as the slapping waves will allow. "This is definitely the mouth of the Fleet, right?"

Hunter scans the Embankment wall. "Got to be. The RET info said the Fleet flows into the river directly from a tunnel next to the Thameslink exit to the station—and that's here. The trouble is the river's too high."

Uma frowns. "There's got to be something here. Or I'm finished."

There's nothing for it; to see properly she's going to have to climb on to the iron grille. Jumping sideways from the ladder, she lands on the lowest bar, her fingers gripping tight on the lat-ticed metal. She squints into the dark tunnel mouth. "Wait. There's something—look—on the right side, near the top."

On the ladder, Hunter clambers down to the bottom rung and twists his body to the farthest extent of his reach. She's right; there is something there. Set back high up on the curved concrete is an image of a small red dragon, perfectly sprayed on the stained concrete.

Hunter gasps—the arch of the back, the tail twisting around the body, the familiar curving flame—he recognizes it immediately. Every Londoner knows this. "But that's—"

"—The logo for the Dragon Karaoke Palace. I know."

"What does that mean?"

Uma shakes her head. "I don't know."

"You don't know? This doesn't mean something, y'know...to Outsiders?"

"Nope. Means the same to you as to me. A massive twenty-four-seven karaoke bar in Leicester Square."

"So now what are we going to do?"

"No, what am *I* going to do. You promised."

Hunter glances at her. Ah no, there's a hard look to her eyes that he knows he's not going to be able to defeat this time.

He clears his throat. "I know, but I thought I'd be leaving you . . . y'know, with a plan. This thing doesn't mean—"

"Hunter. You've got to listen to me. There is no safe, not for me. And you can't help. This isn't your thing."

He juts out his jaw. "What if I make it my thing?"

Uma gazes at the bridge, at a train rolling across the river. It's only her. Zella may be dead, and she ordered her to find the Keeper and tell no one. Uma pats her jacket for the thousandth time, feels the small heavy shape inside. She looks at Hunter. This boy, there's something real about him, something she can trust. But trust is a luxury she can't afford. Uma injects a harsh note into her voice. "Oh, and I thought you were different. But in the end you're just like all the other Sleepers. Always going back on your word."

Hunter's heart twists. She's not backing down this time. He's going to have to get on his bike and go home. He tries one last time. "But is this it? I mean, we can't ever see each other again?"

"I don't know. Maybe, when this is all over." Uma reaches forward, touches his cheek. "But thanks. I really mean it."

Hunter is drawn forward, closer, as if magnetized. All he can see is *her*, her face, her eyes, her lips. And then out of the corner of his eye—a flash of movement—a blinding flash of pain in his head—and suddenly everything goes black. His hands lose their grip on the ladder and he falls, a dead weight plunging into the river below. Uma stares down, frozen, and for a second she clings to the grille, too shocked to move. What just happened? Was he shot? Heart pounding, she scans the bridge, the Embankment walls, urgently trying to make out who did this. She has to get out of here. She's a target. But she can't just leave him in the river.

"Hoi, Uma!"

Her head twists round. The voice comes from the direction of the bridge.

"Uma!"

And then she sees her. Rose standing above the central arch, waving her arms.

"Stay where youse are. I'm comin' over."

But Uma is already in the water, swimming with long strokes toward Hunter's lifeless body.

Hunter suddenly comes back to consciousness as the rushing cold water drags him down once again, sucking him under, twisting him in circles. He can't breathe, he's sinking...And then somehow he's back on the surface, sucking in a raw, ragged breath as the waves slap his face. A voice calls his name. But he can't react, he can't understand what to do. He dips under the surface again. He can see his own body twisting, his arms and legs working frantically against the current, but he can't seem to take control. Then suddenly there are hands reaching for him. Uma! He turns, blind, splashes out his arms to grab her, but misses and is swept away.

Thrashing, gulping down water, he starts to go under again, but this time, as his body descends yet again, a feeling of peace envelops him; it's like he's an observer, watching his own body roll in the water. He relaxes his limbs and for a moment, he drifts on the tide, caught in this beautiful feeling. Then his survival instinct cuts in again. No! Fight!

Uma's voice comes again. "Hunter! Where are you?"

He forces himself to the surface once more and this time he turns against the current, kicking furiously, clawing at the heavy wall of water.

From her vantage point on Blackfriars Bridge, Rose can see the struggle all too clearly. The boy and Uma are both being swept toward the whirlpools under the central arch. They've got to be stopped. Sighing, Rose slots her crossbow into her belt. Then she lets go of the metal scaffolding and, leaping into the river, she lands only a few meters away from them. Surfacing quickly in the brown swirl, she turns. Hunter is clawing, dragging at Uma's throat and chest, while she desperately tries to break his hold, but to no end, he won't let go, he's gripped by pure fear.

Setting off with powerful strokes, Rose brings herself alongside and pulls out her crossbow, reversing it so the handle is foremost. Then she lifts her arm high and lands a stunning blow to Hunter's skull, just behind his ear. His body immediately goes limp. Rose grabs the boy's inert body as it begins to sink. Then she turns, takes in Uma's shocked face. "Can you make it to shore by yourself?"

Uma wipes her hair out of her eyes, nods.

"Sure?"

"Yeah. Go."

Rose points toward the Embankment. "C'mon then, let's go back to the north bank. There's a wooden pier there where we can drag this eejit out of the water."

Over in the Isle of Dogs, Guido sits in Harry's terraced house, a cup of steaming dhal in front of him, as the old man tends to his wounds. He shifts in his seat, staring out through the broken wall toward the Thames. "So what news does the river bring you today, father?"

Harry dips a cloth into a bowl, glances out of the window with clear blue eyes. "Today and every day. He is an old, old thing, this river. He carved a path out for himself thirty million years ago." Harry sits back on his heels, his frayed slippers slipping slightly on the crooked tiles. "Ah, he was a tropical river then, flowing straight into the Rhine, fringed with palms and citrus. Crocodiles and turtles swam in his depths. It wasn't till much later that people came."

Guido shifts slightly in his seat. "Yes, but is there any news *today*? I mean, about what the Kossaks plan to do to us? They are using this nuclear breach to wipe us out, father. They want their London clean of Outsiders."

Harry shakes his head. "All of this death. The river, the land was here long before people came to work it, to call it their own. *London.* But it belongs to itself, not to us. We've made it many things: a road, a boundary, an attack route, a playground, and a cesspool. But in truth, the land and the river made us."

Guido sighs. It's all very well old Harry being mystical, but where's Uma?

Fifteen

On the pier, Rose crouches on the lower step and scans the river-bank as Uma drags the boy into a sitting position on the wooden boards. She lets out a breath. No Kossaks in sight, at least not for now.

"Y'know this boy then?"

"Yeah. His name's Hunter. He's been... helping me."

"Some help. The bugger nearly drownded you."

"After you knocked him out with your crossbow. What did you do that for? You could've killed him."

"I din't know he was all right. He was kinda leaning over you, bit menacing, like. So I shot. Like a Kossak. *Shoot first, ask later.* Anyways I used a blunt dart, I wasn't meaning to kill." Rose leans forward, clicks her fingers in Hunter's face. "Can you hear me, mate?"

He gives a faint nod.

Rose holds up two fingers. "How many fingers I got here in fron' of youse?"

"Two."

"Where you live?"

Hunter's head is swimming, but he tries to stop his teeth chattering, to keep his voice clear. "Apartment 1028, Battersea... Power Apartments..."

She sucks in a breath. "A Citizen? Ah jeez, Uma. With all that's goin' on, you got to go and pick up a Sleeper!"

Uma frowns. "He was just about to go. . . . Look, just leave it, it's been a long, long night."

Rose glances at her friend. "I know. We're all out searching for youse. Guido's orders."

Uma's heart lifts. "Guido? Is he free?"

"Aye. Pretty beat up, but he'll live. The Kossaks dropped him along with a bunch of other beat-up prisoners back in the favela."

"And Zella?"

"Not back when I left."

Uma closes her eyes. She's got to keep it together. Rose scans her gray face, the dark circles under her eyes. "C'mon, girl. Let's get you to Guido, you look like you need some sleep." She turns back to Hunter. "You all right now, feller? Jus' rest up here for a while, then get yourself home, right?"

But Hunter doesn't answer. The dull ache in his head has suddenly transformed into a searing pain, ripping at his eyes. His stomach heaves. Rolling onto his side, he pukes up a great jet of river water across the wooden planks of the pier. Uma bends over him, her face full of concern.

"I—I can't leave him like this. I want Harry to look at him. This is the second time he's been punched out in two days. Most likely he's got a concussion."

Rose shakes her head. "You've got to leave him. There's no way I'm taking this boy back with us."

"Then I'll do it myself."

"You can't. Not today. Not unless you're jumping high. There's roadblocks everywhere."

Uma smiles. "Ah, but today I've got a Sleeper secret weapon. Tech Class 1 ID and a scooter."

Rose's eyes widen. "You'll not bring him to our place. Guido'll kill yer."

"I can't take him back to *his*. Not like this. His dad's out at work all day."

"Well, what about a friend, then?"

An image of Leo comes to Uma's mind. "No way."

"Then drop him at a hospital. Though it'll be tough enough to get him through the security. You'd have to dump him at the entrance."

"I'm not doing that."

"Uma, listen. He's"—Rose's voice drops to a hiss—"not our problem. We got enough going on as it is."

"She's right." Hunter pulls himself up on to his elbows. "Jus' need to rest a minute. You should get going." He tries to smile.

Uma looks at him closely, sees how he tries to cover his pain. She can't have another death, another bad thing on her conscience today. "I'm doing this, Rose. I got to make sure he's okay. He helped me. It's our way."

Rose knows this expression on Uma's face. She's like Zella. Once her mind is set, it's set. She releases a jet of spit from a gap in her front teeth. "Well, fine, then. You know where we are, in Harry's old house in Mudchute. Aye? An' you better get there in one big piece or I'm gonna get a beatin'."

Uma grins. "I'll be there before you. As long as I can get this boy to sit upright on a bike. You can do that, right, Hunter?"

He nods, euphoria spreading through him despite the pain hammering in his temples. Somehow, he's still in the game.

A quarter of a mile away, on the north bank of the river, Evan paces in his City Hall office. It's not even properly light yet, and he's talking to four people at once. Four people who want solutions *now*. A hospital generator down, the Northern Line closed and the refrigerators out at New Billingsgate Market with ten tons of fish rotting on the slabs. And the questions are always the same. What's he going to do about it? When's he going to get the power back on?

For the tenth time in as many minutes, he glances at his watch. When did time start going by so quick? It feels like he's always playing catch-up, never getting the chance to slow down, take stock, *breathe*. Maybe those Outsiders have got the right idea. I mean, that dock in the Isle of Dogs they've turned into a tide generator. What do they call it? Ah yes, the Royal Docks Wadi—now *that* never packs up. Those people are the masters of microgeneration. In fact, the only place he never gets called out to is the favela. They haven't got a pot to piss in, but somehow they've got themselves sorted out.

He checks his watch again. What's that Hunter up to...has he left Leo's place yet? That crazy Brazilian is a bad influence all right. *A bad influence.* Evan shakes his head with a rueful smile. He's turning into such an old man.

"Mr. Nash!" A grounds worker stands at the door, fluorescent jacket on.

"Eh?"

"We've got to go."

"Yes. Right."

Evan slowly reaches under the desk for his work shoes.

"You all right, sir?" The assistant frowns.

"Yes. Of course. Why wouldn't I be?" Evan bends down slowly, dragging on a heavy waterproof boot—and suddenly bursts out laughing. When he was Hunter's age he wouldn't be seen dead in anything except patent leather Winklepickers. How the mighty have fallen.

Hunter and Uma leave the river behind them as they make their slow way across the busy traffic, heading back to the parked scooter. Hunter tries to keep up as they dodge across the lanes, but he's shivering badly. It's not the pain anymore; that's easing off. It's the images, the pictures that are flooding into his mind.

Uma tightens her grip on his arm as they reach the far sidewalk. "Come on...Nearly there."

"I-I can't go on."

Uma ducks her head as a Kossak van rolls by. "Just a bit farther, we're nearly at the bike." Hunter nods, forcing himself to move forward, but as soon as they reach the alley, he sinks to the ground.

Uma's face clouds. "Is your head so bad? Maybe I need to get you to a hospital after all."

"No."

"But you're really shaking."

Hunter grips his arms, fingers digging into the flesh.

"Hunter, talk to me."

He tries to clamp his teeth shut on the images, the words inside him. "Look, you don't understand—it's the water—I don't go in the water, ever—"

"No kidding." Uma smiles. "You were pulling me under till Rose decked you."

But Hunter doesn't smile back. He clenches the flesh on his arm, gives a vicious twist, but feels nothing. The words are pushing up, past his chest, his throat, he clenches his jaw muscles, shuts his eyes, trying to block it all out. But he can't do it. "It's not that—I *can* swim—but . . . it's my mum. It's because of her I don't go in. She . . . drowned, you see . . ." He speaks without shifting his position, without looking up at her.

For a long time Uma is silent; and in that moment, he imagines her, almost hears her coming close, wrapping her arms around him. Uma sinks to the ground beside him. She doesn't have any words. She suddenly remembers what it's like, the loss, the longing that you can't fill—and for the first time in years, she feels her eyes prickle with tears. Laying her hand on his trembling arm, she sits beside him in silence.

Hunter sucks in a deep breath, trying desperately to calm his booming heart. He's never told anyone about his mother before, never actually said the words. *She drowned.* Either people know or they don't. It feels . . . strange. He looks down at Uma's hand. It suddenly strikes him that he knows nothing about her.

"What about your parents? I mean you've been out all night . . . won't they be mad? Ever since my mum, my dad goes nuts if he doesn't know where I am for more than two hours."

Uma forces her voice to be calm. "My father died when I was very young. Shot in the trade union protests when the first cuts came in."

"Oh."

She shrugs. "It was a long time ago."

She bites back the break in her voice. This is what she always says to people when they ask. She's said it so often she almost believes it.

"And your mum?"

"She's in prison."

Hunter's eyes widen. "When did you last see her?"

"About nine months ago. They don't give much access, not for political prisoners."

Silence falls between them. Then Uma frowns. "What's he like?"

"Who?"

"Your dad."

Hunter thinks. What is he like? "Well, he's out at work mostly."

"But when he's not?"

He flicks through a sequence of images. That's strange, he can't fully focus, get a fix. "I mean he's all right, he's a laugh sometimes, or well he . . ." He falters.

"What?"

"Used to be. Before Mum. Now he's more . . ." Hunter searches for the right word, in the end murmuring, "Quiet." But really he means numb. Him too, for a long time. But at least he's trying to fight his way out, not like his dad. The man's been on autopilot for years and there's nothing he can do about it. Hunter picks up a plastic bottle top, twirls it in his fingers.

"That's got to be hard for you, I mean both your mum and dad—"

Uma shakes her head. "Plenty of people in the favela have been through much worse. I'm one of the lucky ones." She suddenly clambers to her feet, cutting off any more questions. What's she doing talking about this stuff with this boy? She never talks about it with *anyone*, never mind a Citizen who hasn't the faintest idea what it's like in there.

Hunter flattens the bottle top in his hand, a sudden irrational anger flaring up inside him. She's so calm, so distant, been through so much more than him. He feels stupid, weak for telling her. No matter what his story is, this girl's always got one to rival it. Got a distant father? *Try a dead one.* Got a dead mother? *Mine's in prison.* He plants his hands on the concrete, levers himself up, furious.

"Look. I'll be on my way. Don't want to hold you up. . . . You've got to get yourself down to the Dragon Palace, fast as you can."

Uma glances at him in surprise. "Yes, but I'm taking you to Harry's first."

"No need. I can make it home myself."

She frowns. What's with this boy now? His eyes have gone all strange. "No, you can't. You've got a bruise like a tennis ball on the side of your head. You need to get it checked out."

He faces her, mouth thin. "Then I'm driving."

"Hunter, you've just been knocked out cold."

"I know. By your friend Rose. C'mon, Uma. I got my pride."

Uma looks at his pale face. He's in no fit state to drive, but if she says no then he might leave. A strange desire, to not let him go, to keep him close for a little longer, steals over her.

"Hunter, if it helps, Rose *is* the Bow favela arm-wrestling champion. I've seen her grind grown men into dust."

A beat and then he smiles. A thrill jags through Uma. She's done it, she's changed his mood. He's not going to leave, not quite yet. Hunter crosses to the bike and activates the starter. The engine bursts into life.

"It doesn't."

"What?"

"Help."

Uma climbs behind him, and this time, when Hunter turns the scooter on to the main road, she allows herself to lean toward him. Just a little.

Up in his bedroom, Leo lies on the scruffy mattress, a gentle stream of light falling onto his retina from his RETScan. With his brother away on the wind rigs off Scotland and what's left of his family back in Brazil, truly the 家 is Leo's family. He doesn't mind. It's better this way. No one telling you to clean your room, what time to go to bed, no one bugging you about where you're going, where you've been. Leo sighs, yeh, this life is definitely better. All the laughs, the information, the games, and the friends you need when you want them.

But that girl has gotten him all nostalgic about the favela. Just seeing her has brought it all back. He's spent so long cussing his old life, adapting to being a Citizen, that he's almost forgotten about the good stuff, the sweet woodsmoke and the smell of rain on hot streets...and the *closeness*. On his old street in the Streatham favela everyone looked out for each other, they shared everything...what little they had. And they had so much freedom, too. Much more than wimped-out Sleeper kids. And the parties! Leo grins. Favelados, they know how to party in style.

He draws his foot away from the sun into a patch of shade cast by the ratty sheet hanging over his bedroom window. He wills himself into sleep, but he knows it'll do no good. He hardly sleeps at all these days. He glances at the wall clock, wonders about maybe going down to the 家 Bar, maybe hunt a few of his all-nighter buddies up to play a game or two.

But despite himself, his eyelids start to flutter as a softly modulated female voice fills his earpiece, narrating over the sequence of old movies, drawings, black-and-white photos that he's just called up.

The voice is telling him about the buried rivers of London. The Fleet, Wallbrook, Tyburn, Westbourne, Peck, Neckinger, Effra, Falconbrook, Moselle, Langbourne. Rivers that used to shine and shimmer, feeding pure wells, flowing free alongside us, but now reduced to shadow status. And the Thames, the daddy of them all. Nobody knows the origin of the name for sure, maybe it comes from the Celtic word *tam*, meaning smooth, and *isa*, running water. But the name could be much more ancient, springing from languages of the lost Indo-European cultures that spread across the world long ago. Hundreds of thousands of years of human history, a long, long love affair with the natural world, gone, forgotten, turned into stinking sewage and buried under brick. All in the name of progress.

In the listening post deep in the bowels of the Kossak HQ in Vauxhall, the crawler assigned to Leo's case once again activates, logging the date, time, and access code of the Citizen under surveillance. Another illicit search, another dangerous area. What Citizen would search out the ancient buried rivers of London?

Sixteen

As soon as Hunter cuts past the last skyscraper of Canary Wharf, the road beneath his scooter wheels begins to disintegrate. A few minutes later he and Uma drive into the Isle of Dogs proper, threading their way slowly through the crowded heart of the favela toward Mudchute. Hunter grips the bars tight as he negotiates a series of deep ruts, narrowly avoiding a rolling dogfight that breaks out across the street. Behind him, Uma watches the tense faces around her. Why's it so packed? Then it hits her. All these people must have fled here from the raids. She narrows her eyes. How can they do this to her friends, her people? Even if they did shut down the reactor, this is too brutal.

Twenty minutes later, Hunter turns on to a derelict street of houses bordering the Thames, and as he swerves to avoid a giant pothole, a dog suddenly darts out and rushes up to the bike, snarling.

Uma's hands dig into him. "Lyuba! Stop, Hunter, we're here."

He pulls over, and Uma jumps off, rolling the dog onto the sidewalk in a wild caress. But Hunter sits for a moment, taking it all in. He's never truly been inside the favela before. So strange; it's so clear from here where the privileged Citizen areas are, rising up like fortresses out of the city—shining tower blocks, polished windows, wind turbines, solar-paneled roofs.

The city is so divided. Like a medieval stronghold with rich ID elites blockading themselves behind their gated communities, while the favelados starve outside the walls. No, that's not true either, most Citizens are struggling to get by too. It's *his* world, the 2 percent, who live in luxury. The rest of the people are screwed, Citizens or not. A flush steals across his cheek.

"Hunt, you coming?"

He pulls himself to with a start. Quickly he pulls off his helmet and gulps a sudden, surprised breath—the scent of frying fish and grilled corn hangs heavy in the air. He's never smelt anything so good, it almost makes him forget his pounding head for a moment.

He glances at Uma. "Is it always like this?"

She smiles. "Is this your first time in the favela? Thought you were a jumping pro."

"Well, no, I've only ever been on the edges."

Uma digs him in the ribs. "Rich-boy slummer."

A head emerges from a bedroom window above. "Uma, girl. 'Sthat you?"

She glances up, shading her eyes, "Yes, Mr. Ali!"

The old man leans far out of the windowless frame, cups his hands round his mouth.

"Allahu Akbar! Here's Uma! Our girl is home to us!"

The cry is taken up along the street and a gang of kids come flying over from the corner, but they stop short when they see Hunter, drawing back in suspicious silence. Then a solid, beefy-looking young man jumps down from a nearby roof, his boots sliding on gravel as he lands.

"Who's this, then?"

Uma glances over. "Chill, Little Fats. He won't bite."

His lip curls. "I ain't shook."

Uma rolls her eyes. "D'you know where Guido is?"

Fats jerks his thumb behind him, his eyes never leaving Hunter's face. "He's at Harry's place. Number thirty-three, innit?"

"Cheers."

"He sent us out lookin' for you earlier, y'know that?"

"I do. I saw Rose."

"Yeh, I just run into her. . . . She told us to stop lookin', that she'd found yer . . . down by Blackfriars . . . with a Sleeper."

"Yeah, this is Hunter."

Fats scowls, flicks some dust from his pinstripe sleeve.

Uma turns. "Look, I've got to see Guido now, but thanks for searching for me."

She sets off along the sidewalk, Lyuba trotting by her side, and Hunter goes to follow, but Little Fats suddenly blocks his way. For a long beat they stand face to face, the chill favela wind spinning grit in the air around them.

Uma glances over her shoulder. "Oh, leave it, Fats."

The boy fingers the heavy gold chain around his neck, his face set solid like a breeze block.

"Fats, I mean it. He's with me."

He sticks a finger in Hunter's face. "Just make sure you stay with her, Sleeper. I find you on your own and—"

Hunter scowls. "What?"

But with a flicked glance toward Uma, Fats turns away. Hunter watches him jog down the street toward the gang on the corner. His heart sinks. What is he doing here? If he was a favelado he'd probably feel the same way. He crosses the road, catching up with Uma as she nears a row of terraced houses set hard against the river.

Hunter shakes his head. "I know Rose told Fats I was a Citizen, but it's like my ID is burnt into my forehead. Am I so different?"

She shrugs. "Well, we pretty much know all the people round here."

"You can't know everyone in London. There must be thousands of you."

"Yeah, there are. But it's kind of like a big tribe. I mean, I can travel all over the city and be safe. Outsiders have all got one another's backs."

"But I could be an Outsider from another city, another country, right?"

Uma bites her lip. Not in a million years could Hunter be taken for one of them. He hasn't got that look in his eye. He's not *driven*, *wild* enough. Reaching a battered red door she pauses, looking up at the collapsed front wall.

"We're here."

Hunter's eyes widen. "This place is a wreck."

"Snob." Uma walks up to the front door, kicking off her sneakers at the entrance.

"I'm just saying—"

But she has swept aside the heavy fabric hanging over the door frame and disappeared inside. Hunter stands on the step for a moment, looking back down the road. The gang is gathered around Little Fats, looking in his direction with a long, menacing, cold glare.

Hunter pushes the door open and as he steps inside the hallway, it's like he's walked into another world. The walls are crowded with swords, their blades bent back in the Roman style—and above the living-room door, three human skulls guard the entrance to the room. From inside he hears a sudden cry.

"Uma!"

Hunter goes to the doorway and sees a shaven-headed young man struggling to rise to his feet, a flash of joy jolting across his dark, bruised face. By his side Uma gasps, her hands flying to her mouth.

"Oh, Guido! What have they done to you?"

The man waves her aside. "Ah, it's nothing. I spent the night in the cells, but they let me go without charge this morning. I knew you were split from Zella, so as soon as I got back I sent crews searching out wide for you."

"I know. I saw Rose."

Guido frowns. "Ah, good. Did you come back with her?"

Uma motions for Hunter to enter. "No...I came with him."

Hunter takes a hesitant step into the room. Guido switches his gaze toward him for the first time.

His dark brows draw down. "Who are you?"

"He's—"

Guido chops the air. "He has a tongue, no?"

Hunter grips his scooter helmet. "Hunter Nash...sir."

"*Sir?*" The dark eyes are very black now. "Are you a Citizen?"

"Yes."

Guido whirls around to face Uma. "Have you lost your mind, girl?"

"He hurt his head really bad; he was trying to help me...and so I wanted to bring him to Harry."

His eyes bore into hers. "We are fighting for our lives. And you bring a Sleeper here? To a secret place?"

A strand of hair drops in front of Uma's eyes as she lowers her head, never breaking eye contact with her cousin. "He helped me. And so I help him now that he needs me. It's our way."

"That's not for Sleepers. They have no...respect for us. Look at what they've done in Bow favela this last day. And *Zella*—"

Uma's voice starts to tremble. "Don't tell me what I can and can't do. He is my guest—"

Hunter's fingers whiten around the helmet rim. He should go. It hits him what a massive risk Uma took to bring him here, to help him.

The room falls deathly quiet. And then, suddenly a tiny, frail old man bursts into the room, a delicious, spicy smell coming from the dish he carries. Harry nods toward the table in the corner.

"Clear a space over there, please! We are all here at last!" He plonks the dish down on the table and then, seeing Hunter, he runs his expert eyes over the boy's face. "You are also hurt, my son."

Uma nods. "Yes, I brought him to you, father."

"I will tend him, then."

Guido shakes his head. "No, Harry, he'll not stay here a minute longer!"

Harry bursts out laughing. "Come, Guido. Eat. Men always growl on an empty belly. Fill yourself, and after smoke...your mind will be more clear. And look here is Uma, she is safe!"

Guido's brows lift a little. But he has not stayed alive for so long, or led the battle for survival so well, by letting his guard down. He gives Hunter a long, searching look. Hunter returns his gaze. Guido's is not the kind of face you see so much in his world. It's a face that's seen things. Scarred, swollen, with the same dark eyes as Uma's, the same fire.

Guido sighs, flicks a glance at Harry. "I am not hungry. But let them eat and then tend to the boy." He shakes a finger at Uma. "And then we must talk. I'll be upstairs."

Twenty minutes later, Uma licks the last red smear of the spicy fish curry off her fingers as Harry looks on. He leans forward, dipping a spoon in the dish.

"More?"

Uma groans. "No! Not another thing."

Harry turns to Hunter. "You, boy?"

He shakes his head. "No, thanks." He's starting to feel sick again, his head firing fresh waves of pain down through his spine, into his guts.

Harry nods. "Then come, I will look to your head."

Hunter looks down. "Nah, I'm fine."

The old man smiles, points upstairs. "Then I won't take long."

There's something about the gentle way he speaks, a kind of hidden power, there's no way Hunter can refuse. Uma nods for him to follow, and a minute later he finds himself sitting on a thick blanket in an upstairs room while Harry bends over him, examining the swelling on his right temple with gentle fingers.

"Hmm, you have a tough head, son. Hard like a big stone. But still it's not good to rattle the brains like this."

"I didn't exactly have a choice."

Harry gives him a sideways look. "If you say so." And then he turns, fingers searching along a row of jars that line a low shelf beside him.

Hunter blinks. What's this old geezer saying, that he wanted to get into trouble, that he wanted to get knocked out and nearly drowned? Fat chance. But he says nothing; it's too weird here, too otherworldly. Harry lights a bunch of herbs inside a brass holder, then reaches for a pinch of something from another jar, mixing it with the contents of the first before starting to grind the mixture in a stone bowl. As he works he sings a soft, almost inaudible song, aromatic smoke rising around him.

Hunter watches closely as he works the mixture into a paste. "What's that?"

"For your head. These are all good herbs gathered from along the river."

"The Thames?"

A clear glance. "Of course yes, plenty growing there if you have the eyes to see. For many, many thousands of years we've been healing ourselves this way."

"Who has?"

"Us."

"But I thought you were...I mean, the Outsiders...you've only been here a short time...since the crisis and the evacuated estates."

Harry cocks his head and smiles, revealing a set of beautiful white teeth. "The Outsiders are many different people drawn together in one goal. But we are all ordinary people, thrown out of work, struggling to get by, sick of politicians' false promises, but all united under a common cause—to fight the mad regime, to build a new world before it's too late."

Hunter frowns. "The way you talk it's like all Citizens are the enemy, that we're doing nothing. We don't all agree with the sick things this government does in the favelas. And we're not just sitting by and doing nothing either...my dad is working twenty-four-seven to fix up the energy gap, to get past oil."

Harry frowns as he adds some drops of oil to the paste. "I am sure your father is a good man, but it is not enough to patch up the system. We must live differently. Here we fix things ourselves, grow things ourselves, make things ourselves, and by doing this we have made ourselves strong again."

Hunter snorts. "So basically, your plan is for us to give everything up and go back to living in caves again? No way."

Harry's face splits into a grin. "No caves for us. Outsiders are masters of technology. But that's just it; we're *masters*, not slaves. We use it to bring us together, not to make us stupid and separate like you do." The old man taps Hunter's chest lightly. "And tell me, son, what is it that you are so afraid of giving up? Working seventy hours a week, half dead, your senses dulled by virtual reality, afraid to speak your mind for fear of losing your ID status…what's worth keeping in that life?"

Hunter leans back against the wall. "You only say that because you don't have anything."

Harry bursts out laughing and strikes his own chest a solid blow. "It's true I'm poor in terms of possessions, but I'm a free man. It's wonderful, Hunter, to own yourself and your thoughts and feelings. This favela life, it's addictive. Once you are here, you cannot go back…and soon you'd rather die than trade your freedom for possessions. Ach—they fill men with fear, and the more they have, the more they are filled with fear."

"My friend Leo, he says loads of the favelados hate you—"

"That's only because we won't submit to their gang laws. We are our own people. We want no part of drugs and violence."

Hunter shifts, restless. "But—"

Harry raises his finger to his lips. "Come, you must hush now. I cannot heal you if you keep on asking questions. You Younger Brothers are forever chitter-chattering." He begins to sing a gentle song, a whisper almost, over the bowl, before dipping a red cloth inside and raising it to Hunter's temple.

As soon as he feels the cool paste on his skin, Hunter experiences a tingling, a wave of energy spiraling outward, spreading through his head and along his neck and spine. His chest rises, it feels like a great weight has been lifted and his eyes close in relief.

Harry pauses for a moment, gazing down at the boy's face. He nods. There's something about this one. A glint, a fire, something that can't be taught. A willingness to go all the way.

Seventeen

Hunter wakes with a start. Harry is gone, leaving only a faint scent of incense lingering in the air. How long has he been asleep for? Struggling upright, he runs his hand over his head. It's amazing, but the pain is gone; all he's left with is a dull ache in his shoulders. He stretches. Through the patched-up window he can make out a Kossak chopper hovering in the distance. When will these raids stop? What are they looking for? He can see Outsider watchers posted nearby on the rooftops, but down in the street a bunch of teenagers are laughing and climbing along the walls of a ruined building.

A graceful Asian boy takes a flying leap upward, catches hold of a high wall and backflips onto the top before walking on his hands along the narrow strip as if he was on the ground, not ten meters up in the air. Down in the alley, another kid lets fly with a crossbow bolt and it slams into a sagging roof, sending a tile crashing down on the boy on the wall. Without missing a beat, he straightens, catches the tile in his hand—and with a fast, accurate whip of his wrist, he hurls it at the crossbow shooter, knocking the bow clear out of the boy's hand—an action that's met by a roar of approval from the others.

Behind the group he sees a girl and boy pressed up against an old car, caught in a passionate kiss....Hunter runs his hands through his hair, grins. Man, he's going to have some tales to tell when he gets back to the 家 bar. Who else of his mates has even set foot in the slums, never mind hanging out with full-on Outsider rebels?

From a warehouse on the opposite side of the road, Rose peers through a grimy window, watching the boy who watches them. And then her quick ears catch a stifled groan. Quickly crossing the room, she kneels down beside her brother, who lies in a mess of blankets in the corner. She puts her hand on his forehead; he is burning up. Only a month ago, plastic surgeons cut down to his skull, moving and reshaping the bones—and already the pressure is building again. Crouzon syndrome, that's what the doctors call it; distorting his face, fusing and twisting the bones. Rose shakes the tears out of her eyes. He's reached crisis point, and only last week she had an emergency meeting with the doctors, when they told her he must have a string of operations if he's to survive at all.

Ray Ray presses her hand, his eyes apologetic. Under cover of straightening his blankets, Rose turns her head so he can't see the jolt of pain blurring her face. To see your own little brother crying and not be able to take the pain for him. . . . She would take his place in a heartbeat. But there's only one thing she can do. Get the money for the next operation and then the next and then the one after that, till he's better.

Hunter moves away from the window. Picking up his jacket, he heads toward the stairs; it's time to find Uma and get out of here. But as he approaches the door he hears low voices coming from the next room. Is that Guido? He stops, suddenly listening intently because another voice has just cut in—Uma's. Without knowing quite why, Hunter presses himself up against the wall.

Uma sits opposite her cousin at a low table, Lyuba lying on the bare floorboards beside her. "So you've heard nothing about Zella?"

Guido sighs. "Still in Belmarsh. That's all we know. Maybe they suspect her of being a Council leader. It seems strange that it's just her. Almost like there's an informant." He narrows his eyes. "How did you escape?"

"Lyuba. She must've followed me all the way from the bridge after I was arrested. She attacked the guards when they pulled me from the jeep."

Guido's face lights up. "Is that so? It was a good day I found this one." He reaches out to rub the dog's ears, wincing slightly as he bends.

Uma glances at his shoulder. "How are you?"

"Well, I've seen better days. But them Kossak bullets only clipped me." Guido flashes a quick grin. "And let's face it, my face was never that beautiful to begin with." He picks up a penknife, starts to dig a curved groove in the table surface. "So what's the story with this boy?"

Uma shrugs. "Hunter? Remember on the boat when Zella ordered me to take the package, climb the bridge?"

Guido nods.

"So...when I finally got to the top I threw myself onto the metal struts...and he was there too, hiding—"

"What in God's name was he sitting on the roof of Tower Bridge for?"

"He'd been watching us, the funeral."

The knife jags in the wood. "What?"

Uma waves her hand. "I know, I know...but he's not a spy. He's helped me a lot."

"How d'you know he isn't?"

"He just isn't. He was going to the favela to jump."

A moment's silence, then Guido bursts out laughing. "家 boys don't jump."

Uma flushes. "He does...."

"Ah, come on, Uma. I understand he helped you, but get real. When he wakes he's got to be history. I'll get one of the boys to see him out safe. He's lucky to be alive, coming here on a day like today." Guido leans forward. "Just how did he help you, anyhow?"

Uma looks down at her hands. "He hid the package that Zella gave me. He slipped it into his pocket, lied to the Kossaks. And after I was arrested he took it to his house."

Guido's penknife sticks in the wood, quivering. "You gave Zella's package, the one she told you to guard with your life, to a *Sleeper*?"

Uma glares at him, defiant. "Yes, Guido. I did. And you and Zella can shout at me all you want, but it wasn't you staring down the barrel of a Kossak gun."

Under the table, Guido balls his fist. He looks at her carefully, his little cousin, trying to work out what she knows. He's not going to find out what's going on if he makes her mad. Sometimes she gets a look in her face like Zella, and there's no crossing his aunt. He shifts in his seat.

"But you've got it back now?"

"Yes."

"Can I know what it is?"

Uma drops her eyes. Guido, her big cousin. The only steady thing she's ever known. Her mum always away—protests and marches and running the school—and then put inside. Through it Guido's always been there, making sure she's got enough to eat, looking out for her, backing her up, pushing her on.

She sighs. What should she do? Zella said to tell no one, not even him, for his own safety... but what choice does she have? She glances at his swollen eye, his crooked nose, the great blood-red bruise spreading across his cheekbone. What is he? Twenty-two? He faces death every day on behalf of the rebellion, and here she is, hiding things from him like he's the enemy.

Guido reaches across the table, taking her hand. "Look, I have to know what's going on, Uma. Whether it's safe to use the Dream-line. I need to contact the leaders in the world Councils. I hear stories about raids all over Europe, but I can't coordinate anything unless I can talk to our brothers and sisters directly. Now's not the time to keep secrets from me—and I don't even know why you'd want to, unless Zella ordered it."

Uma runs her hand through her hair. "Why do they hate us so much?"

"Who? The government? Well, this time it's because they think we blew that damn reactor up."

"*Did* we?"

Guido's eyes widen. "Of course not. That's the coward's way, to destroy things, to put people in danger. I don't know why they had to close it down, it could have been anything—a plutonium leak... groundwater contamination. Who knows?"

"Why are they blaming us, then?"

"If they didn't they'd have to blame themselves."

"But Citizens, they're not all bad, Guido. I mean, Hunter... he's—"

Guido grins. "Very cute."

Uma flushes. "No, it's not that. He's...they're not all the same, Guido. They are trapped too."

"I know. But they've got to untrap themselves." He leans back against a cushion. "Come on, Uma, tell me what's in the package."

She can't delay any longer. She reaches inside her jacket, pulls out the case.

"The Encryption Codes. Zella is, *was* the Keeper."

Guido's heart flames. The Codes, here in this room? This is top-secret data, way out of his league. He strives to keep his voice level. "So! Zella was a *Keeper*. Incredible." He holds out his hand. "May I?"

Uma slides the metal case across the table, experiencing a beautiful sense of relief as Guido's fingers close around the case. Now he must think what is best to do. He must make the decisions.

Guido narrows his eyes. "Does anyone else know about this, apart from you and Hunter?"

"Another boy, called Leo."

"Who's he?"

"A friend of Hunter's....He...stole the Codes, tried to break in—"

"Unbelievable!" Guido brings his fist down hard on the table, sending a glass flying. "What have you been playing at? The Codes are the key to our encryption system that conceals all our true identities on the Dreamline. If this data fell into Kossak hands, our whole global communication system would be cracked wide open. Thousands exposed, tortured, imprisoned around the world....The movement would never recover."

Uma cuts in. "I know...but it happened before I got there. Leo stole them from Hunter, patched himself *inside* with a fake patch. Nearly killed himself, I only just pulled him out in time."

"But how did he even get *inside*? Is he some kind of hacker? Not even a pro Kossak code breaker would get that far without a lot of Outsider knowledge."

"All I know is he used to work with a favela kid who was obsessed with hacking the system. He got in, but it shut down on him."

"Of course it did."

"No. The Code program didn't just shut him *out*, it *completely* shut down, crashed. At least that's what Leo said. I tried to test it myself, but I burnt my retinal implant out when I pulled him from *inside*. I must've pushed it too hard." Uma looks down. "I need you to test it, Guido. Because Zella...she told me if anything happened to her, she'd lock the progam down. So if it *has* crashed, it means she's in bad trouble."

Guido's face creases. "And if she is? What did she order you to do?"

"To get the Codes to the new Keeper."

"How?"

"She didn't know, just said some kind of directions would still be traceable. The only thing I've got to go on right now is a stupid logo."

"A logo?"

"Yeah, I got it by following directions from *inside*. I don't even know if it's going to lead to anything concrete. It comes from these two lines of verse that Leo found, before the program crashed.... Then we decoded the directions, followed them down to Blackfriars Bridge—"

Suddenly a siren, a great whooping mechanical claxon explodes across the favela.

Guido leaps to his feet. "Raid!" He reaches for his gun. "Don't move, right? The boy too."

Uma frowns. "You're not going out there with the Codes on you?"

Guido gasps. "You're right." Bending down, he raises a section of floorboard and drops the case inside a dark square before slotting the board back in place. At the door he turns. "Stay here, Uma. I mean it. Harry will take care of you."

The front door slams behind him, and Uma drops her head in her hands. Now she's told someone, it's suddenly all so real, everything that's happened with Zella. Uma squeezes her eyes shut, urgently trying to block the pain of losing someone *again*.

As soon as Guido leaves, Hunter moves out into the hallway with only one thought in his mind. Escape. What has he got himself mixed up with? This is crazy dangerous. But as he tiptoes past Guido's room, he catches sight of Uma through the few centimeters of open doorway. He pauses, staring for a long moment. Awkward. A trespasser. He shouldn't be here, but he is here…and she is so alone. He shakes his head. *He's such a fool.* This is the time to leave now, while everyone's tied up with the Kossaks. But suddenly, somehow, his hand is on the door handle and with a rapidly beating heart, he pushes it open.

"Uma?"

At the sound of her name, Uma is suddenly unable to hold back any longer. Hot tears well through her fingers. What is it about this boy that makes her cry? She turns her head away. "Go away, please."

Suddenly the favela siren stops, the silence almost as stunning as the noise. Gunfire is now clearly audible, flaring up from the streets below. Hunter hesitates. He can't leave her like this. He goes over to her side and gently touches her arm. "But it's me, Hunter."

"Leave me alone."

"I want to help."

"You can't."

"Won't you even talk to me?"

Uma's eyes blaze. "What is it with you and helping me? I'm not some project, you know. I can take care of myself; I've been doing it a long time."

Hunter draws back. "Okay."

"Okay *what*? My dad died when I was a baby, my mum's been gone for years, my aunt's just been taken to Belmarsh, and the Kossaks are outside trashing my home. So what are you going to do to help me, Hunter? What good Citizen stunt are you gonna pull to make everything okay?"

Hunter flushes. "Quit beating me up about that. I'm here, aren't I? I've never let you down."

Uma's voice suddenly turns flat. "Guido's men will get you out of here once the raid is over. You've got to leave."

Hunter shakes his head. "I go when I want. I'm my own man."

Uma sighs. What was she thinking, bringing him here? Now that she's back in the favela, reality has come crashing down on her with a vengeance. "For the last time, Hunter. This is not a game. I've got to do this thing and fast. And you...can't help."

The silence that falls between them is so heavy, it feels like it's crushing him down like a great stone. Her face is so hard. She wants him gone. Now. But somehow he can't break contact with her eyes, glittering, massive, full of rage. He reaches out, dragging her to him, and then his mouth is on hers. Her lips part and they kiss. A long, savage kiss; their fingers digging into each other's flesh, their bodies pressed tight. But after a moment Hunter feels her pulling away, struggling to break free.

"No! This doesn't change anything."

He stares at her, wild. "How can you say that?"

"It's—*we're*—impossible."

"No, it's not. We live here, in London. We can do what we want."

"Can we?"

"Yes."

She shakes her head. "You see how it is here. My world hates you...and yours hates us. Listen to the guns outside! And there's nothing we can do about it. You're a *Citizen*, Hunter."

"And you're an Outsider! So? Is that all we are?"

"No, but in the world, the real world, that's how it is. It's a war, and I don't belong to your side."

"But I don't belong there, either."

Her face blurs. "I know. But there's no way out." Her voice drops almost to a whisper. "You *have* to leave me alone. *Please*."

Eighteen

Suddenly there's the sound of heavy boots pounding up the stairs. A voice comes from the hallway outside.

"Uma! You in there?"

She doesn't have time to answer before Little Fats pushes inside. He stands there a second, chest heaving.

"Fats! What're you doing here?"

"I've come...to get him. Time to...move...mate."

"Guido didn't say anything to me about this."

Fats shrugs. "Must've changed his mind. Just saw him on the corner, he ordered me to get the boy out of here straightaway."

"I don't understand."

"Girl, it's a dogfight down there, but the lines have just shifted a few roads up the island. We got ourselves a window. If this feller's gonna leave, it's now. We can't be caught holding a Citizen. They'll call it kidnapping and it'll be hell to pay. Plus he'll lose his ID for sure." He glances at Hunter. "You want that?"

Hunter shakes his head.

"Jump to it, then."

But Hunter hesitates, takes a step toward Uma.

Little Fats's hand moves toward the gun holster slung around his hips. "Now. I'm sorry, but I ain't telling you again." He glances at Uma. "Don't worry, he'll be safe with me."

She bites her lip. "You promise?"

Fats's eyes widen. "'Course. We'll take his bike through Mudchute, round the east side of the island toward Wapping. Easy."

Hunter scarcely has time to grab his scooter helmet before Fats hustles him down the stairs and out through the front door.

Pressing herself against the bedroom window, Uma watches as he trails Fats along the row of terraced houses. But as Hunter reaches the corner, he stops, turning to look back up at her window. Just in time, she ducks out of sight. She lets out a breath. Enough, now. She can't let herself get close to this boy, not now, not ever.

From her hiding place in the warehouse, Rose watches Hunter as he trails Fats up the deserted main street. She clenches her hand. What now? Turning to look at Ray, she sees he's fallen into an uneasy sleep. She's got to make a decision, and now. Something's going on here, something she needs to know about. With a last look at her brother, she reaches forward, pushing the window open, and then swings herself out of the window. Sliding silently down a gutter pipe, she drops into a low crouch on the street below. Up ahead, the two figures suddenly disappear. They've darted off to the left, into an abandoned garage. Rose frowns. Why aren't they going straight to the bike? Hugging the far wall, she sets off after them.

Hunter frowns. Why are they running into this gas station when his bike is only a few meters farther up the road? But Fats mouths, "Kossaks!" and signals for him to run to the abandoned garage shop up ahead. Hunter follows the order, running in a fast diagonal behind the boy across the asphalt toward the store's broken door. As he enters the gutted interior, he senses—he knows—something is wrong, but it's too late and the blow from Little Fats sends him slamming into the far wall. Gasping in pain, Hunter spins around as another blow comes flying in—but at the last second he manages to swerve sideways and Fats's blow lands wide. He's pressed up hard against the wall; he's got no room to move, let alone swing his arms. Twisting his shoulders, he throws all his weight into a vicious headbutt to his opponent's face. With a grunt of pain, Fats falls forward, but as he hits the ground, he swings his right foot out, taking Hunter's legs out from under him.

Rolling sideways, Fats makes a grab for his gun. Hunter's arms flail wildly, searching for some kind of weapon on the garage floor. His fingers touch an old oil can, and gripping it tight, he brings it down with all his strength, just as Fats is raising the gun barrel to put a bullet between his eyes. Hunter catches the gun, hard, with the can, partially breaking Fats's grip on the weapon. And then immediately he strikes again, bringing the metal container down a second time, this time catching Fats in a glancing blow to the side of his head. The boy reels back, desperately trying to get his grip back on the gun, but now Hunter lunges at his hand, trying to force the barrel upward, toward the ceiling. Screaming with fury, Fats slaps the gun into Hunter's face. *Don't let go, don't let go*, Hunter screams inside his head, but he knows the other boy is an Outsider, a street fighter. It isn't enough to hold on, he's got to unbalance Fats, surprise him, if he wants to get out of this alive.

With desperate strength, he reverses direction, ramming the gun handle downward into Fats's neck, jamming it into his windpipe while simultaneously drawing his right leg back and kneeing him full in the stomach. Fats gasps, recoils, but he's too strong; he snatches his left hand free and locks it onto Hunter's wrist, desperately trying to prise the gun free of his grasp. Pressing down with the full weight of his body, he forces Hunter's arm up and backward, twisting it to its highest arc and bending it back to the screaming point before smashing Hunter in the face with his elbow. Hunter's head smacks against the floor and Fats scrambles to his feet and buries his boot in Hunter's belly, sending the boy sprawling faceup on the dirty oil-stained floor.

Fats raises his gun, screams, "Turn to face the wall, hands on the back of your head."

Hunter's gut twists. "No!"

"Do it!"

"You got this wrong. I came here with Uma—"

Suddenly the gun is in his face, the cold metal pressed hard against his temple.

"Yeah, well. I don't take orders from her. So turn, or I'll blow your face off right now."

Slowly Hunter shuffles around on his knees. This can't be happening. He's going to die, here, in this trashed-up garage.

"Hands on the back of your head. Slow."

In spite of himself, Hunter raises his arms, feels his biceps bunch, his fingers interlock. He can't breathe, can't see, can't...he squeezes his eyes shut against the horror. A sharp metallic *fsst*—he screams in pain, falling forward on the concrete. Everything is black. A long, dark beat. But he's breathing, his chest still rises and falls. He's alive.

Suddenly there's a hand on his shoulder. "Get up, youse."

A girl's voice. What?

"*Move!* Now."

"Rose?" Hunter twists on to his side. Little Fats is stretched out on the floor, unconscious.

"Is he dead?"

The girl bends over the boy's neck, checks his pulse. "No. Lucky sod. I caught him just right." She sheathes her crossbow and pockets Fats's gun. "We got to tie him up." Running her eyes over the dusty shelves, she spots a loop of rusted wire hanging behind the counter. "Pass me that, Hunter. Then come over and get his arms behind his back. Quick, 'fore he comes round."

Hunter jumps up and grabs the wire before crossing the floor to roll Fats's inert body over, pushing the boy's arms back and together.

"Soon as we do this we got to get you hid from the rest of Fats's gang till we work out what to do. It's too dangerous to move till the raid has died down."

Hunter stares into Fats's unconscious face. "You think Guido knows about this?"

Her eyes spark. "Dunno. Maybe Fats was doing it for his gang. But I wouldn't bet against Guido either, eh?" She twists the wire around Fats's wrists in tight circles.

"But why?"

"Maybe he figures you're too dangerous to let live. If you haven't noticed there's a bit of a war on out there and you've seen our faces, where we live, like. Anyways, get a move on. We can talk after." Rose twists a rag and stuffs it in Fats's mouth. "That'll keep yer quiet for a bit, you fat pig." She straightens. "Right, Hunter, follow me. What I do, you do. Right?"

Hunter nods. This girl's his only way out of here. Rose goes to the door, pauses, scanning the forecourt before sliding onto her belly and setting off across the pavement. Hunter follows, the rough concrete scraping his hands as he drags himself forward. They'll not get very far like this. But as they reach the row of gas pumps in the middle of the forecourt, Rose halts, and for a few seconds she fiddles with some kind of lock set into the ground before levering up a small hatch. A strong stench of gas rises into the cold air.

Rose gestures. "Down you go."

Hunter peers downward. "What the hell is that?"

"Gas storage tank."

"But how deep is it?"

"No more'n a few meters. C'mon, it's been empty for months and anyway you got no choice. I got to hide yer while I go get Uma."

Hunter grits his teeth. Swinging his legs inside the hatch he lowers himself down into the tank. For a moment he hangs in the rising fumes, before forcing himself to let go—dropping into the black pit and landing with a heavy splosh in the thin layer of gas coating the bottom.

Hunter straightens, gazes up; Rose's face is outlined in the square of light above. She grins. "Be back soon as I can."

And with that the hatch drops with a dull metallic clang, leaving Hunter alone in the dark. The stink of gas is overpowering. Ripping off his jacket, he wraps it around his face to block the fumes out. He lifts his hand to his chest, gently rubbing his bruised muscles. It feels like someone's tried to rip his heart out. A stinging gash throbs across his neck, blood oozing through his T-shirt. He's got to keep calm, not think about being trapped here. Because if Rose doesn't make it back, he's got no way of getting out of this place. What a way to die, in an empty gas tank. Hunter smiles grimly. Pretty funny when you think about it.

Down at New Billingsgate Market, Evan stands in a great stinking warehouse of rotting fish. Ten tons of decomposing flesh, the ice melted, the stench unbelievable.

Evan shakes his head, wondering for the millionth time if human beings are worth the effort. Oil. This cheap energy has turned us stupid, no different than a bunch of fruit flies who've found a pile of sugar: a mad feeding frenzy, an exploding population—and then horrible collapse once we've sucked the sugar dry. So much for us being superior to other animals.

He glances up at the sky as a new platoon of Kossak choppers fly eastward. Operation Clearwater, that's what they're calling it. The mission is to flush out the Outsider ringleaders behind the reactor shutdown. Evan frowns; they love their little code names, these Special Forces.

He checks the time. Midday. Weighs up whether to call Hunter. He taps his teeth; he's got to trust the boy; he's almost a man now. But Evan can't get rid of this feeling that he's not being straight with him. Reaching for his RET, he punches in Hunter's number, promising himself to keep his voice light, casual. The number dials, then dies. He tries again. Dead. This isn't an engaged signal, this is a network *disconnect*. Where in London can't you get network these days? The 家 never goes down. His chest tightens; something's not right. Well then, he'll call Leo. Wherever he is, Hunter is sure to be.

Evan calls Leo's number, but it goes straight to voice mail. Evan frowns. If Hunter is up to anything like yesterday's bridge stunt the Kossaks won't be so lenient this time. Activating his RET again, Evan punches in his full Tech Class 1 ID. He's got to do this.

A voice comes online. "You're cleared for security. What search do you require, sir?"

Evan frowns. He can't find Hunter if he's offline or damaged, but

Leo is another matter. His RET is at least *connected* to the 家. He clears his throat.

"Yes, I want a GPS fix on Leo da Silva. Address: flat fifteen, Union Grove SW8 5BN." Evan stares down at a box of cod, the fish stare back at him.

After a moment, the voice returns. "That citizen is currently logged in at IP 20078455//ws."

"Address, please?"

"The 家 Bar. 232 Oxford Street."

"Thank you."

Evan disconnects, furious. Downtown at that stupid bar. Hunter's bound to be there too—and after he promised. Evan looks at his watch again. Right, he's catching a rickshaw downtown. He can make it in half an hour if he pushes it.

In the Kossak listening post, the crawler sends a message. Three alerts on Leo da Silva in twenty-four hours. A Code 3, High Priority, is initiated and on the twenty-fourth floor of the Central Military HQ, the message is received and in seconds a search warrant is processed, issued, and activated.

Nineteen

Uma pads over to the sink in the corner of Guido's room. Splashing cool water on to her cheeks, she stares at her reflection in the oval mirror hanging above the tap. Everyone says she looks just like her dad. Uma leans in closer, examining her face....she'd like to be more beautiful like her mum...but her nose, that bump halfway up, there's no escaping that. Maybe she could get a bit of reconstruction work done, like a Sleeper girl, the kind that Hunter probably goes with....What would it be like, to be with him? Her eyes harden. *Stop it.* She glances outside, impatient. As soon as Guido comes back they've got to test the Codes and then get on their way to the Dragon Palace. There's no time to lose.

Suddenly there's a sound, a tap at the window. Lyuba trots over, whimpering. Now what? Uma peers down at the street below, but it is deserted. Little Fats was right, the fighting has moved away for now. She lifts her gaze to the warehouse windows opposite, but there is literally nothing and nobody to see. Everyone is either out fighting the Kossaks or inside, hiding. And then a small stone bounces against the window ledge. Uma ducks down, her eyes now sweeping the rooftops...until...on the slates, *there*, she suddenly catches a movement. A hand. Waving. She looks closer. It's Rose, pressed flat against the gutter, signaling for her to open the window.

Heart racing, Uma yanks the windowpane as high as she can. Rose straightens, and, steadying herself on the cracked slates, she sizes up the series of jumps to the window. A moment later Uma steps back, watching as her friend flashes through the frame, tucking her body into a tight curl as she rolls across the wooden boards with noiseless precision.

In a second Rose is on her feet again. "You got to get out of here, girl."

Uma sticks her hands on her hips. "Why? What's going on?"

"No time. Move."

"But Guido told me to stay."

"Guido just ordered your friend killed."

Uma closes her mouth with a snap. "No he didn't."

"I was there, I saw. Little Fats, it was. I stopped it happening. I mean it's either Guido who ordered it or Fats working for his gang. But either way, they done it."

Uma gasps. "I don't believe you."

Rose shrugs. "Believe, Uma. I got your boy hid round the corner."

Fear surges through Uma. Did Guido order this? Why? Because he couldn't let Hunter live because he knew about the Codes? But, no, Guido wouldn't, *couldn't* do that. Not to her friend. Could he? Guilt crashes over her.

"Where is he?"

"In the gas station."

Uma digs her fingernails into her palms. Of course there's a chance that Little Fats was working on his own, but she can't take the risk. She's got to get out of here. How can she trust her cousin now? Uma fights back tears. *Guido.*

Rose crosses over to the window. "Ready?"

"Wait!"

"What now?"

Uma kneels down and, levering up a loose plank, she reaches inside, snatching up the metal case in the dark space beneath.

Rose's eyes blaze. "What's that?"

"Never mind." Uma slots the board back in place before bending down next to Lyuba and softly stroking her ears. "Don't follow me this time, okay?"

And then, jumping lightly on to the window frame she follows Rose out on to the roof.

Hunter stands in the pitch-black gas tank. Only a quarter of an hour has passed, but it feels like a lifetime. He's already done a dozen circuits of the metal container walls; he's tried to jump, to climb up to the hatch, but the cool, smooth surface defeats him every time. He's trapped. This can't be happening. For the millionth time Hunter tries to activate his RET, but he gets nothing but a silvered-out lens and a blank tone. Stupid slice of chip and plastic. What he wouldn't give for a ladder.

A memory, of going on a day trip to the beach with his parents, suddenly flashes into his mind. Hunter half smiles. It was a really hot day and his mum'd got him one of those blow-up crocodiles to get him in the sea. What was he, five, six? He wasn't crazy about the water, even before... But anyway, there they were, mucking about in the waves, his mum messing with him, playing really fierce. She was doing this thing where she'd sneak up on him and push him right under. Hunter's face splits into a smile. He can still see the crocodile's wicked rubber teeth snapping in the air above him as he went under the waves. But he loved it, loved the terror of her coming after him... and then her arms around him, lifting him, whooshing him up into the air... and after, laughing, laughing.

Deep in the tank, Hunter takes a breath. That's what he's got to do now. He's got to get control of this panic. Turn it into a game, one that he can win.

Fear. He's been training in the gym for years to beat it. He first started training not long after... he had to do something, the dreams got so bad and he needed to tire himself out, to drop exhausted into bed. And then one day he saw these favela kids through the gym windows.... They were leaping across tower-block roofs— and they looked so wild, so free, that he felt ashamed at his little bench presses and programmed fight sequences. And that's when he started to go down to the edge of the favelas, to jump in secret—and over time it became an obsession, his secret from the world—to train himself to be a true free runner, as good as the Outsider kids.

Hunter shivers, wraps his arms around his body. *Fear.* It's there to protect him; it's like an old friend; it'll never go away; it'll never get weak even if he does. It's formidable. And then he is suddenly hit by a wave of remorse. What if he dies down here and his old man never finds out what happened to him? It'd kill him. Literally.

And then a square of light appears above.

"Hunter! Youse down there?"

Relief pumps through his veins. "Yeah."

"Hang on, we're getting some rope sorted."

On the garage forecourt, Rose slips the end of an old frayed blue rope through a loop, and pulling tight, she finishes the last of a series of six similar knots each set about a meter apart. Enough for Hunter to rest a foot on, if the rotten thing will hold. She glances over at Uma.

"Done?"

"Yes." Uma loops the other end of the rope around a battered diesel pump and passes it back to Rose, who lowers the cord down into the blackness. Hunter watches as it descends, makes a grab for it, misses. He reaches out again and this time his fingers tighten around it. He starts to hoist himself upward. One, two, three lifts—nearly there—he can feel the air on his face. Raising his arms through the hatch, he reaches for the rough concrete but just as his head clears the tank, the dull roar of a chopper engine comes overhead and he's suddenly slammed sideways by a heavy weight.

He loses his grip and suddenly he's falling again, landing heavily on his back in a pool of gas. Winded, Hunter can only stare upward as the hatch drops above him, shutting out the light again. And then, next to him, a shift, a groan. Someone else is in here! Hunter drags himself to his feet, groping for the other body. He's got to attack first. His hands bump up against something, and he hurls himself forward.

"Hunter, no!"

He pulls back his fists. "Uma?"

"Get off...of me."

Hunter relaxes his muscles, rolls to the side. "What's going on?"

"Kossak chopper came out of nowhere. Rose pushed me sideways into you and then dropped the hatch."

Hunter stamps his foot. What madness has he gotten himself into? Three times in two days this girl has nearly got him killed. If he gets out of here alive, he's driving straight home, back to where he belongs. Squatting on hands and knees in the shallow pool of gas, he faces her in the blackness.

"You people are crazy. Is it worth all this danger? I mean, d'you really believe this stuff, or is it just something you've grown up with, like a cult? C'mon, the Dreamline, Outsiders, the rebellion. It's a fantasy."

"No more than your crazy life. Least we're fighting for something real."

Hunter grabs her arm. "I overheard you and Guido. I know what you've got to do...with the Codes and the Keeper. How can something so massive be down to you? It's too big, Uma."

A sharp intake of breath. "You were listening?"

He swallows. "Yes."

"Then how do I know Guido's not right, that you're not a spy? You're always in the right place at the right time, Hunter."

"And how do I know that you didn't let Guido kill me? That you didn't just watch me walk away to my death with Fats?"

Uma gasps. "You think I could do that? It's only you and Rose I can trust now. And answer me this, what am I doing down here with you if it's true?"

Hunter stretches out a hand in the dark. "Look I never said—"

Uma slaps it away. "Yes, you did."

The sound of the chopper is fading. Hunter looks down and desperately tries to control his breathing in the silence. This girl is no good for him.

Uma clenches her jaw tight, staring straight ahead. Is he abandoning her as well as Guido and all the others? Can she blame him, though? She's pushed him away; why should he come back for more? Maybe it's better this way. Cleaner.

Suddenly the overhead hatch opens and Rose's head appears once more. "All right, guys. Out and fast!"

Uma lets out a breath. "All clear?"

"Aye."

"Good." Uma reaches for the rope and clambers to the top in seconds.

"Where did you hide?"

Rose jerks her thumb backward. "Just behind the pumps there."

"And they didn't see you? Lucky."

Rose snorts. "Luck's nothing to do with it. When I hide, I stay hid."

Moments later, Hunter emerges from the tank. He stands dead still, taking a long, long look at his scooter, parked meters away on the main road. One curl of the throttle and he'll be on his way, back home. He glances at Uma and his heart twists. She's got no one, not even her cousin anymore, to help her to get the Codes safe. His head says one thing, but his heart says another. Hunter pushes his hair back. Well, better get to it. Striding over to his bike, he flicks the ignition and the engine purrs into life.

"Well, come on, what you waiting for?"

Uma stares at him. "Thought you were leaving."

"Yeah, but you're coming too. I-I'm not leaving you here like this!"

"I don't want your pity."

"That's good, cos I'm not offering it. I'm doing it because *this*...," he flicks a hand around the deserted favela, "is wrong, and...I owe you for coming back for me." Hunter swallows. "So let's get moving. But from now on, we do this together, right? No more secrets."

Uma's eyes drill into his. What would Zella say? *Trust your instinct.* That's what she's always taught her to do. Her head says ditch him, but something about this boy *feels* right. Suddenly her face softens. Look at him, all serious in his stupid Sleeper-branded *free runner* trainers. But he's never let her down. Not once in these last mad hours.

She nods. "All right."

Rose takes a step forward. "Uma, where are you going?"

"I can't tell you."

Her friend's face sets in defiant lines. "I'm coming with you."

"You can't. We've only got one scooter and we've got to get out of here, fast."

"That ain't the real reason, though, is it?"

Uma sighs. "No. But I don't have time to tell you."

Rose flicks a glance at Hunter. "But *he* knows?"

"Yes."

Rose spits. "You'd trust a Sleeper over me? After all we been through?"

"It's not that simple."

"Nothing ever is. But you'll not be going without me, will you now, Uma girl?"

Uma stares at her a long moment. There's no way she can do this on her own, she's got to trust *someone* if she's to stand a chance of finding the Keeper. And this is Rose, her best mate, the girl who grinds grown men into dust. She and this boy are all that stand between the Kossaks and the Codes.

"The Dragon Palace, Leicester Square. You know it?"

Rose nods. "Course."

"How long will it take you to get there?"

"An hour, give or take."

"We'll wait for you out front, by the statue of Charlie Chaplin."

"And you'll tell me what's going, then?"

"Yes."

"Fine."

Uma slips behind Hunter on the bike seat. She holds Rose's eye for a long moment. "Tell *no one*. Promise?"

The girl nods. "On my life."

Rose stares after them for a long moment, watching as Hunter takes the corner at a low angle, heading away from the river toward the city. Rose dashes away the tear that slips down her cheek, cursing the favela, the life, for what it's done to her. And then she sets off toward the West End, a girl on a mission.

Twenty

High in the ruined apartment, Leo lies, belly down, his right eye glued to the telescopic sight. The armored jeep swings around the corner onto the Ratcliff Road. Finally he's got a clear shot. He squeezes the trigger, firing the bazooka directly at the nearside flank. The recoil knocks the boy backward, the rocket fizzes through the night air, and *BAM!* Impact! The jeep flips over, engulfed in a great ball of fire. Black smoke billows from the interior and a door opens. Soldiers emerge, desperately struggling to drag themselves away from the burning wreck.

Face blank, the boy ditches the rocket launcher and reaches for the rifle lying on the burnt carpet alongside him. Pressing the butt tight into his shoulder, he activates the digital crosshairs and zooms in on his first target, an officer crawling along the ground. He sees the man's face, magnified, twisted in pain. The boy takes a breath, and holding the air in his lungs, he positions the crosshairs directly over the officer's skull. His index finger tightens on the trigger.

Suddenly a great rip tears across the landscape, the rifle crosshairs dissolve—

—and Leo bunches up in agony as his RETScan is ripped off his eye. The apartment around him folds in on itself, disappears, the walls fading to black.

"Hmm. That's not nice, is it . . . ?"

"No, mate, looks like we got ourselves a little wannabe cop killer."

On the floor, Leo gives his head a sharp shake, opening his eyes to narrow slits. The apartment, the ruined urban landscape has vanished, replaced by the stained purple ceiling of the 家 Bar. Two heavily armored Kossaks bend down over him. This is not good. Leo tries to pull the corners of his mouth upward, in what he hopes is a law-abiding Citizen smile, and is rewarded by a sharp cuff to the head.

"What you smiling for, you loser? You think it's funny to kill cops?"

Leo struggles to his knees. "It's only a game, officer."

The man, close-cropped hair, a scar running from ear to chin, looks down at him in disgust. "To you maybe. Get up, Leo da Silva. We want to talk to you."

Leo's mind reels. This soldier knows his name. This isn't just some random raid on the bar. They've come for him specifically. He takes a long moment to move, trying to steady his nerves. Is it that bit of hacking he did down at Mile End two weeks back? He must keep calm. Slowly he raises himself to his feet. For the first time in living history, the 家 Bar is silent; all the kids stand mute, backed up against the wall, network-disconnected, Beijing Techno paused, Sims unplugged, as they take in the full live 3D situation in front of them.

"Chop, chop, boy, we're taking you downtown."

"No!"

"Excuse me?" The scarred officer whirls around.

Leo clears his throat. "I mean, could I know on what charge, sir?"

"ID offense, 261."

A sharp intake of breath around the bar. Everybody knows this is serious. This isn't just a black mark, a demerit. 261 is a homeland security charge. Leo looks around the room. No one will meet his eye, not one of his 家 buddies. But he is desperate. Once he gets in the back of that Kossak wagon, all his witnesses are gone; he's got to force something to happen out here.

"Can't I at least make a call?"

The officer grabs his arm, pins it back, hard. Leo grits his teeth, but plants his heels on the floor.

"It's my right. You gonna throw me in the wagon without a call?"

The soldier exchanges a glance with his partner. This is the kind of bar where high-ID kids come to slum it, snotty little kids with ideas about police brutality. Not that they look like they care too much right now, but still....Reluctantly he nods.

"One call. Now."

As Leo reaches for his RET, the officer tuts. "Nah-ah. Tell me the number and I'll make the connect."

Leo squeezes his eyes shut. Hunter's offline...so there's only one person he can think of to call...but he can't remember the number, it's...ah...he runs through all the lists he's got stored in his brain, desperately seeking the answer.

"Come on, boy."

Leo jogs from foot to foot. His brain is like the Darknet, there're things submerged down there that haven't surfaced since the Jurassic Age. Streams of digits flicker in his brain...no, no, no... yes!

"It's 093B744GU."

Inside the rickshaw, Evan frowns as his RET buzzes. He scans the lens, *secure number.* Now what?

"Hello?"

"Mr. Nash, this is Sergeant Lane from the Fifth Military Police battalion. We just arrested a Leo Wellington Santiago da Silva in the 家 Bar, Oxford Street. He says he knows you. This true?"

"What?" Evan straightens in the back of the rickshaw.

"Sir, I need to confirm you know Leo—"

"Yes, yes I do, officer. I was just on my way there. Is my son with him also?"

"Don't know nothing about no other boy, just this one. We are taking him down to Vauxhall HQ for a few questions."

"Is he in trouble?"

"I can't reveal that to you at this time. This is his permitted call. If you want to know more, come down to the HQ." The officer disconnects, grins at Leo. "Done."

Leo stares. "I don't get to talk to him?"

The officer comes close, whispers, "Nope. You been watching too many cop shows, son. That there talking to your lawyer stuff's fairy tales, least for us Kossaks. Now get in the van."

An hour later Evan Nash sits on a hard plastic chair in the overheated Military Police interview room on the twenty-fourth floor of the Central Military HQ in Vauxhall. It's boiling in here. He permits himself a small smile. Trust the Kossaks to keep themselves warm even in a crisis. No funding cuts here. He pushes down the bad things he's heard about the force, the stories about how brutal they are, how they won't even use handcuffs in the favela because they don't bring out anyone alive....

Evan shifts, restless in his seat, and glances at the digital clock on the wall, watches as the milliseconds climb into seconds and the seconds bloom into minutes. He hasn't got time for this. He's got a 3:30 emergency meeting with the mayor about the power shortages. There are rumors that the gas pipeline from Russia has just been cut by rebel forces in Chechnya. If it's true, that, on top of the reactor shutdown, is going to cripple the city.

Suddenly there is the faint hiss of the lock release; the door slides open and a heavyset man strides into the room.

"Mr. Nash. I'm Commander Clarke."

Evan gets to his feet. "Is Leo all right?"

Clarke nods. "Yes, we've questioned him and are happy to release him with a caution."

"May I see him?"

"Of course."

"Can I know what the charge was?"

"We questioned him under ID offense, 261."

Evan's eyes narrow. "But that's a security charge."

"Well, he was engaged in some unusual Darknet activity we wanted to discuss with him. Leo has explained himself clearly and we shan't be needing him any further at this time."

Evan glances at the commander. "But you might later?"

"Everything is possible. The Military Police unit is always on full alert." Clarke pauses. "This boy, he's not a relative, is he?"

"No. He's my son's friend, but he has no close family in London, his brother works on—"

"—The wave rigs off the Hebrides. We know." Clarke runs a shrewd glance over Evan's face. "Sir, if I can make a suggestion, maybe keep your son away from someone like Leo da Silva. . . . Did you know he has previous form in the favela?"

Evan hesitates. "Yes, Hunter's told me something about it. But he was very young at the time and I'm sure—"

"With all due respect, you can't trust anyone or anything in the favela, sir."

Evan drops his gaze from the professional face of the officer, squashes down his dislike. He doesn't like this man, but he is doing an ugly job, cleaning up the mess in the slums. Rising to his feet, he offers up a blue-chip Evan Nash smile.

"But he's free to go now, right?

"Yes."

"Then if you can take me to him, I'm kind of pushed for time."

Standing at the end of the ruined terrace in the Isle of Dogs, Harry's place is utterly silent. The raid is finally over, leastways there's been no gunfire or screams for at least an hour. Down in the kitchen, Harry stretches, rises to his feet, and shuffles to the foot of the stairs.

"Tea, Uma?"

There's no response. Harry cocks his head, it's very quiet up there; she may be asleep. Climbing the stairs, he knocks gently on the bedroom door, but still she doesn't answer. He turns the handle, peers around the door. The room is empty, the window wide open. With hurried steps Harry crosses to the window, peers out, but the street is deserted too. Maybe she slipped out after Guido? He frowns. What is happening this day? Many lines are crossing. With a fast-beating heart, he looks out over the ragged skyline of Canary Wharf.

Suddenly from below the front door slams, followed by heavy footsteps climbing the stairs.

Harry whirls around.

"Father, where is she?" Guido stands in the doorway.

"Isn't she with you?"

"No. I've been down at the Crossroads."

"Then I don't know, son."

Guido's face pales. Crossing to the far side of the room, he bends down to rip up a loose floorboard before peering down into the space below. Nothing there. Thrusting his hand into the cavity he searches every corner, but the case is gone. He stares round, bewildered.

No Codes and no Uma. Will *nothing* go right today?

"Did you not hear anything, Harry?"

The old man shakes his head. "No! I was mixing herbs downstairs, waiting for the raid to finish."

Guido aims a savage kick at the floorboard, sends it slamming against the wall.

Harry lays a trembling hand on Guido's shoulder. "I will send out messages to our people. She'll be found. But, Guido, I counsel you not to use the Dreamline yet, it is not safe." His mouth puckers into a worried smile. "Even without it I can reach many people. It's not only down to you, Guido."

Guido sighs. He'd give anything to confide in Harry, to tell him about the Codes, but it is too dangerous. What's Uma playing at, disappearing like this? He runs his hands over his face. He is twenty-three, but he feels like an old man already.

Twenty-one

In the Kossak cell, Leo sits, hunched over on the bare metal bunk, dreaming about his favorite Wo Han Hubei place in Soho. Leo's mouth waters. What he wouldn't give right now for some super-dry, peanut butter–flavor noodles, served with hot pickled carrots and chili sauce. The hotter the better. Suddenly the cell door opens and Evan Nash stands at the entrance. Leo's face lights up. "Mr. Nash! They locked you up too, huh?"

Evan shakes his head. "Very funny. They've just told me they are releasing you without charge."

"For real?"

"Yes." Evan stares at the boy's face. A dark bruise is starting to form under one eye. What have they done to him? Despite himself his anger starts to melt. "Did they hurt you?"

Leo shakes his head. "Nah. It's nothing. They pushed me about a bit when I first got here, but after that they jus' went through a bunch of questions, wrote my answers down on a disk and then stuck me in here."

Evan frowns. "They picked you up on a two hundred and sixty-one, Leo. Are you crazy? You can kiss good-bye to a good future if that gets tagged on your ID."

"I wasn't doing nothing bad. Honest. I was just fooling around in the Darknet, is all. Last I looked that wasn't a crime."

Evan leans against the cell wall, lowers his voice. "Well, it's not that smart either. Anyway, this time you're lucky. But, Leo, you've got to level with me.... Where's Hunter?"

Leo's throat tightens. "I don't know."

"Oh, come on. You can't expect me to believe that. You're his best mate." Evan rubs his forehead. "Look, I know I'm not home as much as I should be ... and with his mother gone ... I just need to know he's safe."

Leo shifts on the bed. Hunter is lucky to have someone to look out for him like this. "On the level, I don't know where he is right now. All I know is ... he was with a girl ... an' he wanted some time alone, y'get me?"

"A girl?" Evan sticks his hands in his pockets. "This is the first I've heard about this.... Who is she? And why's he got to disappear off the face of the earth? I haven't been able to get hold of him all day." His voice hardens. "After you both promised to stay put at your place."

"I know, I know ... and I'm sorry 'bout that. But truth is I really don't know where he is at."

"Come on, Leo, you know more than you're telling me. You lied this morning about an epilepsy fit to cover up for him, didn't you?"

Leo reddens. "Well, yeah, that was the girl thing."

"Tell me the truth. Is he mixed up in any of this Outsider stuff? You've just been questioned on a very serious charge. Is Hunter involved?"

"Nah, nah, it's nothing like that. And I shouldn't've been brought here neither, these Kossaks they're crazy paranoid. Honest, Mr N., Hunter jus' wanted time alone with her; he really likes her ... an' he's definitely gonna call you in a couple hours, you'll see." Leo forces his voice to be calm, neutral. Argh, normally he'd have no problem lying like this. But to this guy, it's killing him.

Evan shakes his head, grim-faced, he's not getting anywhere

here. Well, after this stunt Hunter is going to be grounded for a month. No scooter. No 家. No nothing.

His RETScan buzzes. Evan stares at his lens. Surely it must be Hunter this time? But no, it's the mayor's office. Bringing the meeting with the mayor forward by an hour. The news has just been confirmed. The gas supplies from Russia are down.

"Leo, I'm sorry, but I've got to get back to City Hall immediately. Are you fine to get home by yourself? Want me to call your brother?"

Leo shakes his head. "Nah, I'm cool, thanks for comin' down—and don't worry about nothing. Hunter'll be back before the day's end."

Evan looks at him a long moment then presses a buzzer mounted on the right-hand side of the cell wall. In a few seconds the door slides back and a uniformed guard stands at the entrance.

Evan smiles. "Officer, can you make sure this young man gets home safe and sound?"

The man nods. "Yes, sir. I'll escort you to the exit, and then we'll take Leo through his release paperwork."

"And then he'll be free to go?"

"Yes, sir."

Evan takes one last look at the boy. He feels terrible leaving him here. "Bye, Leo. Call me as soon as you're home, right? And when you speak to him, tell Hunter to call me immediately."

The door closes behind him and Leo slumps onto the metal bunk. He sighs. Call his brother? The man must be crazy. If Paolo got caught up in this, he'd be off that wave rig tomorrow. Dirty ID in the family, job over, and thirty other people desperate to take Paolo's place. Just like it used to be in Brazil, now here too. Evan is a good man, but he don't know how it is. The Kossaks, they call him sir, they're all in this together—the people on the *right side*.

From his office, Commander Clarke monitors a bank of CCTV screens, watching as Evan Nash steps out of the lift—crosses the lobby—returns his security card—steps out through the main exit—before finally disappearing into the lunchtime crowd.

Clarke massages the back of his neck. He's so near to breaking the Outsider communication network, but he's got to be so careful, so delicate. The Outsiders have outmaneuvered, outsmarted, and outclassed every investigation he's worked on for years. He's been close before, but not this close. He's going to use this Operation Clearwater for all its worth. Normally he doesn't get resources like this, and he isn't going to miss, not this time.

Leo stands up as his cell door slides open, but it's not the young officer returning; instead a stocky man stands in the doorway, behind him two soldiers in Kossak field uniform.

"Hello, Leo."

Leo frowns. "Yeh, hi. You come to get me out of here?"

"Certainly. Just another short interview and then we're done."

"But that's not what you told Mr. Nash. . . ."

Commander Clarke frowns. "Really? Well, we thought it was better for him to leave happy in the knowledge you're *all safe and sound*." He steps inside the cell, sits on the edge of Leo's bed. "So, about the Darknet. Tell me again, why would a boy like you be accessing it? And so close to a Dreamline hot spot. How did you know to do that? That's more than we can do and we've got a whole department working on it."

"I don't know. It was a mistake, a lucky guess, like."

"Oh, come, that might work with Evan Nash, but you're dealing with us now. We know you've got hacking form from back in the favela." Clarke's eyes drill into the boy's. "And like Evan, maybe we'd also like a little chat with your friend Hunter."

Leo jumps up. "Did you bug this cell?"

Clarke puts out a hand. "Calm down, son. We may have picked up a few words here and there—so we decided to run a quick check ourselves on Hunter Nash. Turns out he's also been making some interesting RET searches today—and the most recent GPS fix we have on him indicates he's in the Isle of Dogs favela. Now what business would a good Citizen have down there? Especially today."

Leo makes a sudden dart for the door, but a sharp blow to the neck sends him sprawling. At a nod from Clarke, one of the officers shuts the cell door while the other grabs Leo's rough-chopped hair, slamming his head down on the stone tiles with brutal force.

The hydro tram picks up speed as it lurches on to the Strand. Hunter grabs hold of a rail to steady himself. He and Uma had to ditch the scooter back in Holborn about twenty minutes ago when their luck ran out and they were waved into a checkpoint queue. They did the only thing they could. Slipped off the bike and dumped it behind a bunch of arguing rickshaw drivers. Another thing for his dad to be mad about. The man must be going nuts by now.

Hunter drums his fingers on the tram rail; he's got to do something to buy more time. There's only so long he can ignore the man before he'll do something stupid like contact the police. He's going to have to ask Leo for help again. Epilepsy, Act II.

He reaches up to power up his RET, then frowns. Something is wrong; instead of loading, his lens is rolling and flickering in and out of focus. He unclips the device, brings it to his eye. Damn, there's a crack, right across the laser pad. It wasn't working before in the gas tank, but he thought that was because he was so deep underground. Now he realizes it must've been damaged in the fight with Fats. Well, there's only one way to see if it'll still connect. Punching in Leo's number, Hunter holds his breath. One second, two...then the click of the pickup tone. Yes!

Hunter blows his cheeks out in relief. "Leo, my man, is that you?"

A pause. "No, Hunter, this is Commander Clarke."

He gasps. "Excuse me?"

"From the Fifth Military Police battalion. Unfortunately Leo can't come to the phone right now. In fact I'm very pleased you've called, as I'd like to clear a few things up with you...so if you could pop down to the station in Vauxhall, I'd appreciate it, as would your father."

"My *father*?"

"Yes, he's just been in to see us...but everything's fine. You're not in any trouble, we'd just like you to come in."

Hunter swallows. "But why have you got Leo's RET? Is he hurt?"

"No...just a little faint after helping us with our inquiries."

Hunter mutes his RET and turns to Uma. "Kossaks. They got Leo.... What do I do?"

She frowns. "Keep calm, like there's nothing wrong. Find out what they want you for."

Hunter turns the volume back on. "Sorry, officer, you cut out for a moment. Can I ask what this is about?"

A note of irritation creeps into Clarke's voice. "A few routine questions we need to ask you to corroborate Leo da Silva's statement."

"What kind of questions?"

The voice turns suddenly harsh. "Look, Hunter, we ask the questions, if you don't voluntarily come in, we'll have to activate a GPS arrest on you. You choose. According to my live data, right now you're on...the Strand...traveling toward Trafalgar Square. We have several units in that area—"

Hunter leaps out of his seat, fumbling to power off his RET. "Move, Uma!"

She gasps. "What?"

"They got a GPS fix on me. Go!" He starts to run for the exit. Uma glances out of the window, they haven't got time to wait for the scheduled stop. She stabs the emergency button and the tram brakes engage, hard. Up ahead, Hunter is thrown off balance, catapulted sideways into a bunch of schoolgirls, and for a second he's trapped in a whirl of flying hair and screams and chewing gum before he manages to pull himself free.

Staggering to his feet, he joins Uma at the doors. Ignoring the shouts of the colliding passengers around her, she is trying to prise the emergency doors open. Hunter throws his weight against the doors too and they part, and together they leap into the traffic-clogged lanes, with Uma stumbling, nearly falling into the path of another tram as she lands. Hunter grabs her hand, yanking her upright as they force their way across the traffic; tires squealing, horns blaring, angry faces all around till finally they stand gasping on the Strand sidewalk.

Directly in front is a narrow stairway leading toward the river and they cut down it, emerging moments later in a manicured city park backing on to the Thames.

Uma puts her hand out. "Wait! What's going on?"

Hunter props his hands on his knees, sucking in great lungfuls of air.

"Don't know... Kossaks ordered me... in for questioning... threatened a GPS arrest if I didn't come voluntarily."

Uma blows out her cheeks. "Maybe they just wanted to question you about some of his hacking or something that's nothing to do with... us... with last night. I bet he's up to illegal stuff all the time."

"Don't know... they've never wanted to talk to me before. We can't take the chance." Hunter's stomach drops. What has he gotten his friend into? And his dad, he'll be beyond mad now, he'll be moving into an out-of-body experience. "Come on, Uma, we've got to keep moving. Leicester Square is close enough to walk... Rose'll be there before us at this rate."

"Okay, but stop breathing like an old tramp. You got to be more normal, so you don't attract attention."

"But how can they find me now that I've powered off my RET? I'm not on the 家 anymore."

Uma shakes her head. "This isn't a Citizen thing now. This is the Kossaks. They'll have our ID images already, and it won't be long before they flash it on to the whole 家 network. Get ready to get famous."

"Should we try and change how we look or something?"

Uma slaps her forehead. "Damn, but I left my fake beard at home...."

"All right, all right."

"Our best disguise is to act normal. Like some Sleeper couple from the 'burbs out Saturday shopping."

Hunter smiles despite himself. "Yeah, cos that's so us."

"I'm serious."

Hunter rolls his eyes, tries to remember what a normal person looks like, acts like. He hasn't been around normal for quite a while now.

"Fancy a snog, then?"

Uma glares at him. "Not so deep into character, Hunt."

Sighing, Hunter catches up her hand in his and together they set off through the park, looking every inch the Citizen couple they aren't. And as he steps out of the gates, Hunter feels a surge of energy, momentum, connection. They're both naked now. Not an implant or a live RET between them. Just him and her and the city.

In the cell, Clarke tosses Leo's RETScan down on the table. "Hung up on me. Now why would a boy with nothing to hide hang up on an officer, Leo? What's the big secret, hmm?"

But Leo doesn't answer. His face a smear of blood, he's fainted again. Clarke closes his eyes, takes a deep breath. He hates it when kids are involved. And these Outsider kids are tougher than most soldiers. He didn't sign up for this when he joined the force, but this is what he's got to do to get the job done. The network must be broken. The country must be kept united.

He's got a son, a boy Leo's age at home. If anyone so much as touched a hair on his head... Clarke sighs, pushing the thoughts down, willing his brain to get in the right place again. Then, scooping up a water jug, he turns and tips the freezing contents over Leo's head, bringing him back to choking consciousness. Clarke bends down low. "Come, my little immigrant friend. You'll have to do better than this. Want your brother to keep his job on the rig? Want to go back to the slums?"

Leo eyes him with rage, but inside his heart sinks. There's no way out of this. He's screwed.

Twenty-two

Uma and Rose stand beside the statue of Charlie Chaplin in Leicester Square, gazing across the paved expanse toward the vaulted double doors of the Dragon Palace. Uma's gaze travels up the stone pillars to the high pointed Chinese roof before settling on the great red dragon that dominates the entire square with wings outstretched and tail curling down to the ground.

She's forgotten how massive this place is. Completed only five years ago, the building soars twenty stories high, housing two thousand separate karaoke booths and twelve monumental luxury gambling rooms, each with its own zodiac-sign motif. But the heart of the building is the Dragon Hall, where the superstar diva Sita Devi reigns supreme. Luminous eyes, ivory skin, and a voice like pure silk, she is the undisputed queen of the Dragon Palace, and every evening, as the world's largest shimmering gold stage curtain lifts on her, every karaoke booth empties and every card table clears as the crowds stampede into the hall for the performance of a lifetime.

Uma shivers. What are the chances of finding a clue to the Keeper in this place? Then her quick eyes catch Hunter as he crosses the square toward them. In a few seconds he is by her side, holding three tokens in his open palm.

"Well, I got us tickets…but it cleared my account out. I had to bribe the ticket guy €2,000 just because I couldn't show ID."

Uma smiles. "Welcome to the Outsider world, my friend."

Rose drags her gaze away from the Dragon Palace entrance. "You got any ideas about what we've got to do once we're inside this piece of madness?"

Uma shakes her head. "No. You?"

Rose turns slowly, her eyes still wild from the story Uma has just poured in her ear. *The Encryption Codes for the Dreamline.* This is the stuff of legend. She forces herself to focus.

"Nope. You sure there was nothing else in the Fleet tunnel other than the Dragon Palace logo?"

"Not that we saw. Mind you, Hunter did get knocked out by a crossbow bolt, remember? Bit distracting."

Rose's eyes flicker. "Then we've *got* to try entering the Code program again. Otherwise what's the plan, to go 'round asking every fool singing Frank Sinatra if he knows who or where the Keeper is?"

Uma shakes her head. "That's the problem, I can't. My implant is burnt out."

Rose stares. "So you haven't been back inside? What about with Guido?"

"We were about to, but the siren went off—and you know the rest."

"Then I'll do it."

"No, Rose, it's too dangerous. Leo nearly died in there."

"So?"

Uma searches her friend's face. "Let's at least look round first before we think about going back *inside*." She runs her hands through her hair. "Am I okay to go in? I can't even remember the last time I changed my clothes."

. Hunter steals a sideways glance at her; even with her old dark hoodie and her pale, exhausted face she is extraordinary. There's a grace, something indefinable about the way she holds herself; she's just like no one else. Uma catches his look, blushes. Then she throws her shoulders back—and together they walk across Leicester Square, into the Dragon Palace.

Uma hands her token to the doorman, steps into the marble foyer and stops dead, stunned by the shimmer and dazzle of light playing over a great fall of water that plunges a full twenty meters from the ceiling. The interior is lavish beyond belief, the curved air staircase, the jungle palms, the jewel-studded walls—but dominating all—the centerpiece—a gigantic bamboo Chinese water clock. Uma gazes up in wonder. As the vast torrent of water begins its descent from the ceiling, it is funneled through a series of bamboo tubes that dip and rise as they fill and empty, the movement driving the massive time mechanism forward with breathtaking, perfect accuracy.

From behind, Rose pushes her in the small of the back and Uma walks on, following Hunter across the smooth marble tiles toward the nearest of the gambling lounges, the Capricorn Hall. A group of giggling women emerge from inside and Uma catches a glimpse of the interior, where a dense crowd of people surge and flow around endless rows of green baize tables. It suddenly hits her, how split the city is, how truly massive the gap is between the Citizens and the Outsiders. She glances at Hunter, realizes with a shock that this is *his* world.

And then from the foyer behind them comes a sudden roar. Uma and Hunter spin around. Twelve jets of water are now spurting high into the air, aimed directly at a silver tank suspended from the ceiling. In seconds it fills and, tipping forward, it releases a hammer. This swings forward, gathering momentum until it hits an enormous dark bronze bell hung from a ceiling beam. A deep booming note sounds through the building and silence falls for a moment on the Dragon Palace. A voice comes through on the address system.

"Ladies and gentlemen, the matinee performance commences in ten minutes. Please take your seats in the Dragon Hall for Sita Devi."

And then, like an ant nest stirred up by a stick, the crowd froths forward; its one purpose, to get to the hall, to hear the diva sing.

Near the doors of the Capricorn Hall, people are suddenly thronging all around them and Rose's eyes sparkle. "Sita Devi! This Dragon Hall might be a good place to start, no?"

A tingle runs down Uma's spine... to see Sita Devi, live? She grins—and some five minutes later they reach the dark-paneled doors of the Dragon Hall. As they step inside Rose stumbles, nearly going down under a bachelorette party. Swearing under her breath, she picks herself up from the crush of pink skirts and casts her eye around the auditorium.

"This is stupid. Let's climb up to that balcony overlooking the right side of the stage and hide in one of the fancy boxes. At least we'll be able to see what's going on from up there."

Hunter swivels round. "But the stairs to the balcony level are all the way on the other side. It'll take hours to get there in this crowd. '

Rose grins. "Ah, come on now, Hunt. You're one of us for today at least."

Elbows angled, she pushes and shoves through a wall of sweaty bodies until she reaches a section of oak-paneled wall. Sizing the climb with expert eyes, Rose leaps upward, her fingers outstretched to catch a low carved ledge. Following this with a rapid series of upward leaps, in seconds she reaches the balcony, vaulting neatly into the velvet-lined interior of the box.

Uma follows. Catching hold of a wooden balustrade, she launches herself upward, and within moments she, too, slides out of sight. Hunter curses, he hates it that she's so good. He reaches for a hold, pulls himself up on to the first tier, but then someone yells from the dress circle above. A guard leans over the edge, shouting at him to get down. Blocking him out, Hunter reaches for a carved centaur head and drags himself into a trembling crouch, before flinging himself sideways onto an ornamental grille directly beneath the balcony. Steadying himself above the crowd, he stretches upward, ready for the final move into the box, but then a whisper comes from behind the curtain that hangs over the edge of the stage.

"*Sst*. Hunter. Here!"

Twisting his head, he can just make out Rose's sneakers perching on a narrow wooden balcony. Changing direction, he slides under the curtain and clambers onto the ledge alongside the others. "What happened to the hiding in the box idea?"

Rose shakes her head. "U.S. ambassador jus' walked in. An' what happened to not gettin' seen by any guards? Are they after you?"

"Don't think so." Hunter peers around the side of the curtain. The guard seems to be gone. His heart sinks. How are they going to find any clues in all this mess?

He glances at Uma. "I think you've got to let Rose go *inside*. Once the show starts, everyone will be distracted, and if we get a clue we can at least move around without all these people bugging us."

Rose nods. "He's right."

Uma's mouth tightens. "But it's dangerous."

"But I don't hurt so easy, girl—an' I won't take a second longer than I have to." Rose shrugs. "We got no choice that I can see."

A beat and then Uma nods. Reaching inside her jacket, she draws out the metal case.

"But you pull out if anything goes wrong, yeah? Even the smallest thing?"

"Aye." Rose's eyes dilate as she opens the case, her fingers fastening around the delicate shell inside. She blows out her cheeks. "Well, so much for me catching Sita Devi. Enjoy for me, willya?"

Uma gives her a long, steady look. "Yes, Rose."

And then suddenly the lights dim and the noise of the crowd changes to a low hum of expectation. . . . This is it, the event of a lifetime, the chance to experience Sita Devi live. Inside the Dragon Hall, ten thousand people adjust their RET Enhancement levels, joining the millions already online on the 家, and the hum builds to a moan, a roar, a foot-stamping thunder until finally the glittering gold curtains sweep open, on a dark stage, illuminated by a single point of light that picks out a delicate figure seated at a baby grand piano. Uma gasps. The woman is like someone come down from another world; her face painted like a courtesan, her hair piled high in a white-powdered Georgian wig, a heavy sapphire brooch sparkling on her deep-slashed vintage Vivienne Westwood blood-red dress, revealing supple dark skin. She's beautiful.

And then Sita Devi begins to sing. In the hall every RET lens fills with the image of her face, her eyes, her lips—and in seconds the audience is completely swept up in the flow. They are on the stage, they are the music, they are the performance, and as Sita Devi swirls up into a high alto, they surge forward, flailing, screaming, fainting, whirling in ecstasy.

Uma grips the balcony rail tight. She's never heard a sound like this. Even though she's naked, listening with no enhancement, the force of the woman's voice overwhelms her. Pure joy, clear like spring water, floods into her heart, and suddenly the tears are streaming down her face.

Twenty-three

As Sita Devi's voice sweeps across the auditorium, Rose takes one last glance around. Then she lifts the delicate shell code and moves it across the implant above her right eye. Hunter watches her closely, sees her eyes blur, and he reaches out his arm to steady her.

He nods at Uma, whispers, "Take her hand, in case she falls." But Uma doesn't respond. Transfixed by Sita, her focus is only on the stage below. Hunter sighs, tightening his grip on Rose's sleeve. It's like both the girls have vanished somewhere, leaving only their bodies alongside him on this tiny balcony rail.

Rose is *inside*. She stands on a long carpeted corridor that runs through an open-plan suite of offices, the room dominated by a huge digital screen at the far end where numbers flicker and roll in constant change as the dollar, the yen, the rupee, the euro fluctuate in the marketplace. Rose blows out her cheeks. At least the Code program is functioning, she's got something to work with. Now all she's got to do is find the clue. It should be near the Dreamline. She peers through the leaves of a potted plant at the office workers in the nearest section.

This is her first time in a Citizen office. God, everyone looks so bored and gray, pretending to work, dragging their saggy arses around the place.

A woman suddenly comes around the corner, heading toward the water cooler. Rose presses up against the wall, but the woman looks straight through her like she doesn't exist. Can't she see her? Rose pads over to the nearest workstation where a paunchy guy is tapping in database figures. She touches him on the shoulder, but gets no response. She reaches over and hits a couple of keys, but the man doesn't even look up. She's invisible all right. Rose looks around again, and this time she sees the junk. She can't believe she didn't see it before, maybe it's because the office workers are acting as if the piles of paper, documents, forms, and emails that spill out on to the floor don't exist. Well, one thing's for sure, this is the Darknet all right.

Rose rubs her nose, what's going on? Normally once she's accessed the Darknet she knows how to find the Dreamline easily; she's an Outsider, she's been taught the signs—but in this place, she's got no clue how to find it. It's like the Code program's partly shut down, leaving only a small part functioning. All the usual signs are missing. Rose juts her jaw, well, there's no point wasting time here. Taking the first area on her left, she searches booth after booth, office after office. Outside, the sun shines, but no one looks out; everyone's tapping at screens, faking work, secretly hooked into the 家. In fact the whole thing feels fake, even the plants seem made of dusty plastic, and on every desk, on every screen is a clock. Time is money. Benjamin Franklin rules. Okay.

Rose finally reaches a set of heavy doors at the far end of the room. She peers through a circular window cut into the doors. The room beyond is a cafeteria, filled with rows of colored tables and chairs, and as she pushes the door open, a microwaved food smell hits her.

The room is busy—a long queue snakes around the edge, but again the workers look half-dead. There's no animation and *everything* looks plastic somehow. People queuing up to buy plastic food with plastic tokens to eat at plastic tables. Reaching forward, Rose swipes a chip from a nearby tray. Urggh, plastic too. She chews thoughtfully. What does it taste like? What actual living thing? The taste of Zukko's shish kebabs down on the Bow main strip sizzles into her mind. Explosive, full of zing and enough chili to blow your lips clean off your face. Kebabs that come from his family's lambs that graze on the old Mile End Park; they're flaming on the barbecue coals before they know what's hit them.

On the balcony, Hunter watches Rose carefully as she murmurs and twitches, her eyes rolling back in her head. He touches her shoulder, whispers, "Rose?" But she doesn't respond. Over to his right, Uma has eyes only for the performance as she leans out dangerously far over the stage. Hunter frowns, willing himself to concentrate on Rose, to ignore the singer down below. At least one of them has to be focused.

Each and every RETScan lens in the Dragon Hall fills with images of Sita Devi's neck, her breasts, her delicate fingers on the keyboard. She is joined onstage by dancers. A young man runs to her and as the singer turns to him, he lifts her high and she throws her head back in pure pleasure. The dancers now surge toward the crowd, lights strobing and arcing across their fabulous bodies. A flawless union of actor and crowd, the perfect symmetry of the 家, the *family*.

Uma watches, captivated. So this is what it's all about. . . . She cannot feel exactly what the crowd feels, but she can guess. Emotion, unity, togetherness—and all so perfectly unreal. She's always wondered how the Sleepers could be so blind to the world. She always thought they just didn't care. But now she sees. They've just invented a new one.

In the cafeteria, Rose checks the time. She's got to make something happen, find the clue before the Code program shuts her out. What's with these people, this place? She needs to stir things up. Crossing to the food counter, she picks up a handful of chips, flings them at a knot of businessmen. Nobody even looks up, so she stomps to the counter and hurls a tall stack of dirty trays to the ground. Nothing. She's invisible, inaudible. And then something happens. From the far side of the cafeteria, Rose catches a janitor looking directly at her. Can he see her for sure? Maintaining eye contact, Rose picks up a pizza slice and smears it into a balding guy's face, and the janitor frowns, setting off across the hall toward her while raising a walkie-talkie to his lips.

Rose hasn't stayed alive as long as she has by waiting for men in uniform to catch up with her. She breaks into a light trot, heading for a set of fire doors, but as she pushes through them onto the stairs, she hears shouts—and turning, sees armed guards bearing down on her from the stairs above. Rose hesitates, she doesn't want to quit the program, but she's got to get away from these guys, and with a movement born of pure instinct, Rose vaults over the iron railings down onto the floor below. But as she jumps, an explosion of energy blasts through her as a giant shudder runs through the program—

On the balcony, Rose tips forward—and before Hunter can grab her, pull her back, she leaps clear of the gallery, landing heavily on the stage below.

Landing on the stairwell, Rose screams as her ankle buckles under the impact. Why can she feel pain? She reaches up to disconnect her implant, but it isn't there, it's disappeared somehow. She's trapped inside! The soldiers are closing in on her. She forces herself to her feet and sets off. Bursting through a set of fire doors, she charges into a bustling cafeteria kitchen and, narrowly avoiding a vast tray of pink blancmange, she hurdles over a bank of microwaves.

On the balcony ledge, Hunter shakes Uma.
"Hey!"
Uma gasps. The hall is in uproar. Sita Devi has half-risen from her baby grand, and around her performers stare in openmouthed shock as Rose careens across the stage before finally hurling herself over a synthesizer bank near the left wing.

Rose barges out through the rear of the kitchen and as the doors slam behind her, the lights suddenly blow, plunging the place into total darkness. She trips, falling heavily, and her right hand smashes against glass. Rose feels the blood spurting from her wrist. How can she be bleeding? This is no ordinary program. If she gets hurt in here, it's for real. She's got to get out. Once again she tries to exit, to access her implant, but the program won't respond. The guards will be here any minute, she's got to hide, to buy herself more time.

Staggering to her feet, she stumbles forward till she feels a wall in front of her, and using her outstretched hands, she sweeps the surface for a light switch. Her hand brushes against something and she slaps her fingers against it. *Yes!* The light flickers on, revealing a filthy backroom; dirt and scraps on the floor, washing hanging from a line and a row of soiled mattresses stacked against the far wall. Rose scans the room. Her heart sinks. There's no exit!

In the hall, Uma grabs the balcony rail. "We've got to get her out of there."

Hunter nods toward a group of security guards running toward the stage. "I'll target them, you get Rose, right?"

Uma nods. "Bring down as many as you can. I'm going round the back to cut her off by that synth bank. I've got to smash her implant. It's the only way to get her out."

Together they leap from the balcony. As he lands, Hunter hears the hiss and angry roar of the crowd, aims for the knot of security guards streaming onto the stage steps. Behind him, Uma darts behind the curtains, making her way toward the synth racks where Rose hides.

In the backroom Rose has only a few moments before the guards catch up with her. At the far end of the room is a toilet block; maybe there's an exit in here? It's her only hope. She runs over, throws her weight against the door, but it's locked. Looking up, she takes in the high rectangular windows running along the top of the row of stalls. Whirling around, she drags a table under the window then slams a chair on top of it. Then climbing up she grabs the bathroom window ledge and, using her other hand to unlock and raise the window, she kicks the chair away from under her, swinging her legs through the gap. A hideous stench rises up to greet her as she lands inside. Rose stares around, wild. *There is no through door here either.*

Her only chance of escape has gone. She can hear the guards outside. The only thing she can do is hide. Pray they don't check in here. Rushing into the nearest cubicle, she eases the door shut behind her and then squats down on the rusty, feces-spattered toilet bowl, desperately trying to stifle her breathing, to calm the beat of her own terrified heart. A bullet in here is death for sure.

The Dragon Hall is utterly silent. The performers frozen, the crowd stunned, fuzzy, coming down off their RET Enhancers. In the silence, Rose dives from behind the synths and her momentum carries her forward across the stage, slamming her into the legs of the baby grand. For a second she lies there, dazed, before hunching herself into a tight ball and wrapping her arms around Sita Devi's legs. The singer's face contorts in terror and she motions for the guards to back away. Who knows what this insane girl will do to her?

Hunched over in the stall, Rose hears the footsteps of the guards, the burst of gunfire as the bathroom lock is destroyed. She hunkers down in pure terror. There's no escape, no jump, no leap she can make. She can't get out of this. All that stands between her and a bullet is this rusting, filthy door. Her eyes sweep over the broken frame, over the stained metal, over the graffiti verse cut deep into the surface right in front of her.

There Chairon stands, who rules the dreary coast…

Her eyes widen, is this it? The clue? She tries to take in the rest of the lines, but there's no time.…The stall door buckles, slamming inward, and suddenly she's staring up at the Kossak, into the barrel of a Heckler & Koch MP7.

On the Dragon Hall stage, there is a sudden flash of movement from behind the left curtain as Uma races across the space, aiming for the baby grand piano. Dodging two guards, she throws herself on top of Rose. Her fingers reach for her friend's forehead—

The guard smiles down at Rose, his finger tightening on the trigger. Rose screams in terror—but then suddenly the soldier's body is ripped in two, his rifle clatters to the ground, his face contorts in pain, and he screams.

A heavy fist connects with Uma's jaw, knocking her sideways. The guards are on top of her, pulling her away from Rose. Spitting, twisting, Uma desperately struggles to break free. She almost got her fingers on Rose's implant, dislodged it. Her friend is going to die if she doesn't destroy it.

Rose's stall smashes onto its side as it is hit by a great sloshing wave of sewage that surges and boils through the bathroom. She makes a desperate grab for the toilet bowl as the weight of the water crashes down on her. But she can't hold on, her hands slip on the bowl, the force is too strong, and suddenly she's falling, choking, plunging down, down, down, carried at breakneck speed along pipes and buried streams; the great brick tunnels in the earth rushing up to meet her.

Rose braces herself for the killing impact, the spike of stone and steel through her guts—and then, suddenly there is no impact—and she is somehow still falling. She's in the water, she's in the river. She's still alive. How? Down, down, down again she falls, plummeting deep into the abyss. And then with an explosion of light the Dreamline appears beneath her.

There it is! Spiraling down toward it, Rose fumbles to catch hold of the pulsing network. A brilliant jolt of pure energy jags through her body and for a long, timeless moment she is *there*—connected to every point in time and space, plugged into the mainframe. And then it's gone and blackness envelops her once more. Rose's body plunges straight through the other side of the Dreamline, and seconds later she hits the riverbed; striking the soft, slimy, treacherous base with massive force, a great cloud of mud billowing up around her. She lies there, unconscious. She hasn't got the will to rise again.

Rose lies motionless on the stage. Uma, pinned down by guards, screams, a wild animal scream—and on the far side of the arena, Hunter drags himself clear of the knot of guards surrounding him and races over to Uma. He launches himself at her guards and unleashes a rain of blows and kicks on their bodies.

The heavy current beats down on Rose's body. Eyes staring, heart frozen, the last beat of warm blood leaves her heart.

Suddenly Uma is free. Squirming out from under the tangle of limbs, she hurls herself at Rose, her fingers tightening like a vise on her friend's forehead.

"Rose! C'mon. Up!"

But now another guard's hands are on her throat, tearing her backward. Uma delivers a final despairing smack across her friend's white cheek. And then the guard grabs her by the hair and slams her against the piano legs. For a moment Uma lies still, stunned. But behind her Rose moves. Her body bucks, her hands spasm upward.

On the riverbed the girl's eyes open. And with the last bit of will, with the last remaining dregs of air in her lungs, she launches herself up to the surface of the water, kicking her legs like a maniac, reaching, grasping for the air as she explodes through the surface.

Onstage, Rose's eyes open, she draws in a great ragged breath and screams at the top of her lungs—

"*There Chairon stands, who rules the dreary coast!*"

—before she collapses back on to the boards, a great burst of pain ripping through her right eye as her implant rips free.

For a moment all is silent in the Dragon Hall, all eyes on the girl at the center of a group of angry guards.

"Wait!" Sita Devi stares at Rose, wild-eyed. Suddenly she throws her body between the girl and the men. "Don't touch her."

And then she rises. Turning to the audience, she bows. "Ladies and gentlemen, the show is over." And indicating to the guards to bring along the intruders, she sweeps off the stage.

Twenty-four

At the base of the stage steps, Sita Devi turns to the senior officer.

"Bring them to my room."

He frowns. "With all due respect, ma'am, we can't do that. This is a serious breach of security."

Sita Devi's lip curls. "Three teenagers?"

"They attacked you. Favelados by the look of them."

Sita draws herself up, flashes him a look. "Officer, they did not attack me. Do as I say. These are only young people, and I do not wish them to be caught up with the police."

The guard swallows. "As you please, ma'am, but it's against my advice."

A smile sweeps across her beautiful face. "That has been noted. Now please, to my suite. *All* of them."

Hunter and Uma carry Rose between them, with Uma holding the girl's hand up high to staunch the flow of blood. After a few minutes, Sita arrives at her dressing-room door. Hustling them inside, she slams the door, barring the guards outside despite their protests.

"Lay the girl down here." She indicates a low divan in the corner of the room.

Hunter and Uma gently ease Rose onto the bed and, as Sita

bends down close over her, Uma watches her, magnetized. If anything, she's more beautiful offstage, more real. Everything about
her shimmers softly, as if her dress is made from candlelight. Pushing Rose's hair back from her forehead, Sita, in perfect clear tones,
slowly begins to chant.

> *There Chairon stands, who rules the dreary coast*
> *A sordid god: down from his hairy chin*
> *A length of beard descends, uncombed, unclean*
> *His eyes, like hollow furnaces on fire;*
> *A girdle, foul with grease, binds his obscene attire.*

Rose's eyes widen in amazement, her good hand reaching out to
grip Sita's forearm. "That's it...the verse, the graffiti...on the toilet
door...Before Uma ripped me out."

"Easy." Uma frowns. Rose's eyes flutter shut again. Then Uma
turns, staring full in Sita's face. "What's going on? How could you
know that?"

The woman holds her eye. "Because I hold one of the Keeper
directions. This verse is my activation."

Uma gasps. "You're one of us?"

"Yes."

Uma and Hunter exchange shocked glances. Is this real?

"So do you know what we must do next?"

Sita nods. "You must go to the Ferryman's Seat."

"What's that?"

"It's an old resting place of the watermen, down by the Thames."

Uma frowns. "Where?"

A shake of the jeweled head. "I don't know."

"But how can't you know?"

Sita drops her gaze. "I'm sorry, but I only know one element. It's
the Keeper system, to guard against—"

Uma closes her eyes. "Betrayal. I know."

The singer looks from her to Hunter. "You seem very young for
this. May I ask please your names?"

"My name is Uma . . . Zella Shater is my aunt and Guido Fernandez is my cousin. This girl is my friend Rose McGuire from the Bow favela—and he is Hunter Nash, a . . . friend."

Sita's eyes widen. "Ah, so you are Zella's girl? I know of you. But why in Shiva's name are *you* taking on this burden? Where are your aunt and cousin in all of this?"

"Zella was taken to Belmarsh yesterday . . . and Guido . . ." Uma's voice drops. "He was in the Isle of Dogs when I last saw him."

Sita glances at Hunter. "You are a Citizen, yes?"

Hunter nods. He doesn't know how they know, but they all do.

"And forgive me, but how can we know to trust you?"

Uma's face flushes. "Because we can. He has shown himself completely true in the last two days."

Sita stands. "Uma, I must speak with you alone for a moment."

Uma flashes a glance at Hunter. They promised to do this together. No more secrets.

"Please, Uma."

He nods slowly. "Go, I'll stay here with Rose."

Uma rises and follows Sita into a costume room leading off from the main suite. The singer closes the door behind her. "Surely you must take this to Guido?"

"No." Uma hesitates. Can she tell this woman the truth? She wants to so much. She perceives Sita's clear mind, it reminds her of Zella. A cold, steely will to survive, to win.

Uma swallows. "I think Guido ordered Hunter killed as soon as my back was turned. I'd just told him about the Codes and I guess he was trying to cover the traces. Either that or he wanted them for himself. I don't know . . . but my cousin was released from Kossak custody very soon for someone so senior." Uma flushes a deep red. "I mean, I'm not saying Guido's been turned, but I don't know . . . and I've got to be sure."

Sita sighs. "Are you sure you are thinking this through? It *must* be he ordered this killing to cover the traces. Guido is Outsider in his blood. He is on the Council. Every day he must make strong decisions to keep us safe, to keep the movement alive. Being a leader means hard choices."

"To kill my friend? Who I brought to the favela as a guest? I don't want any part of that movement."

"Maybe he felt he had no choice. We are threatened on all sides and the boy could have been a spy. Are you...sure you're taking the right way here?"

Uma finds herself starting to shake. There's nothing she'd love more than to be rid of this weight, to trust her cousin and be free again. But she made a promise to Zella...and she can never forgive Guido for what he did.

Suddenly there is a knock at the door. Sita moves to the wall and activates the corridor scanner. The sweaty face of the Dragon Hall stage manager appears onscreen. From behind him, Sita catches a movement—a glimpse of a soldier in Kossak uniform—as he moves into the shadow of the passageway.

Sita deactivates the monitor. "Quick, you must get out of here. They have brought soldiers in! Go through this window into the alley below!"

"But what about Rose? I can't leave her here."

Another knock at the door, more urgent this time.

"Don't worry. I'll protect her the best I can." Sita's face melts into a self-deprecating smile. "I am not a diva for nothing."

Uma stands motionless. Rose! What has she done to her? Letting her go unprotected inside the Code program—and now leaving her here to face the Kossaks. But the woman's right, Rose is in no state to run. And she, Uma, must run now as if her life depends on it. She flings the connecting door open.

"Hunter, we've got to get out of here!"

Hunter quickly crosses the room and, joining Uma at the window, he helps her ease the heavy pane upward. Another knock at the door and this time Sita Devi reactivates the scanner.

"Yes, what is it?"

The manager's anxious face fills the screen. "Ma'am. Are you all right? May I come in?"

"Really, Paul, it's not a good time."

"Yes, but I was told there was trouble."

"We are all perfectly fine...and I'd prefer to be left alone."

His eyes flicker, but his voice remains steady. "But it's only me, ma'am. I'd feel a whole lot easier if you'd just let me in for a moment."

Out of the corner of her eye, Sita sees Uma make the jump. She can't delay too long, or they'll break the door down. "Well, if you insist. Please give me a moment to dress." She disconnects, just as Hunter is swinging his legs through the open frame. Sita runs to his side, snatches at his hand. "Don't leave her, Hunter. Promise me this."

He turns to gaze into her huge kohl-lined eyes. "Are you really... an Outsider?"

"Yes."

"But you seem just like one of...us."

Sita Devi cocks her head. "On the outside, yes. Maybe you too, Hunter? Now go, and God speed!"

Hunter nods and lets go. Sita Devi watches his body plunge downward into the rat-infested alley below, sees him land and roll before setting off at a fast run toward Uma at the back-street end of the alley. She closes her eyes against the rising tears. Then closing the window behind her, she fixes on her most imperious face as she turns toward the door.

In the military HQ at Vauxhall, Commander Clarke strides into the cell. The nearest of his men has Leo in a brutal headlock. Clarke steels himself. He hasn't got the time to break the boy slowly. He needs him to deliver a message. Word's just come through that Hunter and the Outsider girl have escaped capture again.

He nods to the other soldier in the cell who pulls out a pair of serrated pliers and, grabbing Leo's hand, positions the metal teeth over the base of the boy's thumb.

Leo screams in terror, "No!"

Clarke flings his hand up. "Tch, all this noise. I'm tired of your pathetic lies. So this is how it works from now. You help us and we help you. Or one word from me and he'll rip your thumb off and toss it into the bin. All you need to do is make the call, Leo."

The boy suddenly collapses, breaking into great sobs, and at a sign from Clarke, the soldier releases his hold. For a fraction of a second, the Commander closes his eyes. Thank God he doesn't have to take this further. He spins Leo's RETScan across the table. "Do it good, son. Your life depends on it."

Hunter and Uma race across the back of Leicester Square, cutting through Chinatown before turning into the intricate network of back streets of Soho. Hunter suddenly grabs Uma, pulling her to a stop.

"We have to know where we're headed. This blind running is no good."

She nods. "But how?"

"I'm going to power up my RET. Pray it works one last time."

"No, it's too risky. The Kossaks will track us immediately."

"No choice, Uma. We've got to know where the Ferryman's Seat is."

Uma wipes her forehead with the back of her hand. He's right. But she's sick of her friends going into danger. She glances at Hunter. What is he going to do once all this is over?

"Okay, do it, but go as fast as you can."

Hunter flicks the device on, waiting for a moment for the lens to power up. It flickers, blurs, but he can just about make out the 家 symbol. *He's connected.*

"I'm in."

Quickly, he punches in the name, frowning impatiently as the information feeds on to his lens. "Got it! *The Ferryman's Seat*—it's on Bankside, next to Southwark Bridge. You know the way?"

Uma snorts. "I was born knowing this city. When you Sleepers are all tucked up and dreaming at night, this is our place."

Hunter grins. "Yeah, yeah…" He reaches for the power-off switch, when suddenly a piercing tone rings out: *AAAEEEEEE-EEEEIIIIOUUUUUUUUUAAAAA!*

Hunter freezes. Leo?

Uma chops the air. "Don't answer it."

His finger is on the power button. But this is Leo. He can't just ignore him. He's got to do it. He hits *connect*. "Leo?"

Leo's breezy voice fills his ear. "Yo, amigo, where you at?"

Uma's hand falls to her side in disbelief.

Hunter takes a step away. "Are you free?"

"Yeah, man, them Kossaks can't keep a man like me inside for long. Questioned me, but I told 'em nothing and so they had to let me go, innit? But look, I got to talk to you, urgent."

"I can't."

"But I *got* to speak to you. Something I have to tell you. *Now.* Not here, on the network, in case they're listening. Where you at?"

"I—I can't tell you."

In the cell, Leo glances over at Clarke, who mouths, "Keep him talking."

The digital crosshairs of his GPS tracker narrow in on Soho.

Leo swallows. "Hunter, you owe me big times, they kicked me around good and I din't tell them or your old man nothing. So I'm not askin', I'm telling. I got to talk to you. Couple minutes is all I need."

Uma grabs hold of Hunter's shoulder, gesturing for him to hang up.

Hunter frowns. "But, Leo..."

"Would you shut it? I ain't slept for twenty-four hours, I'm starving—and I'm willing to haul myself over town to save your ass. You owe me a beer...and a bowl of sweet-bean noodles at the minimum."

Hunter presses his fingers to his temple. "Hundred percent this can't wait?"

"No!"

"And you can't tell me now."

"No way."

"All right. But on my life I can only give you five minutes. I'll be down on Bankside by Southwark Bridge. By the Globe Theater, in half an hour. Can you make it?"

"Sweet. See you there, brother. Thanks."

Hunter disconnects. Uma pushes him in the chest. "What are you playing at?"

His eyes blaze. "He's my best friend and he was *begging* to see me. It's not only you in the world, y'know?"

"We can't trust *anyone* today. The Kossaks might have been listening in. Did you ask him why they let him go?"

"You mean we can't trust your people. Leo is sound. He'd never let them listen into a call between us."

"Sound? He stole the Codes before, remember?"

"Yeah, but he made a promise not to mess up again. Did it on Paolo's life."

Uma whirls around. "Listen. Sirens!" She reaches for a drainpipe.

Moments later the Kossaks flood into the Soho back streets, but Hunter and Uma are already sliding down from the roof into a courtyard on Glasshouse Street.

"Follow me," whispers Uma, and together they set off toward the Haymarket, heading south, in the direction of the river.

Twenty-five

Sita Devi paces her room. Despite all she could do, the Kossaks have dragged Rose away for questioning. She's got to do something, clearly the Codes are not safe in Uma's hands. She's too young. But who can she trust with this level of information? Him! He's the only one. Closing her eyes, she accesses her implant, calls up his number, and after a moment a familiar voice answers. Sita Devi takes a deep breath. "I have news, father...."

Some five minutes later, as she finishes pouring out her story, Sita pauses. "Did I do the right thing in telling you?"

In the old tumbledown house in the Isle of Dogs, Harry nods. "Yes, Sita, you did well. Don't worry, my child. I will send help."

Disconnecting, he turns, face somber. "Well, it seems we have found Uma. Why did you not tell me that she had the Codes?"

"I—I wanted to, but..."

Harry sighs. "I know. You wanted to keep the secret close. You did right, son."

"Where is she now?"

"Heading for the Ferryman's Steps, with the Kossaks in pursuit."

Guido rises quickly from his seat. "Where's that?"

"On Bankside, by Southwark Bridge. As I recall it is set into a wall, just along from the Globe Theater. Watermen have rested there since time out of mind. Go quickly."

Suddenly there comes a loud knock at the front door and Fats steps into the room.

Guido glances up, takes in his bruised face. "You hurt?"

They exchange a long glance. Fats looks down. "I'm fine, it's nothing."

Guido snatches up his rifle. "Come with me now." He nods at Harry as he strides out of the room. "I'll bring her home safe, father."

Little Fats wheels around after him, massaging his bruised wrists as he runs to keep up with Guido.

After they leave, Harry sinks down on the ratty pink sofa and sits quietly, listening to the river. Why must there always be so much violence and fear? It seems to him that man is going backward. An image of the river at Vauxhall comes to his mind. The "Celtic golgotha' they call it—a place where thousands of skulls were thrown into the river after the great battles with the Romans. Death and destruction for sure, but at least in those days there was honor. And humility. When the fighting was over, men returned their spirit to the water and their bodies back to nature. Now the fighting never stops and the bodies are left to rot in the street.

Hunter presses himself flat against the wall of the Globe Theater and lets out a long, slow breath. They've made it. That last run over the Millennium Bridge; a frantic ten-minute burst on the exposed footbridge all the way from St. Paul's down to the Tate was the worst part.

He shivers. Evening is fast approaching; a cold mist is rising and the final lurid rays of the setting sun cast a strange light over the surface of the river, the last bright tints flickering over the inky shadows. The Thames seems out of another time, flowing onward, carrying smells of the past—tobacco, rum, coffee, spices, oranges, sugar, tea, wine, brandy—and older, forgotten things, past lives uncounted. Hunter checks the time and peers up and down the riverbank. Leo ought to be here by now. He frowns, something is nagging at him, but he can't work out what it is.

He glances at Uma. "Where now?"

She nods toward Southwark Bridge. "Don't know. Maybe somewhere along that row of cafés?"

Keeping close to the wall, they take to the cobbled street. In the fading light, there are a few people around, mostly tourists, but no one lingering, no one hanging around in the chilly evening air. Hunter and Uma walk quickly, scanning the buildings, the walls, until suddenly Uma stops, pointing to the corner of a restaurant, where a small rectangular block is cut low into the side of the wall.

"Look!" They start to run.

In a few moments they stand in front of a stone recess with a heavy slate slab across the base. Above it, a plaque is screwed into the wall, bearing the words, *The Ferryman's Seat.*

Hunter balls his fist. "Yes!"

"Shhh." Uma frowns, nodding toward an old lady in a heavy coat and red scarf who sits, huddled over a chestnut brazier, a few paces to the left. "Yes *what*? What do we do with this now? Where's the clue?"

Hunter grins. "Bring the mood down, why don't you? We found the thing after getting across London with a zillion Kossaks at our back. At least be happy for one second."

Uma pulls her lips back over her teeth in a Hollywood-style grin for a fleeting moment. "Enough?"

Hunter rolls his eyes. "More than."

They both turn back to the seat and for a while they pore over the wall, the surrounding stone blocks, the sign. Frowning, Hunter begins to read out loud. . . .

This ferryman's seat, located on previous foundations on this site, was constructed for the convenience of the Bankside watermen who operated ferrying services across the river. The seat's age is unknown but it is thought to have ancient origins.

He taps his teeth with his knuckles. "Maybe there's something hidden underneath the stone?"

"Move it if you can, but I reckon it weighs about a ton, Hunter."

"All right, then, what about the watermen bit? Maybe that's the clue."

"You know any watermen to ask? Got a number in your RET? Watermen Limited, for all your secret-clue requests?"

Hunter eyes the old lady warming her hands at the brazier. "You got any better ideas?"

"No. I thought there would be another sign here. We haven't got time for these games." Uma throws herself down on the old stone seat, suddenly furious. "What kind of crazy system is this? You'd think we'd work out something more sophisticated. No wonder everyone thinks we're backward."

"Works pretty well, seems to me. It's impossible to follow these clues unless you've got serious Outsider knowledge and help from the community. You see why the Kossaks get nowhere with cracking the Dreamline. They'd have to infiltrate the movement big time—the people, the life, the world—to ever stand a chance of getting anywhere."

But the anger bubbles up inside Uma. Springing to her feet, she spreads her arms wide, shouts: "*There Chairon stands, who rules the dreary coast!* Anyone got any ideas? Anything at all?" Her voice bounces off the walls, and a few people turn to stare at the strange shouting girl, but Hunter isn't listening. A strange sense of dread falls over him. It's Leo. What is it? He said something weird. Hunter goes back over the RET conversation again. *Kossaks—in overnight—owes him—got something can't say online—starving—sweet-bean noodles—meet in half an hour.* Then it hits him. Leo hates, literally *pukes* around sweet-bean noodles—last year he ate a bowl and threw up on Hunter's jacket. So why did he say it? Because he *couldn't speak freely.* He was trying to warn Hunter. And that must mean the Kossaks still have him. Hunter stares round wildly. It's a trap!

A shout comes from the river's edge. Hunter turns his head and sees, as if in slow motion, a scuffle breaking out by the pier. A boy is struggling with an armed soldier. Hunter catches sight of a ragged Mohawk. It's Leo! And then from beyond him, high up on Southwark Bridge, he suddenly sees the soldiers racing across the walkway.

Fury blazes up inside and he races toward Leo. As he draws alongside, he lashes out his left foot, catching the soldier in the knee before pivoting and slamming his heel into the man's groin. Taken by surprise, the Kossak staggers off balance, his gun clattering to the ground, and before he knows what he's doing, Hunter lunges for the weapon, scraping it up in his right hand. But as he raises it, the soldier springs forward, his hands closing like a vise around Hunter's wrist in a desperate attempt to wrench the gun free. Bending the boy's wrist inward, the soldier yanks his forearm diagonally, dragging him off balance.

Hunter lurches backward and the soldier presses home his advantage. Still gripping Hunter's hands around the gun handle, he pushes Hunter backward, sending him crashing down onto the pier steps. But as Hunter lands, with the full weight of the man on top of him, he is suddenly jolted through with a violent explosion. Above him the soldier's eyes widen and then he collapses, his body falling lifeless onto Hunter's chest, pinning him underneath. Hunter stares up in blind shock. What just happened? The gun, his finger—it must have hit the trigger as he fell on to the steps. What has he done? But it was a mistake. Hunter stares up in utter shock, transfixed by the unconscious man who sprawls over him, blood pouring from a great hole in his chest.

"Hunter!" With a great effort he turns his head. Uma. He can't work out what she's saying. Lifting his head, he peers woozily along the riverbank. Fighting has broken out all around him. A group of ragged men are exchanging fire with the Kossaks from behind the restaurant terraces. Who are they?

Uma pulls at his arm. "Come on, get up!"

Hunter drags in a ragged breath, starts to squirm out from under the soldier, and, as he kicks his way free, the man's inert body rolls down the pier stairs and falls into the Thames.

Uma grabs him by the shoulders. "Leo's gone. Ran off behind the theater. Come on!"

Hunter stares at her, dazed. "Where?"

"The boat."

But he can't move somehow, he can't make his muscles obey him. Uma shoves him forward, literally forcing him in a zigzagging run along the pier walkway, out over the river, to where the woman in the red scarf crouches at the water's edge. She clutches the side of a motorboat with clenched hands.

"You!" cries Hunter.

She nods. "Yes, I heard it all. So's I called the Ferryman, brung our people out. No time. Jump, boy!"

Bullets ring out on the wooden pier slats. Throwing himself forward, Hunter lands heavily in the boat. He catches a brief glimpse of an old man in a long, dark coat before the engine roars to life and the boat surges forward, gunfire spattering in the water all around. Hunter crouches down—every moment expecting to feel the bullets rip into his flesh—but suddenly the city around him plunges into total darkness. Every light in every streetlamp, every room, every building dies. A massive power cut; it's as if someone's thrown a great black curtain over the fog-bound city. Hunter gasps. Suddenly they've got a chance. They are invisible on this dark water.

Over by the Millennium Bridge, Commander Clarke smashes Leo's RETScan on the jeep dashboard in rage. He was too cautious, wanted to lure them in with the boy. Well, this isn't over. He's got a backup plan. He knows now what they are carrying and he's not going to let it slip through his fingers. But which way are they headed? You can't tell with these damn people. Activating his secure comms line, he barks into the speaker. "All units on the north side proceed east. All units on the Southbank proceed west. The target is on the river. Do not allow them to land." He turns to the officer next to him. "And someone get to the boy's father. Break him."

Lying flat on a scaffolding board just beneath the central struts of Southwark Bridge, Guido stares through his rifle sight as Uma's boat disappears from sight. His dark brows draw down as the Kossak jeeps start to pour east and west. He's got to slow the police down, buy more time. He *knows* she's heading east. He can feel it. Stifling a grunt of pain, he adjusts his body postion, now taking careful aim at the fast-moving traffic above him.

Pressing the rifle sight to his eye, he waits for a moment until he is securely locked onto the HGV. Then he squeezes the trigger. He waits, face impassive, as the lorry skids hard across the road, coming to a jackknifed halt across the bridge, its front tires blown to shreds.

Beside him Little Fats whistles in appreciation. "Nice shooting, mate."

Guido nods in satisfaction. The truck has completely blocked the traffic in both directions. That should hold back the eastbound Kossaks for a while. Shouldering his rifle, he reaches up for the metal struts of the bridge railings. "Move! We can't allow them to get out of sight."

Twenty-six

City Hall stands in darkness. In the mayor's office the emergency energy council sit in silence, waiting for the backup generator to kick in. Evan Nash takes off his glasses and rubs his sore eyes. When will this day end? Somehow, he can't shake off his earlier visit to the Kossak headquarters. Commander Clarke's cold smile is sticking in his throat—and the way he talked about the favelas, like the people there were scum—when did we start giving men like him so much power? When did we get so scared? He can't get Leo's bruised, frightened face out of his mind. Evan shakes his head, tries to push down the anger, but he can't somehow.

How many times has he sat through a moment, a meeting like this? He's served under three mayors and he's sick of them all. He glances toward the head of the table, where the mayor sits in darkness—and he feels his anger grow. It's because of short-term idiots like him that we're in the mess we're in. They knew about peak oil in the first decade of the twenty-first century. But every political leader, every chairman of every oil company denied it or ignored it, leaving countries helpless when the crisis finally hit.

The lights flicker on as the reserve power kicks in. The mayor sweeps the room with a reassuring smile. "So, back to our targets. . . .

Despite today's crisis, we predict that both the Russian gas and Bradwell B will be back online in the next few days and London will—"

"—What?"

"Excuse me?"

Evan shifts in his seat. "London will what? Be back to normal?"

The mayor frowns. "With the new capacity coming online from twenty new nuclear power stations in the next two years—yes, the country will be on track to return to normal energy levels. I don't think now is the right time to—"

"Question what we're doing? Oh, I think it's a pretty good time." Evan waves his hand at the dark city all around. "Normal? There is no normal anymore. That's all gone now. Look at us—dependent on Chinese aid, up to our necks in debt, under the rule of the harshest peacetime government in history. We're trying to build a new energy system here, sir. Would it kill us to stop for a second and ask who we're building it for and why? This time it's our duty to create something fair, something that works for ordinary people, that will be fair for their children's children too. Like the Outsiders do."

The mayor glances at the shocked faces of the meeting group. "You need to calm down, Mr. Nash. We have to work on the best way to give people energy now."

Under the table, Evan clenches his fist. The mayor's right, he really needs to get control of himself, but somehow he can't do it, he can't hold the words back any longer. "What have I got to be calm about? Why should I trust the government to do anything right? Fifteen years ago they panicked and went for nuclear power to bridge the energy gap. And what have we got to show for it? We've waited five years for this first one, the overdue Bradwell B, it's cost billions in taxes we don't have...and we've still got no power! Apparently all it takes is a small group of dissidents to shut it down, if it *was* them that closed it. I haven't seen any evidence. These massive power plants are too dangerous, too vulnerable to be reliable. We've got to get people making their own energy...like they do in the favelas."

The mayor slams his hand down on the table. "For God's sake, man, get a grip."

Evan picks up his glasses, clamping his teeth down on the words that are pushing up, past his chest, his throat. There's a roomful of guys ready to take his job if he gets out of line.

"With all due respect, sir, I think I've got a grip. I live the reality of this energy gap. I clean up your dirty stinking mess every day I come to work. It's you who needs to get real."

In the silence that follows, Evan picks up his papers and marches out of the room. As he shuts the door, a wave of panic engulfs him. What has he done? Heart pounding, he catches the elevator down two floors before turning into the corridor leading to his office. And then he stops dead, transfixed by the breaking news feed on the widescreen monitor on the wall, his son's face staring back at him from the screen, a line of scrolling text updating underneath—*Hunter Nash wanted in connection with the shooting of a military police fifth batallion officer.*

Evan fumbles for his RETScan and punches in Hunter's number, praying, screaming inside, for him to pick up. But after a few moments the call dies in dead airspace. Oh, where is he? And then he turns, sees the three officers moving swiftly down the hall toward him.

In seconds they are upon him, the lead man flashing a police badge in his face.

"Mr. Nash?"

Evan narrows his eyes. "Where's my son?"

The detective frowns. "Can we move into your office please, sir?"

"No! I have to find him."

The man signals and the armed constables spread across the hallway, blocking Evan's way, hustling him back inside the room. The detective follows, quietly closing the door behind him.

Evan is pressed back against his desk, his chest heaving. "Why are you treating me like this?"

The detective holds out a hand. "Sir, we don't have time. We ask the questions, understand?"

Evan takes a breath, tries to control his breathing.

The detective nods. "That's better. Your son, Hunter Nash, shot an officer—"

Evan grips the wooden edge of his desk. "I don't believe it."

"It happened barely ten minutes ago, just on the pier by Southwark Bridge."

"It's a lie!"

"No. There are at least a dozen witnesses who saw Hunter fighting with the officer. There was a gunshot and then your son fled the scene in a boat on the river. We need to know where he is heading."

"How should I know? The first I knew about this was on the monitor."

"You're going to have to do better than that, Mr. Nash."

Evan slams his hand down hard. "Screw you."

The detective nods, and the nearest officer strikes Evan a hard blow in the face that sends him reeling back against the desk.

"Don't be stupid. Just answer our questions." The detective glances around the open-plan room. "Nice office. Good job. Rare as hens' teeth these days."

Evan's eyes flash and he spits out a mouthful of blood. "Are you threatening me? I am a Technical Officer, Class 1, a senior energy advisor to the mayor of London."

"Then why is your son up to his neck in it with an Outsider girl? A girl who's connected to the group we're hunting for the Bradwell B blowout? Operation Clearwater. You do want to help us with that, don't you, sir?"

Evan swallows. "I don't know anything about any girl, any Outsider. Hunter has never been involved in anything like this before. If you want to know the truth I'm worried sick, I haven't seen him since last night."

"So you say. The dissidents have infiltrated many layers of government."

Evan stares at him, amazed. "Are you accusing me of being an Outsider?"

"I'm simply asking you if you have information about them or your son that you haven't shared with us."

"Of course not."

"Your son killed an officer. You know what that means. You must cooperate."

"I don't believe that he did it."

"Twelve witnesses."

"Kossaks, all of them!"

The detective sucks in a sharp breath. "What the hell's that supposed to mean?"

Evan drops his gaze. He's got to be smart now. He puts on his best, most assured Evan Nash smile. "Officer, I-I *am* cooperating. I want to find him as much as you do and get this thing straightened out." He reaches for his jacket. "So, if you'll excuse me, I'm going to start searching. I assure you that I'll inform you the moment I find—"

The detective takes a swift step forward and whips his arm upward, his fist smashing into Evan's windpipe.

"Let's try again, shall we?"

Evan staggers backward, choking. "I . . . have . . . Citizen rights."

The detective takes out a Taser, brings the base down hard across Evan's forehead, opening up a bloody gash. "Sir, with all due respect, you have the rights we give you. Now where's the boy?"

Evan falls to his knees. "I—don't know."

"Oh, come on, you're his father!"

Evan glares upward, defiant, blood oozing down his cheek. "Don't tell me who I am."

The detective's cold eyes bore into his. "You leave me no choice. Evan Nash, I'm arresting you under the ID offense, 300. Conspiracy to harbor, aid, or abet enemies of the state."

One of the constables grabs Evan's arms, lashing his wrists together with electronic cuffs.

Evan rises to his feet, struggling. "You can't do this! I demand a lawyer!"

Suddenly the detective raises the Taser and leveling it he fires, dropping Evan to the floor like a stunned animal. He looks down approvingly. Silence. That's better. Why does everyone get so shouty about lawyers?

Mist rises from the river all the way up to the gleaming entrance of the Kossak Headquarters in Vauxhall. Rose pauses for a moment on the top step, cursing the conditions. Nighttime, a citywide power cut, and now this fog to finish the job. How's she going to find Uma in all this? But she must. And if anyone can do it, it's her. She knows as much about how Uma's mind works, how she jumps, where she would hide as anyone else in the world. And she has other information. . . . She'll find her all right.

Wiping her swollen, tear-stained face, Rose looks down at the street below, watching as a man leaves his scooter with its engine running as he strolls over to a news kiosk. She smiles grimly. Ah, Citizens, God bless 'em. It's like taking candy from a baby. Rose checks left and right before skipping lightly down the stairs. In a few paces she's at the bike, and before the owner even opens his mouth to yell, she's roaring off down the road, hugging the white riverbank, heading east. She blocks out the pain in her cut right hand as she twists the throttle. She's got to do this, she's got to find the Codes and deliver them safe. She has no choice.

Twenty-seven

In the boat, Uma drags herself to her knees, peering over her shoulder at the bearded old man hunched over the tiller behind her.

"Are you the ferryman?"

He nods. "Aye."

"How did you get to us so quickly? The woman in the red scarf said she called for you... and there you were."

"I got my ways. Bin preparin' for this moment a longtimes."

"Where are we going?"

He scarcely glances at her, keeping his eyes glued to the white wall in front of the boat.

"The Prospect. Down Wapping way."

"The what?"

"Prospect of Whitby. Oldest pub in the city, useta be the Devil's Tavern, hundreds o' years back."

"And then?"

He shrugs. "That's my fare. The old lady heard the verse, called me from the Ferryman's Seat. I don' know no more, jus' to get you to the steps of the pub."

Uma's head is reeling. They are almost back where they started, the Isle of Dogs. She glances at Hunter. He sits bowed, his head sunk between his knees. She touches his cheek. "Maybe the soldier will live? You've got to have hope, Hunter."

Uma wraps her arms around his rigid body. If he did kill the soldier she knows the Kossaks won't stop until they hunt him down. In forty-eight hours this boy's thrown away his whole life for her. She closes her eyes. And it's not even over. What next? Will there be someone waiting for them at the Prospect? Surely they must be getting close to the Keeper by now. Zella! Suddenly an image of her aunt rises up, of what she must have suffered in the past nights. Uma tightens her grip around Hunter's chest.

Behind her, the ferryman cuts the engine for a moment, realigning the boat in the water. He glances at Uma. "You keep hol' tight of the boat, missy. If them Kossaks come to firin' at us agin, you don't wanter be fallin' in under the bridge here. He's a treacherous river, this'n. Calm enough on the surface, but you fall in and you'll be sucked down right fast enough."

Hunter sits in a dream, the black fog pressing down on him like a heavy weight. His world is destroyed. He killed a Kossak. It's a life sentence. His father can't take care of this; it'll bring him crashing down too. He'd give anything to talk to his dad right now, just to hear the sound of his voice, but his RETScan is gone, lying shattered on the pierside by Southwark Bridge. Oh God, he's brought so much trouble . . . and after his mother, too. What he'd give to be back in his room, *Berlin Brawler* on—and this nightmare over. Hunter bends over. Ah, Leo, too! What will happen to his poor friend?

Again and again, he sees the officer's face, his eyes widening, the mouth going slack—and then the explosion, the blood spattering from his chest. The man's dead all right; Hunter saw him fall into the Thames, the same river he is on now, fast running away with the dead body at horrible speed. He reaches out, clasps Uma's hand tight. They are so small; a speck, floating in the ancient darkness through the city. Just as it was in the beginning, the jungle river.

Up high on Southwark Bridge, Commander Clarke drums his fingers on the jeep steering wheel in impotent fury, glaring at the gridlocked traffic trapped behind the jackknifed lorry. He's tried to scramble up military choppers, but who knows if they can even fly in this fog. He's got to come up with a new plan to get himself eastbound. He's sent units west, but in his bones he knows they've gone east. He's got to catch up with the boat, he can't let these kids disappear into the rat holes of the favelas again.

Clarke takes one last despairing glance at the car-strewn lanes. He's got to move now. Leaping from the jeep, he calls to his officers to follow. "With me. On foot to the other side of the bridge. We'll flag down civilian cars on the other side!"

He sets off at a fast run, cursing the blackout. Just when he needs light and power the most. The Encryption Codes are almost in his grasp!

In the boat, Hunter forces himself to come back to reality. On his left the Tower of London slides by; sections of white tower and battlement flashing out from the gloom. He shivers. London is so different in the blackness, so secret—vague forms appearing from the shadows, every movement, every shape, a Kossak platoon bearing down on them.

And now they are passing under Tower Bridge, the water echoing along the stone arches. This is where it all started, just two days ago. But now he is the enemy. He is the dirty Outsider kid running for his life. It's happened so fast. Started out as a game and now this girl by his side is the only thing he's got left. Hunter digs his nails into the palm of his hand. He's got to pull himself together, to be strong for Uma. Passing the Codes on is the only thing that makes sense now. He can't, he *won't* let them fail now.

A minute passes, then another. Hunter and Uma sit silent in the dark, straining every nerve, waiting for the first shouts, the first burst of gunfire, when suddenly beneath them the boat engine cuts and they can clearly hear the suck and drag of the tide riding up against the stone bank. Hunter leans forward. A silent, breathless glide and then the boat bumps up against something, her wooden sides scraping harsh against concrete. The ferryman reaches into his pocket, and a moment later, he sweeps a narrow flashlight beam over the land, the light falling on a set of rough-cut steps leading up to a warped wooden door. He points. "This is you. Up there . . . see?"

Uma turns to him in the darkness. "What is this place again?"

The man beams his flashlight at her. "I tol' yer, it's an old river pub, the Prospect of Whitby."

Uma nods, her face a pale oval in the light. "And you don't know any more than that?"

The ferryman lays his rough hand on her shoulder. "I jus' play my part . . . an' that's to bring my fare to the Prospect steps. No more, no less."

Uma shrinks down in the boat. This is hopeless.

"Uma!"

Startled, she looks up. Using a metal post to steady himself, Hunter leans out over the boat, arm extended. "Come on."

She stares up into his face—chalk white, but set with a kind of fierce determination. And inside her rises an answering emotion. To fight, to push it to the very end. Reaching up, she grips his hand, and as their fingers meet a thrill runs through her—she's going to see this through, for his sake, if nothing else. On the bank, she turns toward the ferryman, whispers, "Thank you," before turning to follow the boy up the rough-cut stairs.

On the top step, Hunter pauses. Golden lantern light spills from inside the pub, and he presses his body into the shadow of the wall as he peers inside. An oil lamp hangs over a low wooden table, its flame sending long flickering shadows across the room. The table is strewn with bottles and dirty glasses—and hunched around it are a small group of men and women, their faces anxious, their talk subdued.

Uma joins Hunter on the step, whispers in his ear, "What now?"

"Don't know. Guess we go in and see what happens."

Uma nudges him. "We could get a beer for sure. They don't look too picky."

Hunter scans the filthy bar. "Or we could get a smack in the mouth." He sighs. "We've got no idea what we're looking for again, have we?"

She shakes her head. "Nope. It's like the Dragon Hall all over again."

"Well, let's get on with it then."

Moving forward into the golden arc of the lamplight, he puts his hand on the handle and turns it, pushing the door open. Silence falls on the bar, and a tall, ruddy-faced man springs to his feet, tipping his chair backward on the stone flags.

"What you want?"

Hunter takes an involuntary step back, ramming into Uma behind him.

"Hold!"

The man points a pistol at them.

Hunter stops dead, the blood thudding in his ears.

"Wait, Theo!"

A small birdlike man emerges from the darkness behind the bar. He peers at Hunter and Uma curiously. "What you want here? We ain't open for punters tonight."

"We..." The words die on Uma's lips. She gazes at the man in despair. She doesn't know what she's looking for...a clue, a direction, another journey inside the Darknet? What can she say to him?

"We what?" The man's shrewd gaze turns to Hunter. "You're a Citizen, ain't you?"

Hunter nods, wearily. "Yes."

"Well then, I suggest you get your arse out of here, 'fore Theo there puts a hole in your guts."

"You don't understand—"

He raises his voice. "I'm the landlord of the Prospect, in the family two hundred year. I don't need to understand. Now git!"

"No!" Hunter takes a step forward into the bar.

"Don't make another move!"

A shot rings out, the bullet glancing off the floor by his right foot. Hunter throws himself to the ground and lies there, frozen, staring up at the barrel of Theo's gun, now pointing directly at his head. Theo glances at the landlord, who nods.

"Do it. We can't take no chances with a Citizen tonight. Raids are too fierce."

"Don't!" screams Uma, but the landlord steps forward, grabbing her by the arms.

"Now, Theo!" he snarls... and then his eyes widen in shock. He holds out his hand. "Wait!"

Hunter desperately twists his head to see the ferryman standing in the doorway, an old service revolver grasped tightly in his hand.

The landlord swallows. "You?"

The room is dead silent, all eyes on the old man.

"You're the... ferryman, ain't you?"

The waterman pushes his battered cap to the back of his head. "You know who I am, Tom."

The landlord pushes Uma to one side, steps forward, and grabs the ferryman by his coat lapels. "Did you bring these ones?" His eyes jerk toward Hunter and Uma.

"Aye."

"Were you—' his voice drops to a whisper—"called from the Ferryman's Seat by them?"

The ferryman holds the other's eye a long moment. And then he nods.

A tremor runs through the landlord's voice. "Then you all come with me. Let the boy be, Theo."

Hunter scrambles to his feet, catching the others up as the landlord leads the way out of the bar along a stone-paved corridor that opens out into a low-beamed room bordering the river. Once the door swings shut, he snatches up a lamp, and raising the flame, he holds it close to Uma's face, searching her eyes with a long, keen look.

"Is it here?"

She stares back into his eyes, says nothing. He needs to say more than this.

The landlord pulls her to him, presses his mouth against her ear. "When the ferryman is called from his steps, he will come to the Prospect bearing a heavy burden. One that only the Keeper can bear. You carry the Encryption Codes?"

Her heart beating fast, Uma nods.

He releases her, amazed. "But you are only a girl. How do you have this thing?"

"I—I can't tell you that."

The man flicks his gaze toward Hunter. "Is he safe?"

"Yes. He's...one of us."

Doubt flares in the man's eyes. "How can he be?"

She holds his eye. "He just is. You must trust me. I am here on the order of Zella Al-Rimthal."

He drops his gaze. "Then so be it."

Uma frowns. "So is this it? The Keeper will actually come here?"

The landlord runs his hand through his thinning hair. "Yes. I sound the siren. That is the sign."

"But that's madness...I mean, everyone will hear it."

"Aye, but they shan't know what it means. Only the Keeper will understand what to do."

"But the Kossaks are after us, they'll hear it too."

A sharp breath. "They know what you carry? They follow you?"

Uma swallows. "I-I don't know what they know, but they're chasing us for sure. And they're close behind."

The landlord throws his arms up. "Not good! But I got no choice. Kossaks or no, we can't delay in following the order."

"Then do it."

Hunter frowns. "How long do you think it'll take for them to get here?"

A faint, desperate smile tugs at the landlord's mouth. "Who? The Keeper or the Kossaks? I'll sound the siren as short as I can. After that we'll just have to pray." He gestures toward a wooden bench set into the wall. "Sit. Our people will stand guard. Rest assured we are all blood here."

His footsteps die away along the corridor and for a long, long moment Hunter and Uma stand silent in the low bar, the only sound the restless Thames lapping at the beach outside—until suddenly the long lonesome rising whine of an old WW2 air-raid siren cuts through the night air. Only a ten-second burst, but it feels like enough to wake the dead.

Uma closes her eyes. This is the moment.

On the waterfront Harry stands motionless, shrouded in the white swirl. Something is not right; the lines are ringing out dissonance, even here on the river where the misrule of the land is reversed and all things are equal. Suddenly the low mournful sound of an air-raid siren breaks across the night followed by an explosion of dog barks and voices, lights flickering on from windows. Ah, what is happening?

The fog is everywhere. Fog on the dark water, fog smothering the skyscraper buildings, fog on the Hackney marshes, fog rising to the Hampstead hills. But there is no fog in Harry's mind, he can see clearly that he has work to do. Here, tonight, something will happen on the river. He can hear the future, clear as a bell. And then he hears something else that fills his heart with fear, the heavy, throbbing engine of a Kossak chopper as it sweeps up the river.

Twenty-eight

Hunter and Uma stand in complete silence, waiting. A light glints on the river. Heart pounding, Uma presses her face against the glass, but after a moment she pulls away; it is nothing. All the wide world shrunk to this moment—the beat of her heart, the cool metal disk grasped tight in her hand, the boy beside her.

She shakes her head. "I'm so sorry."

Hunter puts out a hand. "Don't."

"But, Hunt—"

And then, carried on the rush, on the wave rising, she turns to him and together they plunge deep into the kiss. There is nothing else, only this; the passion exploding through them, together, at the edge. And then Uma pulls back. Hunter waits, breathless. He cannot, *will* not fight her this time if she doesn't want him. He stands, frozen; she's looking at him with eyes so deep he is motionless under her gaze. Uma stares at him, it is like she's seeing him for the first time. With a thrill she *sees*. She gets it. This boy is standing with her, on the *inside. She has let him in and for the first time, she is not alone.* Uma reaches for him blindly, pulling him close, whispering in a voice so low he can scarcely catch the words.

"I love you."

It is like a lightning bolt passing through him. Hunter stands a long moment, transfixed. It's like his heart has stopped beating... and it feels like a lifetime until he is able to draw his next ragged breath, to feel the familiar thump in his chest once more.

Uma smiles a little under wet lashes. "I can't do this without you...."

And then suddenly, quietly, the bar door opens behind them. Startled, Uma turns to see a slender woman standing on the threshold. She enters the room, her short blonde hair catching the lamplight as she moves forward.

"I heard the call. The landlord told me to come to you."

Uma pulls away from Hunter. "What call?"

"The air-raid siren."

Uma stares at the woman intently. High cheekbones, clear blue eyes. She holds herself like an Outsider all right, but how can she be sure?

"How do I know it's really you?"

The blue eyes glitter. "Because I'm here. When the air-raid siren is sounded from the Prospect I take the passageway under the Thames to retrieve the Codes. I know nothing of how they get here... I'm just one element in the chain, but my very being here is proof that I'm telling you the truth... It is how the system works." Her eyes soften momentarily. "I *am* the Keeper, Uma. And you must give me the Codes right now. I promise I will guard them with my life."

Uma frowns. "You know my name?"

A faint smile crosses the other's face. "You're the niece of Zella Al-Rimthal, she has spoken of you often. I serve on the Council alongside her."

Uma tries to keep the quiver in her chin under control. "Can I know who you are?"

The woman shakes her head. "It is better not... you already know far too much as it is. Come now, there's no time to waste."

Uma slowly opens her hand, revealing the metal case. Stepping forward, the woman darts her hand out, sweeping the container up in a simple, graceful movement, and as it leaves her grasp, an overwhelming feeling of relief, of joy, sweeps over Uma, just as it did when she last gave them away—to Guido in Harry's place. Finally it is done! A slow smile spreads across her face. And then she hears it. The brutal mechanical battering thud of the chopper engine as it descends out of the night air. Kossaks!

For a moment they all stand, stunned, until the harsh voice of the ferryman is heard shouting, "Out! Out!"

The Keeper is the first to react. "Quick. To the cellar! Back along the Thames passage with me!" Running to the door, she motions for them to follow her to the main bar.

Hunter sets off behind her, Uma a few paces behind. Then a huge flash of light rips through the building and suddenly he slams into the ferryman, who blocks the passageway with his body.

"Get out of the way!"

But Hunter's words are drowned out by a deep, booming blast—and he is hurled back, crashing down on top of Uma as chunks of wood and plaster rain down from the ceiling.

For a second Hunter lies there in shock. The bar in front of him is a wreck. Then he forces himself up, he wills himself to go forward, a hollow pain knotting in his stomach as he clambers over the debris into the shattered room. Standing at the entrance, he dashes his hand over his eyes. The ferryman lies there, half-buried under a pile of masonry—killed in the act of pushing Hunter back into the hallway, blocking the blast with his body. And a few paces beyond him, her neck twisted, eyes staring, the Keeper lies motionless.

Oh God. He's got to do this. Hunter claws his way over the debris and twists the woman's arm over, prising her hand open. The Codes are still there, the metal case gripped tight in her warm palm. Muttering a silent prayer, Hunter grabs the case from her hand and drops it into his back pocket.

The Kossaks are beating at the front door. They are trapped—and he's no idea where the woman was leading them. Their only chance is to go back the way they came, out on to the beach, along the shore. Clambering over the rubble, Hunter retraces his steps along the corridor, screaming at Uma to turn, to run with him, but she doesn't respond, she just squats on the floor, clinging tightly to the wall.

He grabs her roughly by the shoulders. "Uma, up now!" But it's as if she can't hear him. She crouches on the floor, motionless, staring. Dragging her to her feet, he hustles her limp body onto his shoulder and sets off toward the little bar. Reaching the long window, he lets her body slide to the floor before ripping off his jacket. Wrapping it around his forearm, he throws all his weight at the glass. A faint crack appears. Hunter curses and punches again. This time a shard of glass shatters. Shielding his face, he lifts his arm again and again until he's smashed a large enough hole to climb through. Then, tossing his jacket over the base of the window frame, he drags Uma to her feet, practically pushing her out of the window before following her through the gaping hole himself and landing on the stinking foreshore mud, just as the Kossak soldiers sweep into the main bar.

The chopper is now nearly overhead. The sound is deafening, the blades churning the air no more than thirty meters above, but for now, its massive arc lights are aimed directly at the main bar of the Prospect, illuminating the Thames beyond in a great silver curve. Hunter grabs Uma's arm, dragging her into the shadow of the wall, and using the rough stone as his only guide in the black night, he sets off across the beach.

To his left, a sliver of light appears. It comes from an oil lamp, hanging high in a narrow alleyway that cuts back from the beach to the road. Hunter hesitates. What is waiting for them on the other side? How many soldiers are on the road out there? But from inside the bar he can now hear the shouts of the soldiers, their search lights crisscrossing the foreshore. They've found the smashed window-pane. Shoving Uma forward into the dimly lit alley, he flings himself after her, just as the Kossak search lights brush the wall behind them.

They land in a facedown sprawl in the narrow alley. Hunter scrambles to his feet and yanks Uma up by the wrist. "You've got to move or we'll be dead!" And this time she nods. Her eyes are clear again. Stumbling to her feet, she starts to sprint alongside him and they clear the passage in seconds, bursting onto the main road. In front of them, two huge Kossak vans are parked at an angle, spaced some two hundred meters apart—and without missing a beat, Uma swerves and cuts straight across the street, heading directly for the warehouses that line the opposite curb.

Racing across the cobbled stones at breakneck speed, she hurls herself at a warehouse wall, her feet running vertically up the brick as she propels herself up toward a great loop of chain hanging down from a set of solid wooden doors on the floor above. Hunter flies after her. He makes the jump, just—and scrabbling for a hold, he hooks on to the chain by his fingertips. But his kicking legs dislodge a slab of plaster, sending it plummeting onto the street. A shout comes from below. They've seen him. Flexing his fingers, this time Hunter gets a firm grasp on the chain and, flinging himself forward, he uses the momentum to propel himself toward the next warehouse building.

At the height of the arc he lets go, throwing himself across the gap between the two buildings. For a second he soars through the black space, before slamming into the third-floor window ledge of the next building. Hunter lands, gripping with his hands, using his legs, his whole body in a desperate attempt to absorb the shock. Locking his fingers on to the rotten wood, he yanks himself upright on the ledge before launching himself again up to the next floor. Only another three to go and he'll be over the roof. Out of the corner of his eye he glimpses Uma, expertly moving across the wall two floors above him. She's nearly there.

And then from the street below comes the spotlight, sweeping the warehouse walls left and right before it finds its mark, fixing on the girl. A burst of gunfire rakes the plaster, but she's gone, vanished into black space once more. The beam swirls again, searching her out. Now it's coming toward him. Hunter twists, makes a diagonal leap to the window above in a frenzied bid to outrun it. Grabbing on to the sill, he swings his legs up on to the rough wooden frame— and then gasps. Alongside him, barely two meters away, is Uma.

She's clamped to the wall, her arms stretched wide as she tries to stop herself sliding down the uneven surface, her splayed feet frantically searching for a foothold, for something she can use to stop her descent. But it's no good, there's no hold. She's slipping, fast. Hunter crawls across the ledge, throwing his arm out to try and take some of her weight, but he can't get close enough. The spotlight races across the wall. It's nearly on them. And then suddenly a voice screams from above, "Take my hand!"

Then the light hits them full on. Dazzled, Hunter can just make out Guido, dangling lethally far over the roof edge, his arms extended to their full limit. Gunfire rips along the wall, shattering the brick. Uma screams. She's got no choice. She lets go of the wall and arches her body upward in a desperate stretch for her cousin. Guido's great hands wrap around her wrists, and twisting his body sideways, using all his strength, he hauls her up onto the flat roof.

As the bullets smash the window ledge beneath him, Hunter makes his own desperate leap for the rooftop. Jumping high, he catches hold of the gutter and drags himself over the top, slamming on to the cold slates as the wall is shattered by gunfire. Next to him, Uma rolls on the ground, fighting to get free of her cousin. Hunter staggers toward them, throws a wild punch at Guido. But before his fist connects, a blow from behind sends him sprawling, and he is crushed to the roof, pinned down by a man's weight.

Guido grabs Uma's right arm and twists it sharply behind her back.

"Uma, it's me! Guido."

She turns, spits in his face. "Let go of me!"

To his left, Guido can see the chopper wheeling toward them, picking out the rooftops in a great curve of dazzling light. There's no time for this madness. He slaps Uma, hard. "Come with us, now. Or we'll all be dead."

Uma's eyes blaze. All she's gone through to be caught again!

Guido drags her to her feet. "Come on! St. Katharine Docks are over there. It's the closest Citizen area. Kossaks won't shoot there!"

And then the chopper is on them. A grenade blasts into the warehouse roof but the four runners aren't there anymore. They are gone, jumping for their lives.

Sliding from the warehouse roof, Hunter lands heavily on the walkway a few strides behind Guido. Staggering up, he gathers himself, muscles tensing for the next move. Uma is already pulling ahead; she's just too good. Gritting his teeth, pumping his leg muscles to the screaming point, Hunter takes on a huge jump, aiming for a concrete overpass jutting from the next building. He's got it wrong. For a moment his body flails in the air. But at the last second Hunter throws his arms upward, catching hold of a metal strut sticking from the concrete, his hands sliding cruelly down the metal until he finally gets a grip.

For a dreadful beat he hangs there, suspended twenty meters above the ground, with the Kossak searchlight sweeping around him. Screaming at himself to hang on, he swings his legs forward, and gripping the concrete with his right foot, he clamps his leg around the pitted surface before hauling his body on to the ledge. Crawling forward on bloody hands and knees, he urgently scans the jagged outline of tumbledown favela buildings before him. He can't see anything in this fog. But he can't lose her. *Come on, Hunter! Move. Do it. By instinct. Trust your body and the training and strength of your mind. This is who you are right here, right now.*

Think! St. Katharine is to his left, that's where Uma's heading. Aiming for the river, he sets off again over the asphalt, making a series of zigzagging jumps over the top deck of a car park. And suddenly up ahead, a building, a ragged 1950s estate block, is lit up in dazzling relief as the chopper comes down low. Hunter's heart lifts. There she is, the second of three figures, jumping in perfect unison as the gunfire flares from above.

His chest on fire, Hunter flies across the car deck. He hurls himself forward, coming to a slamming stop on the estate walkway, landing only a few steps behind Uma as bullets spray the piss-stained wall behind him. He hears Guido screaming for them to jump lower, to get out of the chopper range, and he dives after Uma, catching a rusted water pipe and plunging downward in a spiraling slide to the third floor. Surely the chopper cannot follow them so low.

Uma sways as she lets go of the pipe, then rights herself, ducking inside the stairwell. In seconds Hunter lands beside her and they begin to run again. And now the world is nothing but the slap of hands and feet on concrete as they move together. *Jump, climb, run, leap. No thought, pure flow. How our bodies used to be.* Up ahead he can just make out the looming luxury apartment towers of St. Katharine Docks rising above the marina. If they can make it over there, they've got a chance.

There's only one favela tower block between them and the first Citizen apartments in the marina. The last outpost of the Outsiders. It's so mad that they are running toward enemy ground to escape the Kossaks, but Guido's right, the soldiers won't dare indiscriminately open fire there.

Uma and Guido have now climbed again, they clamber along a railed walkway, while Hunter and Little Fats race up the stairs from the floor below.

Suddenly the chopper is directly above Hunter, the Kossaks taking their final chance in the slum. And that's when Fats makes his move. Sticking out his leg, he trips Hunter, and, as he hits the ground, Fats lands a vicious boot in his guts. For a moment Hunter can't move. He writhes in the dazzling light as the gunfire sweeps down from above.

Fats turns away, racing for the shadows, but suddenly he staggers as if hit by a heavy blow. Desperately trying to keep his feet, to outpace the chopper light, Fats leaps for the edge of the stairs, but the sniper catches him again, the bullets spinning his body against a guardrail.

Behind him Hunter drags himself to his feet, but as he crawls toward the stairs, a sharp pain explodes through his calf. Screaming with pain, he throws himself sideways, making a last-ditch dive for safety under the stairs. Twisting his neck, he can only watch helplessly as Fats is shot to pieces. The boy makes one last desperate clutch at the rail. He sways momentarily at the edge, till with a despairing shout, he collapses forward, disappearing over the edge.

And then the chopper is gone, swallowed up in the black fog

once again. Hunter claws his way out from under the stairs and, dragging himself to the edge of the building, he frantically scans the ground below, but there is nothing to see. It's as if the boy never existed. Hot rage fills his chest. Fats! They killed him like a dog in the street. An eighteen-year-old boy. No matter what he did, he didn't deserve that death.

He can't stay here a second longer. He's got to get to Uma. Lifting the torn fabric of his trouser leg, he bends to look at his calf. It's a mess, blood oozing everywhere. He forces himself to run his hand along the shin, searching for a break, but it feels like it's in one piece. Oh God. Slowly he stands, praying the bone will hold his weight.

Pressing his lips tight against the pain, Hunter straightens. For a second everything goes black, the estate flickers in front of him. Taking a deep breath, he grabs the railing and starts to climb down the stairs again, at first dragging his leg, before slowly forcing himself to bend it, to put more and more weight on it. He's got to keep going. It's him who has the Codes now.

Twenty-nine

Uma's outstretched body soars through the air as she makes the final jump from the favela onto the roof of the Tower Hotel. She's got a chance here, if she moves fast. Keeping her body soft to absorb the impact, she lands just behind Guido, before turning to scan the building behind her for Hunter and Little Fats. But she sees nothing, no twisting, climbing bodies, no movement of any kind; the only sound is the rumbling chopper engine circling away over the favela.

Uma cups her hands to her mouth. "Hunter, where are you?"

Guido chops the air. "Shhh. They'll be here any minute. Come, Uma, away." Motioning for her to follow, he starts to run across the asphalt, heading for the lift block set on the far side of the roof.

But Uma doesn't move. Why doesn't Hunter get over here? And then it hits her for the first time. She hasn't got the Codes. The Keeper took them from her back at the Prospect!

Guido stands at the lift doors. "Uma, now! We've only got a few minutes before we lose our advantage."

Uma sweeps the estate building with desperate eyes. It doesn't matter if the place floods with Kossaks, without the Codes it's all over. Her only hope is that Hunter has them. She calls his name again. Nothing, just the echo of her words bouncing back from the hollow apartments. Racing back to the edge of the hotel roof, she pauses for a second, assessing the jump back to the favela.

Suddenly she hears a faint shout from below. Peering downward, she searches the broken concrete till, there! He stands on the stairwell of the favela building four floors below.

"Hunter, what're you doing? Get over here."

He leans heavily on the railing. "No, you come here...I... can't...keep up."

"Why?"

He gives an impatient wave. "Just come. You've got to take the Codes."

Her heart leaps to her mouth. "You've got them?"

"Yes. Come now."

Uma gasps in relief. But why won't he jump over? Is he hurt? She peers over the side of her building. Three floors down, a hotel balcony juts out almost directly opposite Hunter's stairwell. Uma reaches for a metal conductor pipe, and grasping it loosely with both hands, launches herself downward.

Over by the lift, Guido shouts in dismay as Uma disappears. Now what? With a groan, he forces himself to jog back to the roof edge.

In seconds Uma descends to the balcony level. As she reaches it, she tightens her grip on the metal pole and, spinning her body counterclockwise, uses the momentum to twist her body, angling it perfectly to land on the luxury balcony tiles. And then she runs to the edge, seeking Hunter in the darkness. There he is!

"Are you hurt?"

He fights to keep his voice calm. "My leg. I-I can't jump any more. I've got to head down to street level, find somewhere to hide."

"But it's too dangerous down there, the Kossaks will be all over."

"I know. That's why you've got to take the Codes. You can still climb."

She shakes her head. "Come on, Hunt. I jump with injuries all the time, you can do it."

Hunter swallows. A bullet through the leg isn't an injury he can overcome. He *knows* he can't make it. His fear is telling him the truth this time. The gap between the buildings is too far.

"No! You've got to take the case and go."

Her voice breaks. "I'm not leaving you."

"I've been *shot*, Uma. Go! Otherwise it's all been for nothing."

"I'm not going anywhere without you." Clambering onto the balcony rail, Uma steadies herself for the jump back to the favela.

And then suddenly Guido is there. Hurtling downward on the metal pipe, his heavy boots land on the ironwork, and before Uma has time to react, he grabs her, his heavy hand squeezing her arm, his voice harsh. "What are you doing?"

Uma falls back, trying to free her arms. "Run, Hunter!"

Hunter stares wildly as Guido drags Uma from the balcony edge.

Guido's voice is shaking. "Uma. What the hell is with you? Quit fighting me. We've got to move now. I don't wish any harm to this boy, but he's not one of us. The Kossaks will leave him be when they find out he's a Citizen."

She struggles in his arms. "So did you have to order him killed?"

His face slackens in amazement. "What are you talking about?"

"In the favela, after you took the Codes from me you set Fats on him. . . ."

Guido shakes his head. "I never—"

"Oh, stop pretending. I don't trust you anymore. If you can kill my friend in cold blood, you can do anything. How do I know you don't want the Codes for yourself, that the Kossaks haven't bought you too?"

And then from high above, a crossbow dart flashes through the air, thudding into Guido's belly. Uma whirls around in shock as her cousin releases his hold on her, sliding slowly down the plate-glass hotel windows, clutching the metal bolt embedded in his stomach.

A few seconds later, a slight figure leaps down from the roof, landing with easy grace on the balcony tiles.

Uma gasps. "Rose?"

The girl doesn't answer, just fits a new bolt into her crossbow.

Uma tries again. "What are you doing here?"

Guido half turns his head. "Kossak comms... She must've... followed the chopper reports, isn't it, Rose?"

Uma stares at her friend; her color doesn't change, but a sort of white flicker of anger runs across her face. "But how would she know how to do that?"

"Ask her."

"Toss the gun, Guido. Now." Rose's crossbow is aimed directly at his skull.

He spits. "Ah... I wondered... where you were getting the money. Now I know."

"Do it now. You know I don't miss."

His rifle hits the concrete. Rose takes a pace forward and kicks it away, the weapon clattering against the far side of the terrace.

Rose turns back to Uma. "Let's not make a big drama here. The Codes, now."

Uma's brain isn't working. This *can't* be happening.

"But, Rose—"

"Now."

"Why?"

Rose raises her head quickly, a deep, painful blush rising to her face. "Ray Ray. To pay the doctors."

"For *money*?"

"Where the hell else was I to get it from? You never asked, did you, Uma? Maybe you din't want to know. Nor no one else in the favela did, that's for sure."

Uma shakes her head. "That's not true. We all looked out for you."

"Yeah, but none of you give me what I really needed. Managed myself for years, but just a week back I had a meeting at the hospital. The doctors, they told me he had to have five operations in as many months... The pressure is buildin' too fast inside his skull. An' so I din't have but one card to play, one way to pay for it." Rose's voice breaks. "You don't know how it's like, Uma... to watch him cry and be able to do nothin' for him."

Despite herself, Uma can feel the tears running down her own cheeks. "So you sold us out?"

Rose stares straight ahead. "Aye. I did. And I'd do it again for him."

A groan escapes from Guido's lips. Uma moves toward him.

Rose's voice hardens. "No."

"But he's hurt!"

"No, I said."

Uma's voice suddenly trembles with anger. "Now I know why the Kossaks were so close behind us this last week. The funeral, Zella…" Her eyes narrow. "But I don't understand. Why wait this long? When I told you about the Codes in Leicester Square, why didn't you just give me up then?"

Rose sighs. "If you must know it's because when you and Hunter was hiding from the Kossaks in that gas tank back in the Isle of Dogs…I spoke to Clarke, told him you was carrying something secret. He ordered me to keep alongsides you. An' that's why I went *inside* in the Dragon Hall. I knew the only way the Kossaks were ever gonna break the Encryption Codes was to get an Outsider on the job. Almost did it, too, but then I got injured."

Uma strikes her chest. "But this is *me*! *Us*! Think what you're doing, Rose."

"I—don't have any choice." Rose's face blurs momentarily. "They'll kill Ray Ray. After the Dragon Palace I told Clarke you had the Encryption Codes…and he threatened me I'd never see Ray again unless I found you and got the Codes back. I got to do this."

Uma tries one last time. She stretches out a hand. "Oh, Rose. You see how they are? You can't trust them."

Rose's face stiffens. "No. You'll not do this. It's his life on the line. Now, give me the case."

Uma looks her straight in the eye. "I'm not giving you anything, Rose McGuire. You'll have to kill me first."

To her surprise the girl smiles. "Ah, Uma girl. How do you think I found youse here when all them Kossaks are still runnin' around far behind? Because I know the way you think. They told me you was at the Prospect, but I knew you'd cut across to the marina as soon as you could. And I ain't gonna waste time threatenin' *you*." She tightens her finger around the crossbow trigger. "You've got ten seconds to give me them Codes or I'll put this bolt right through Guido's head. And after you mistrusted him, then to be responsible for his death...can you live with that?"

Uma clenches her fists. "And if I give them to you, you'll let him live?"

"Aye. I'll be on my way."

"You promise?"

"Yes."

Guido raises his head slowly from his blood-spattered chest. "Don't give her nothing, Uma!"

On the stairwell, Hunter tastes vomit in his mouth. It's a five-meter jump to the hotel balcony, but from where he stands it's a lifetime, it's impossible.

Rose shakes her head. "Guido, give the girl a choice over whether you die or live. If she gives them to me quick I'll let you live and leave her the chance to escape."

The heavy beat of the chopper suddenly comes overhead again. Rose jerks her head upward. "It's your last few minutes to escape 'fore they land." Her eyes drill into Uma's. "I'm gonna start counting now. One...two...three."

Uma reaches inside her jacket, her fingers closing on empty space, readying herself for one last fight. She can't look at Hunter, she can't do anything but pray that he'll run away, that he'll have the discipline to go.

"Four...five...six..."

Hunter draws a ragged breath. He's got to keep it simple. Focus on the target, not on the ground or the fall or the pain. He knows what to do, he gets it, he really does. *This is who you are today, Hunter Nash.*

Rose raises the crossbow sight to her eye. "Seven...eight... nine...Don't think I won't do it, Uma."

Uma tenses herself for the jump, the jump that will put her

body between Guido and the crossbow dart. The jump that will save his life and buy Hunter a few more precious seconds to escape. And then suddenly Rose jolts forward as Hunter's knees slam into her back. He crashes down, hurling them both to the ground in a tangle of limbs. But as he clears the balcony rail, his foot catches Uma's head, hard with his boot. Her skull smashes against the sharp metallic edge and her body folds under her.

On the terrace floor Rose struggles to break free. Hunter slides his hands down her arms, and gripping her wrists he twists them inward. Screaming in pain, she pulls her leg back, kneeing him in the gut and almost pulling herself upright before Hunter grabs a handful of her hair and yanks her back down. But Rose now has her legs free and she kicks again, her boot slamming into his lower body. Hunter screams in agony as she kicks once more, pain shattering through his leg. He clenches his jaw. He won't let go, he can't.... He's got to win this fight.

Over by the window, Guido throws himself on to his side. He can barely move, the pain in his stomach is so intense. His vision blurring, he crawls forward, extending his fingers as he gropes for his rifle. His thumb touches something cold, and he forces his hand to open, to grab, to pull the gun toward him. Grimacing with effort, he pulls himself upright and fires. The first shot is wide, the bullet bouncing off the tiles, but the second is true. Rose screams, and suddenly Hunter feels her grip loosen as she collapses on the tiles beside him.

"Enough!" Uma's shout rings out. But the rifle has already fallen out of Guido's hands. Crawling on hands and knees over to his side, Uma crouches down beside him, her hands fluttering when she sees the blood pooling under his body. "I've got to get you help."

He shakes his head. "Go. Now. It's an order."

"Guido!" Uma sobs.

His black eyes harden. "Now." He turns his head slowly, takes in Hunter, standing motionless next to Rose's inert body. "It was me killed that soldier...on the pier...I shot him...from Southwark Bridge. The bullet must have hit just as you crashed down onto the steps. It's not on you." And then Guido gags, falling back on the balcony floor. "Little Uma, go now—" His eyes widen in pain, and he goes still.

Uma grabs his hands. "No, no!"

Suddenly a searchlight comes from the roof. The chopper has landed. Hunter grabs Uma, drags her upright. Reaching into his back pocket, he pulls out the metal case. "Take it!"

She pushes it back into his hands. "No! Not without you. If I take it...I-I can't trust you to stay with me. We've got to do it together."

He shakes his head. "I can't."

She fights to keep her sobs down. "Don't give up on me now, Hunter. It's only me and you now. *Promise?*"

Slowly Hunter nods. This is madness. But it's how it is. He slides the case deep into his back pocket again.

Uma straightens, and with one last look at Guido and Rose, she reaches for the balcony railing. But as she swings herself back toward the favela, a burst of gunfire erupts from the roof. Her fingers tighten on the cold metal as she climbs over the railing, but then from the darkness comes the bullet. She staggers, blood erupting as the steel casing punctures her neck. Her foot catches on the balcony rail, and Uma spins sideways, out of control.

Too late, Hunter switches direction. His arms fly out to catch her, but he's too slow. All he can do is stare as her body plunges over the rail, down toward the river below.

For a moment, Hunter stands paralyzed, his hands still outstretched in the empty air. Kossaks are clambering down the wall. In seconds he'll be caught. And then suddenly he is free to move again—and in the last moment before the soldiers arrive, Hunter grasps the balcony rail, and vaulting lightly over, as if performing a routine gym move, he plunges over the side of the building after Uma.

Thirty

Hunter falls eight stories before his body smashes into the Thames, the pain of impact ripping through him like no pain he's ever known before. Stunned, crushed, breathless, he plunges down, down through the murky darkness until he reaches the riverbed. Winded, he twists his head, searching for Uma, but it's too dark to see anything. Frantically he tries to rise, but he is trapped in the current, pressed down by the hundreds of tons of water above him. Battling panic, he manages to push a few feet up before being caught in a vicious spin, the water rotating him like a toy before beating him back down again.

He's trapped. His throat spasms and he takes in a choke of water...Oh God, he's going to drown. No, no! And then suddenly the river is shot through with light from above—and he catches a glimpse of Uma. The chopper must be directly overhead. She's spiraling, twisting, on the dark brown current a few meters to his left. A pale hand, a roll of hair—and then she is gone again, swept into darkness once more. Clutching at stones, pram wheels, rusted metal, Hunter claws himself toward the place she last was. Nothing. He strikes out in another direction and then suddenly, she is right in front of him again, her eyes blank, her limbs lifeless.

Wrapping his left arm tight around her torso, Hunter pushes off with his feet, aiming at the surface with frantic strokes of his free arm, but the current batters him to the bottom again, this time pulling Uma from his grasp, and for a moment Hunter is swept along at horrible speed, rolling along the riverbed like a dead man.

He kicks out frantically. *No! This isn't it. He won't let this be it.* And suddenly the river changes depth. Hunter is dragged into a whirlpool pocket as the water flow completely changes direction, hundreds of tons now rising in a turbulent upward spiral. And there is Uma above him again.

With the last of his will, with the last dregs of oxygen in his lungs, Hunter launches himself toward her and grabs her close. And then, kicking like a madman, his blood singing in his ears, he rises, reaching, grasping for the surface of the river.

For a moment he lies still, gulping great lungfuls of air, but overhead the chopper light sweeps toward him. From the marina he can make out Kossak jeep lights aimed at the Thames and soldiers shouting, barking orders. He can't be caught. He won't allow it. He's not even thinking anymore, he's working on pure instinct, like a hunted animal. And that's when he sees the barge, looming up out of the mist, ploughing slowly up the river toward the sea.

Rolling onto his back, he cradles Uma on his chest, and crossing his arms firmly over her body, he cuts through the swirling tide to the barge, praying for mercy, that he can cover the distance without being seen. The searchlight is so near, just now sweeping over to his right, the beam missing him only by meters. Driving all his strength into his legs, Hunter kicks again and again, his ripped calf muscle screaming in pain at every movement.

Suddenly he touches metal. Twisting his head upward, he can just make out the great rusting curve of the barge hull rising above him. And here, just a few centimeters above the surface of the water is a narrow metal ledge, enough for one body to hide under, maybe.

The chopper is now directly overhead, the light burning down full on the barge. Dragging Uma's body under the ledge, Hunter scrabbles frantically along the side of the boat to find something to grab hold of, so he can anchor her, keep her hidden from the light.

His fingers hit a bulge—a chunk of corroded metal—and he grabs it tight with his left hand, half rotating his body so he can keep her face above water. But this means his body is dangerously low, his head barely clearing the surface. Wake from the moving ship slops into his nose and mouth as he holds the girl tight. He gasps for breath, his lungs aching again.

The seconds pass like hours. Hunter's only chance of survival is this rusty hook in his hand. The river surface shines unbearably bright as the beam of the chopper arclights burns downward, sweeping repeatedly around the barge. How long will this go on? Despite himself, he gulps in yet another mouthful of water. Uma slips a little in his arms, only her nose and lips are above the water now. . . . He is being dragged underwater by her weight. The pain in his lungs grows unbearable.

His hand. The hook. The barge. This is his only reality. Holding on. He has to keep them both alive. He doesn't even know if she's still breathing, but nothing will break his hold. The river is dazzling bright . . . what's that over there? The Codes? No . . . that's stupid . . . they're in his pocket. His mind begins to drift. Hunter slips under the surface again, his blood beating heavily, lungs full of acid.

He opens his eyes and sees the sun on the waves. His mum is there. Ah yeah, she's got the crocodile float. Good. He can see its shiny plastic teeth, jaws grinning at him. It's his mum, but why is she so angry? She's not playing. She's not laughing like she normally is. She's screaming.

"Hunter. Hold on!"

Hold on to what?

It's too much. All he has to do is relax, open his mouth, let it go. Anything to relieve this pain in his chest.

"Wake up!" His mum is shaking him, yanking his shoulder like she used to when he was late for school.

He closes his eyes, angry, tries to roll over.

"Wake up, Hunter. Now!"

His eyes flick open. He is drifting a few meters from the barge with Uma sinking underwater by his side. He jerks his arm out, pulls her back to the surface. And then the reality hits him. It's dark again. The chopper's gone. Finally. But he's too weak to kick. He's got to grab hold of the barge, it's the only way he can keep afloat. Shivering, he swims over and feels his way along the rusted metal until he finds another hook. Hunter grabs hold and then forces himself to look closely at Uma. Her face is totally lifeless, blood flowing from her throat. He presses his fingers against the wound.

"Uma...wake up. Come on!"

Eyes shut, she drifts beside him. Hunter snatches up her wrist, feeling for a pulse, but after a long slow wait, his fingers tight around her flesh, he feels nothing. She's gone.

And then the fury rises in his chest. She can't be dead. Not after all they've been through. Hunter pounds the metal hull behind him with his fist, screaming with rage at the chopper that still circles the Thames upstream.

"Come on! I'm here. I'm still alive! Come and finish it."

Shouting, sobbing, he pummels the water, thrashing, kicking and hitting out in a frenzy, until with a cry of despair he falls back against the hull, utterly exhausted. The minutes pass as he drifts alongside the barge, alone on the black current, clutching Uma to his body, still desperately trying to warm her, to rouse her. Even she has abandoned him now. He doesn't belong anywhere anymore. He is utterly alone in the black, dark city. He didn't kill the soldier. But the only man who can prove that lies dead. He'll never be able to prove his innocence. Pain rips through his heart. Ah, his old man!

It's time to let go. Yes, a moment of panic when the water will start to fill his lungs, but he's already been so close, it's not so bad... a brief fight—and then peace. And Uma is already gone. He'll throw the Codes away, let them roll to the sea, where no one can find them.

Hunter sets his chattering teeth, willing himself to make the final break. Minutes pass, but still he can't do it. Cursing himself for being a coward, he screams out loud—and suddenly Uma moves—an almost imperceptible shift of her body in his arms.

Hunter grabs her tight. "Uma! Can you hear me?"

For a long moment she lies still again, floating like a dead thing.

He gazes, wild, into her face. "Uma, *please...*"

And then he feels it, her fingers tightening around his right arm—a gentle but definite pressure. She's alive!

His heart, his head explodes with joy. He's got to get her out and now. He scans the dark bank feverishly. Where are they? The barge has moved surprisingly fast. Through the mist he can just make out the pyramid tower roof of Canary Wharf, still glowing in the power cut. They must be nearly back in the Isle of Dogs again.

Hunter whispers in Uma's ear. "Hold on. I'm getting us out of here."

No response.

He tightens his grip. "Uma. You've got to promise to stay with me, right?"

After a long beat, her lips move, the faintest whisper coming from her mouth. Hunter strains his ears to catch the sound.

Uma's lips move again. "Try."

And then with the last of his strength, Hunter kicks away from the barge, aiming his body toward the misty shore.

On the roof of the Tower Hotel, Commander Clarke grabs the outer rail, silently scanning the area below as the military chopper repeatedly sweeps the river. One chopper is all he's got. Central command won't give him any more in these conditions. Cowards. He's millimeters away from the biggest breakthrough of the decade and all they'll give him is one lousy chopper.

His knuckles whiten around the railing. He doesn't even know if the kids are dead or alive. And how did that Citizen boy get mixed up in all this? He's got no profile. Clarke frowns. This better not be the start of Outsider ideas creeping into Citizen kids' homes.

Clarke blows out his cheeks. It's over. No one could survive that jump from the hotel roof. Their bodies are right now being carried away on the tide. He's been defeated in the end by the fog and a power cut. How ironic. Clarke strides over to the far side of the roof, pauses for a minute alongside a medical unit in front of the lift. He nods at the body laid out on the stretcher.

"Any chance?"

The doctor shakes his head.

Suddenly Clarke bends down over the body, dropping his voice to a low whisper. "Well, you were right, Guido. You Outsiders never touched Bradwell B. It was nothing really—just a pinhole leak in the heat exchanges—but I'm sure you'll agree it was just too beautiful an excuse to let go by. Sex up the dossier, throw in a few bits of fake evidence about Outsider sabotage, and suddenly I had Operation Clearwater up and running."

Clarke straightens, flicks a glance at Rose lying on a nearby stretcher, a sheet draped over her lifeless body. The Dreamline is still intact, the Encryption Codes still hidden, the Outsider identities still secret. A once-in-a-generation opportunity to break the network is gone. Two kids. No doubt they'll be washed up on some stinking beach tomorrow.

Clarke slides his freezing hands into his jacket pockets as he waits for the elevator. These Outsiders, they just won't give up. Every favela, every estate is a wasp's nest of rebellion; every year the movement spreads a little wider around the world. The elevator doors slide open and Clarke steps inside, stabbing the ground-floor button. Well, he's not finished. There's plenty of fight still left in him too. He's got Hunter's father in custody . . . and if the boy is alive that may prove crucial. He'll start to build the case again. *This isn't over.*

Thirty-one

Down on the muddy foreshore of the Isle of Dogs, Harry is one of a long line of watchers standing lookout on the Thames. He stares out over the water. The most ancient thing on earth. All our bodies made of the ancient seas where life was born. Suddenly Harry stiffens, feeling their approach before he even sees Hunter's arm cutting through the surface of the water. Crying out, he plunges into the river, wading out waist-deep to meet them.

"Are you hurt?"

But Hunter is too exhausted to answer. Harry takes Uma into his arms, gently rolling her from the boy's grasp before turning and clambering back to the shore. In a few moments he struggles up over the mud, to the dry high part of the beach where he bends and places the girl on her back. His forehead creases in worry as he feels for her pulse.

A few seconds later, Hunter drags himself alongside. "I-I did everything I could." He collapses on the ground, his chest heaving with silent tears. Then the darkness takes him. He tries to rise, but his balance is gone. He's vaguely aware of voices; he falls again, only to be caught; a hand holding him, lowering him. A healing coolness spreading over his body and then—nothing. Hunter drifts, falling deep into gentle currents.

In the dark night just before the dawn, Leo wakes in the alleyway. A noise—something rustling in a mound of rubbish farther down the street. He jerks upright, peering desperately into the night, but he can't see anything. Leo shivers and wraps his thin jacket tighter around his chest. It'll be light soon, and then what will he do? He can't go back home. Not today, not ever. Dragging the back of his sleeve over his eyes, he clamps his teeth shut. Crying won't get him anywhere. And he can't, he won't drag his brother into this. Paolo doesn't deserve to get pulled down again.

Leo's got to take care of himself now. If he wants to stay alive, he's got to disappear...into the favela...he's got to find Hunter and Uma. It's his only chance. Pulling himself upright, he forces himself into a walk, and then into a run, heading east toward the Isle of Dogs. That's where Hunter goes to jump, that's where the Kossaks got the last GPS fix on him. If he's anywhere, that's where he'll be.

Hunter opens his eyes. It's daylight. He frowns, vaguely remembering it being light once before. How long has he been here? He lifts his head, looks around the room. It's some kind of office, the space piled up with old desks and chairs. He is alone. Forcing himself upright, he swings his strapped leg over the side of the mattress. And then a wave of nausea hits him. For a second he grips the sheets tightly. When the wave subsides, he takes a deep breath, and cups his mouth with shaking hands. "Hello?"

Silence.

"Anyone here?"

And then to his relief he hears a faint creak of a door opening and quick footsteps approaching. After a few moments, his door opens and Harry steps into the room. The old man shakes his head and eases the boy back on the mattress.

"Ah, lie down. You are not ready to move so fast, my son."

"Where's Uma?"

"Close by."

"Is she—"

"Yes. *Alive*." Harry grips the boy's hand tight. "I have stayed awake with her these past two nights, but still she must fight some more."

"Two nights? We've been here that long?"

"Yes."

Hunter stares into the man's craggy face. "But she'll pull through, right?"

Harry returns the look. "Fate willing. But you have to understand, we *cannot* take her to hospital, it's too dangerous. . . ."

Hunter sighs, glancing out of a cracked window. "Where are we?"

"The old cinammon warehouse, on the far side of the island. Kossaks raided my house on the first morning, but of course we were long gone by then. They are not far, be assured that they are watching the favela like hawks, even though they have lost their best informant." He shakes his head, a tremor coming to his voice. "You said much in your sleep. Poor Rose. To think what that child suffered."

Hunter falls back against the pillows, reality settling on him again like fallout dust.

Harry glances at his face. "Your leg, does it hurt you?"

"A little. . . . But, Harry, what now? We can't stay hidden like this forever."

"I know. The Council has been called. We must use our network to hide you in deep cover."

And then it hits Hunter. His clothes, where are his jeans? The Codes? He looks wildly around the room.

Harry's face is grave. "I know what it is you search for. I have destroyed them."

Hunter's jaw drops. "You've what?"

"I had no other option. The path to the Keeper had become compromised. Too much was at stake."

"So it was all for nothing?"

"No! The International Council will appoint a new Keeper and a copy of the Encryption Codes will be entrusted to them in the utmost secrecy. There are only three copies in existence, so you can see what a heavy decision it was for me to destroy them." Harry sighs. "But I had no choice. And now we must never speak of this again. Promise me this, Hunter."

Hunter nods. Then suddenly he leans forward. "But, Harry, I can't go undercover. I've got to see my dad."

The old man shakes his head. "You can't. They will find you if you try to contact him."

"But I've *got* to."

Harry spreads his hands. "You'll be arrested immediately. And you will put him in even more trouble. Hunter, I understand.... I have already sent a messenger to your father to tell him you're being protected."

"But I didn't kill the officer. It was Guido! And now he's dead... and I can never prove it."

The old man's voice trembles. "You are sure he is dead?"

Hunter nods. "On the balcony, I saw it myself. I'm sorry..." He drops his head into his hands. It's like a dream. One he's never going to wake up from. *This is it.* Right now he has no choice but to do what Harry tells him. After a long moment he raises his head again.

"Can I see her?"

"Yes, in a little while."

In the Kossak Military HQ, Evan Nash is marched into the interrogation room where the soldier pushes him onto a plastic orange chair before unlocking one of his handcuff bracelets and attaching it to the leg of a metal table. Offering a curt nod to the man sitting on the other side of the table, the officer leaves the room, locking the door behind him.

Evan stares stony-faced at the only lawyer the Kossaks will give him; a fat, sleazy-looking guy who seems barely awake. The lawyer dabs at his soft mouth with a handkerchief before glancing up vaguely.

"Good morning, Mr. er... Nash. And how are we today?"

Evan allows his gaze to travel down the guy's cheap suit. "I want my own lawyer."

The man unwraps a stick of gum, drops it into his mouth. "Yeah well, beggars can't be choosers. . . ." He starts to chew with a disgusting smacking sound. "You're lucky to get me at all with these new counterterrorism laws."

"I didn't have any choice." Evan rubs his tired eyes.

Suddenly the lawyer leans forward, his voice dropping to barely a whisper.

"Choice is an interesting thing. In this crisis the government would have us believe there is only one choice. To do as they say, wallowing in past glories and blaming every other country for all our ills. But some people believe there's another way, one which will save us all—but only if we're bold enough to throw away the old and create a new system for the future."

Evan stares at the lawyer. What did he just say? The man is now scrawling a message on a yellow Post-it. He doesn't look like the same slob who was sitting there a minute ago. Putting his forefinger to his lips, the lawyer slides the paper square toward Evan, who reaches for it with shaking fingers. Is this some kind of trap? Are the Kossaks testing him to see if he holds dissident beliefs? He looks down at the note.

The boy is safe with us.

Evan's heart leaps. He grabs at the lawyer's wrist. "Where?"

The man pulls back. "Shhh. Keep talking about the case; the room may be bugged."

Evan passes his hand over his face, forcing his voice to be calm, as the lawyer begins to scrawl another note.

Evan clears his throat. "So can you tell me how long I'll be in detention for?"

The new note spins across the table toward him. Evan snatches it up.

We are moving him. Will contact you when it's safe. Trust us.

Suddenly the door lock releases and the guard steps into the doorway. With a smooth movement the lawyer darts out his pudgy hand and scrunches up the Post-it notes into a ball before tossing them into his mouth. Ignoring the soldier, he leans back in his chair, his face a bored mask as he chews his gum. "Oh, I don't know, Mr. Nash, detention is a tricky thing. We'll have to wait until we have more clarity on the charge." Casually he glances over at the guard. "Yeah, what now?"

The soldier shakes his head. "Nothin'. But I was ordered to keep the door open, that's all. I'll be standing here where I can see you both. Okay?"

The lawyer waves his hand. "Whatever." Reaching into his bag, he pulls out a yellow legal pad. "So, Mr. Nash, would you like to tell me everything that's happened?" He places the pad on the table. "Let's start from the morning of the twenty-fourth of March, shall we? Everything in order."

But Evan doesn't answer him, and when the lawyer glances up from his pad he sees the tremble in Evan's hand, the hope shining in his eyes.

He frowns. "Mr. Nash, try to control yourself. You have a long, long road ahead of you yet."

In a room high in the cinammon warehouse, Uma lies on a layer of rough blankets, her breath coming shallow and harsh.

Hunter stands in the doorway, his heart pounding. She looks so bad. He glances over at Harry. "Did you...take out the bullet?"

The old man rubs his beard. "No...it only clipped her, otherwise she would surely be dead." A small smile tugs at his lips. "I still have *your* bullet if you want it, though. Well, come in, boy, don't stand there like a wet hen."

Lyuba thumps her tail on the floor as Hunter limps into the room, and bending down he slowly reaches out to take Uma's hand in his. She doesn't look like herself. She looks like she's really going to die. He feels the rage building inside him again.

"Why?"

Harry frowns. "Because some people are people, and some people are wolves. I'm sorry, Hunter; this is a harsh awakening for you."

"She's not going to make it, is she? Tell me the truth."

"There is hope. But even if she gets better it's not over. You are both in great danger."

"But where is safe for us?"

"Nowhere *close*, for sure. The European Federation is ringed by the Kossak network."

"Then where?"

"South America, maybe. There is a strong Outsider network there, where you can build a new life."

Hunter stares at him in amazement. "No way."

"You have no choice."

"But I can't just leave everyone. My dad, my friends...my life is *here*. And I'm a Citizen. I-I've got rights."

"You *were* a Citizen. And maybe you'll be again. But not now. Unless you want to receive Kossak justice for killing one of their own. There are two legal systems in this country, and you don't want to find yourself on the Outsider side."

Hunter explodes. "But I'm innocent!"

Beside him, Uma stirs, tightening her grip around his hand. Hunter stares into her face. How can this be happening?

Harry sighs. "Hunter, you've done what very few of us could do....Not only did you outrun the Kossaks, but you stayed true."

He straightens, slowly. "Harry...I *can't* just become an Outsider like you. I was brought up over there...a Citizen...and I'll never ever learn to hate ordinary people who are scared, just trying to get by."

The old man frowns. "We don't hate them either. Don't listen to the lies about us. The Citizens, the ordinary people, they are our brothers and sisters too. But they are sinking...and if the governments sleep, the people must rise. All of us." Harry suddenly grasps Hunter's hand hard, his eyes turning a piercing shade of blue. "Don't you see you have no choice? Everything starts right here, right now, Hunter Nash. The momentum is with us, we are growing, and we must *fight* for a new future. And so must you. It's the only way."

Hunter's gaze moves from Harry to Uma. He reaches down,

stroking the hair back from her forehead, willing her to open her eyes, to live. And suddenly a lone, last ray of the setting sun cuts into the room, lighting up her face in brilliant gold.

Hunter cups her cheek in his hand. "Come on, Uma. Fight now!"

A long silent moment passes—and then, for a fleeting second her eyes flicker open, and she's there, she sees him! She is fighting to come back. A jolt runs through Hunter's body, a pulse of pure energy. His throat tightens. She is the only thing he has left, the only thing that makes sense. And Harry's right; his old world is gone forever.

Hunter nods slowly. "If she makes it, I'll go with her. But promise me you'll take care of my father?"

Harry nods. "Yes, the Outsiders protect their own. And as for you, if Uma's life is spared, you must go together where the flood carries you. Who knows what the future will bring."

And suddenly the room darkens again as the sun drops out of sight, dipping below the ragged urban skyline. The end of another day in the London favela.